Y0-BCT-813

"He said no?" Raleigh guessed correctly.

"He said he was busy." Beth slumped onto a sofa, swallowing back the tears that threatened. So Mitch had turned her down. Big deal. Beth had been concerned that an office romance might affect their working relationship, anyway.

"He didn't issue a counteroffer?" Raleigh sounded genuinely perplexed.

"Maybe he would have." Beth knew she was grasping at straws. "He never got the chance. His half brother was there, asking a lot of questions about something that happened years ago when Mitch lived in— I can hardly say it. Coot's Bayou. Did you know he was from a place called Coot's Bayou?"

"Seems I heard about it at some point."

"Did you know he stole a car?"

"He was a teenager at the time. The charges were dropped."

"So you did know. You encouraged me to hook up with a criminal, when you know—"

"He's not a criminal. He's a good person, Beth."

"Maybe." Deep down, Beth felt that Mitch was good—not that she could trust her own instincts where men were concerned. "But now he's being accused of murder."

Dear Reader,

When I introduced the character of Mitch Delacroix in an earlier book, all I really knew about him was that he was a charming Cajun and an expert computer hacker. But once I started to research the setting for this book—the bayous of Southern Louisiana—he came to life in a sudden burst of inspiration. His wild past and the reasons for his youthful rebellion, his current, secret life as a mixed martial arts cage fighter, his relationship with his half brother—it all came to me in a clump. The man was just there, fully formed, smiling that wicked-charming half smile, and all I had to do was take dictation from him.

Mitch's story, though, wasn't always easy to write. For one thing, I didn't know beans about cage fighting. Bless my supportive husband, he bought tickets to a live mixed martial arts event so I could see for myself what it's like. I blew my holiday gift cards on MMA magazines and spent hours watching YouTube video lessons on jujitsu and Muay Tai fighting techniques. Then I had my husband—a second-degree black belt in Tae Kwon Do—read my fight scenes to be sure they rang true.

I hope you enjoy the wild ride that Mitch took me on, and that you'll cheer on Beth, his sweet heroine, as she tries to find common ground with a man who turns out to be very different from the computer nerd she thought she wanted.

Sincerely,

Kara Lennox

Outside the Law
Kara Lennox

TORONTO NEW YORK LONDON
AMSTERDAM PARIS SYDNEY HAMBURG
STOCKHOLM ATHENS TOKYO MILAN MADRID
PRAGUE WARSAW BUDAPEST AUCKLAND

If you purchased this book without a cover you should be aware that this book is stolen property. It was reported as "unsold and destroyed" to the publisher, and neither the author nor the publisher has received any payment for this "stripped book."

Recycling programs
for this product may
not exist in your area.

ISBN-13: 978-0-373-71767-5

OUTSIDE THE LAW

Copyright © 2012 by Karen Leabo

All rights reserved. Except for use in any review, the reproduction or utilization of this work in whole or in part in any form by any electronic, mechanical or other means, now known or hereafter invented, including xerography, photocopying and recording, or in any information storage or retrieval system, is forbidden without the written permission of the publisher, Harlequin Enterprises Limited, 225 Duncan Mill Road, Don Mills, Ontario, Canada M3B 3K9.

This is a work of fiction. Names, characters, places and incidents are either the product of the author's imagination or are used fictitiously, and any resemblance to actual persons, living or dead, business establishments, events or locales is entirely coincidental.

This edition published by arrangement with Harlequin Books S.A.

For questions and comments about the quality of this book please contact us at Customer_eCare@Harlequin.ca.

® and TM are trademarks of the publisher. Trademarks indicated with ® are registered in the United States Patent and Trademark Office, the Canadian Trade Marks Office and in other countries.

www.Harlequin.com

Printed in U.S.A.

ABOUT THE AUTHOR

Kara Lennox has earned her living at various times as an art director, typesetter, textbook editor and reporter. She's worked in a boutique, a health club and an ad agency. She's been an antiques dealer, an artist and even a blackjack dealer. But no work has ever made her happier than writing romance novels. To date, she has written more than sixty books. Kara is a recent transplant to Southern California. When not writing, she indulges in an ever-changing array of hobbies. Her latest passions are bird-watching, long-distance bicycling, vintage jewelry and, by necessity, do-it-yourself home renovation. She loves to hear from readers. You can find her at www.karalennox.com.

Books by Kara Lennox

HARLEQUIN SUPERROMANCE

HARLEQUIN AMERICAN ROMANCE

‡Project Justice
*Blond Justice
**Firehouse 59
†Second Sons

Other titles by this author available in ebook format.

CHAPTER ONE

"Ask him now."

Beth McClelland shrank back into the hallway, her mind screaming *Chicken!* "He looks busy."

"He's probably just surfing the web. Computer geeks can always look busy." Raleigh Shinn, Beth's best friend, stood behind her with a hand on her shoulder, ready to push if necessary.

But Beth planted her feet firmly. It had seemed like a good idea yesterday, buying tickets to a zydeco concert, then casually telling Mitch Delacroix she had an extra if he wanted to come with her. She knew he liked that kind of music because he often played it as background noise while he hunted online for elusive data or missing witnesses.

"What if he says no?" Beth knew she sounded like a teenager, but she wasn't ready for rejection. Since her last relationship had been so disastrous, she wanted to ease back into the dating world. Shouldn't her first foray be with someone easier? Someone less complicated? Someone she didn't care about?

She and Mitch had become friends. They had an easy working relationship and she genuinely enjoyed hanging out with him. Taking it to the next level might be a logical choice—or a disaster.

"He won't say no," Raleigh insisted. "I've seen the way he looks at you, and you said he isn't dating anyone seriously."

"Then why hasn't he asked *me* out?" He certainly flirted enough.

"Stop stalling and get this over with, please. I'm tired of watching you make cow eyes at him. If he says no—which he won't—you can at least move on."

Raleigh was a compassionate friend, but she never minced words. Her legal training had taught her to get to the heart of the matter in the most direct way possible.

"Can I help you ladies with something?"

Beth stifled a gasp and took a step back. While she'd been arguing with Raleigh, Mitch Delacroix had come out of his chair and walked over. He now stood less than two feet away, his thumbs hooked into the pockets of his faded jeans.

She tried to say something, but her tongue had grown twice its normal size and her brain felt as though it just went through a blender. She had no trouble testifying in court about DNA molecules and ion exchange chromatography, and normally she could hold her own with men, professionally or socially. But just the thought of asking Mitch Delacroix out on a date—a real date—twisted her up inside. She'd never been interested in someone she worked with before, so maybe her instincts were trying to tell her this was a bad idea.

To hell with instincts. She wanted Mitch and she wasn't going to let anything stop her.

Raleigh leaned in and whispered, "Don't screw this up. I'm out of here." She walked away, leaving Beth and Mitch standing in the doorway.

He looked at her expectantly, a smile playing on his sexy mouth.

Crap. She struggled to come up with a credible excuse for why she'd walked into the bull pen.

Mitch's desk phone chose that moment to buzz. He ignored it at first, but it buzzed again. "Mitch, pick up." The voice of Celeste Boggs, office manager for Project Justice, boomed over the intercom, sounding bossy even for Celeste. No, not just bossy. Tense and worried.

"You better get that," Beth said, pleased she could string words together.

Mitch rolled his eyes. "What now? You think she's mad because I took the last doughnut?" But he returned to his desk and grabbed the phone. "Yo, Celeste, what's up?"

Beth stared greedily as his attention moved to the phone call. His light brown hair, streaked with blond from the sun, was well past his collar and unruly— the kind of hair that was hard to tame so he didn't bother trying. Her perusal moved to his body; his typical geek's ratty T-shirt revealed biceps and a nicely muscled chest that were decidedly atypical, and his tanned skin meant he did not spend every minute staring at a screen.

How was it that he looked so sexy even talking on the phone? He had this quiet confidence that was so appealing—not like the macho guys she'd been attracted to in the past, the ones with swagger and swelled muscles. But she was so over macho guys. A cute geek with a touch of bad boy might be exactly what she needed in her life—and in her bed.

"I'll be right up," he said, looking serious as he hung up the phone.

"Is something wrong?"

"Celeste says there's a Louisiana cop asking to see me."

That couldn't be good news. Had there been an accident? Mitch was from a small town in Louisiana, so he was bound to have some family there.

"Walk with me up to the front desk. You wanted to talk to me about something?"

She didn't want to ask him out on a date if he was about to get bad news. Then again, if she didn't do it now, she never would.

Just do it. This was Mitch, her friend.

"Uh, I have two tickets to see Dirty Rice next Friday and I thought you might like to go."

There. She'd at least said the words, though with far less charm than she'd envisioned. She held her breath, bracing for the blow.

"Oh, hell, Beth, I can't Friday night. I have something planned already. Maybe Billy would take the extra ticket off your hands."

"Yeah, maybe. I'll ask him." Dammit. She was going to kill Raleigh—this was all her fault. Of course Mitch had said no. He probably already had a date for Friday night. Guys like Mitch didn't sit around waiting for women to ask them out. They made plans. They did the asking.

What had she been thinking?

She wanted to run for the safety of her lab, where she could hide behind a microscope. But Mitch would know something was wrong if she suddenly took off like her tail was on fire. So she kept walking with him down the hall to the lobby, pretending she hadn't just had her heart body-slammed.

"Celeste didn't say what the cop wanted?" she asked, desperate to fill the silence. A Louisiana cop wouldn't drive all the way to Houston on a whim; chances were good he was here on official business, and that usually meant bad news.

"The guy wouldn't say." Mitch sounded unconcerned, but Beth wasn't fooled. When he flashed his playful smile at her, she could tell he was forcing it. "So, Dirty Rice, huh? I didn't know you were a zydeco fan."

"I'm not. I mean, I like it okay."

"So you bought tickets because…" He seemed genuinely curious, not judgmental.

She couldn't admit she'd bought them because *he* liked zydeco. Then, inspiration struck. "I won them from a radio station."

"Oh." He seemed to be digesting that. She wasn't the type to call in to radio stations trying to win stuff.

They passed through a door in a frosted glass partition that led into the lobby of Project Justice, the Houston nonprofit where they both worked. The lobby was a large space with cold marble floors and wood-paneled walls, rather stark, Beth had always thought. It was intended to impress, but not to be inviting. Daniel Logan, CEO of Project Justice, didn't want just anyone wandering in off the street and feeling at home. So the only visitor seating was a couple of hard chairs.

The cop had elected to stand, his back to Celeste, studying an arrangement of framed press clippings on the wall. He was a beefy guy, his muscular shoulders straining against his khaki uniform. His dark brown hair was cut very short, revealing a tan line at the margins.

Celeste made a big show of ignoring him, her nose buried in a *Soldier of Fortune* magazine, a large knife out on her desk—just in case.

Mitch picked up his pace, striding confidently into the lobby while Beth hung back. "You wanted to see me?" His voice contained a touch of arrogance.

The stranger turned, and Mitch skidded to a halt. "Dwayne?"

"Mitch. Been a while."

"Yeah. A while."

So, they knew each other. Maybe this was a personal visit, not an official one. An old friend, looking him up... No, that wasn't right. Whatever their relationship, it wasn't warm and fuzzy. The two men sized each other up, radiating tension.

"Why the big mystery?" Mitch asked. "Why didn't you tell Celeste your name?"

"I didn't want you to get the wrong idea. This isn't exactly a social call."

Mitch looked confused. "Did someone die?"

The cop named Dwayne looked faintly amused. "Funny you should ask that. I'm here in regards to an incident that happened twelve years ago. A Monte Carlo was stolen from the parking lot of a Piggly Wiggly. Ring any bells?"

"Yeah, I believe I do recall that incident," Mitch said with an exaggerated Southern accent. "But the charges were dropped. Buried, in fact."

Charges? Mitch had been arrested and charged with a crime? Her throat tightened as she recalled the last guy she'd dated, who'd also had a criminal past. Vince had explained away the assault charges, claiming it was all a misunderstanding, and she'd been stupid enough to fall for it. Until he'd broken her jaw.

She gave her head a quick, involuntary shake. No way was Mitch in the same boat as Vince. He'd freely admitted he'd been a "wild kid," but Beth had pictured him pulling pranks, maybe spray-painting a bridge or decorating trees with toilet paper. She'd known nothing about car theft, but that wasn't violent. Still, it was bad.

"I'm not here about the theft per se," Dwayne said. "You had a friend with you that night. Robby Racine. That right?"

Abruptly Celeste came out of her chair, proving she'd been listening keenly despite her show of disinterest. She was well into her seventies, with wild gray curls and a spare, wiry body that she stuffed into the most improbable outfits. Today it was a zebra-striped, bat-wing shirt, black leggings and red boots. But anyone who knew her was scared of her. "Mitch, don't say another word without a lawyer present."

Mitch turned to Celeste. "This is my brother."

"Half brother," Dwayne said.

Beth thought the distinction odd, as if Dwayne wanted to deny the relationship.

"Whatever, I don't think he's here to arrest me." But when Mitch returned his attention to Dwayne, he looked less than sure of himself. "Are you?"

"I'm just here to talk. So, about Robby…"

"Robby Racine was with me that night," Mitch confirmed.

"You happen to know where he is?"

"Robby? Good gravy, no. Haven't seen him since that night. Getting arrested for stealing a car would have been his third felony. He'd have done time for sure. He took off." Mitch seemed to relax slightly. "I figure he's in Mexico."

"You figured wrong. He turned up the other day."

"No kidding. What's he up to these days?"

"Nothing. That's the point. He turned up in a shallow grave on some land owned by your mother. And you were the last one to see him alive."

Beth's head spun. This could not be happening. Mitch, her Mitch, a murder suspect? She simply could not picture it. He was so nice, so laid-back. He was a computer geek. Since when did geeks go around stealing cars and killing people? It was ridiculous.

"*Where* did you find Robby?" Mitch asked. "My mom never owned any land that I knew of. She and

Daddy were poor as cockroaches at a homeless shelter, you know that."

"Hell, Mitch, I don't know the details. I volunteered to come here, pick you up and take you to Coot's Bayou for questioning. Thought it might go down a little easier if you saw a friendly face."

Mitch looked as if he wanted to spit. "Friendly, my ass. You're loving this. And if you want me to come to Coot's Bayou for anything, you'll need a warrant."

Celeste pushed the intercom button. "Raleigh, wherever you are, get your ass into the lobby. Stat."

"Mitch," Beth said carefully, "don't you think you should clear this up?"

Judging from the surprised look he gave her, he'd forgotten she was there—and didn't seem to welcome her contribution. "I don't owe the Coot's Bayou police anything."

"They just want to talk," Dwayne said.

"That's what they always say," Celeste interjected. "You think we were born yesterday, sonny?"

"Celeste, thank you, but I'll handle this." Mitch focused on his brother. "Dwayne, whatever you're selling, I'm not buying. I haven't even lived in Louisiana for seven years!"

"Doesn't matter. We think Robby died the night that car was stolen."

Mitch looked over at Beth. Gauging her reaction? And what did he see on her face? She could hide her emotions when dealing with the press, or in court, but when dealing with her own life, every thought that whisked through her mind showed plainly in her expression.

The revulsion she felt was for the crime, not Mitch, who couldn't possibly have done it, but would he be able to tell the difference?

"Let me know when you have a warrant." Mitch turned on his heel and sauntered out of the lobby, appearing completely unbothered. But his gait was slightly stiffer than normal, his jaw set more firmly. Anyone who'd spent as much time studying Mitch as she had could notice these things.

Had he fooled his own half brother?

Dwayne looked first at Celeste, who stared back with open challenge, then switched his gaze to Beth, perhaps seeking someone with a more open mind. "It's in his best interest to cooperate," he said. "There's gonna be a warrant, and I'll have to come back with it tomorrow." He turned and exited to the street.

By the time Raleigh arrived, whooshing into the hall with her pen, notebook and digital recorder ready for battle, it was all over.

"You're too late," Celeste said. "Missed the show. Did you know our Mitch has a half brother? And a cop, at that?"

"No, I didn't. What happened here?"

"I'll explain," Beth said. "But let's go to the ladies' room where I can have a meltdown in private."

Raleigh said nothing until they were safely inside the ladies' lounge on the second floor. Raleigh and Beth had held quite a few cry fests in here over the past few years. It was furnished with tufted sofas and gilt-framed mirrors, but its best feature was a big box of Kleenex.

"He said no?" Raleigh guessed correctly.

"He said he was busy." Beth slumped onto a sofa, swallowing back the tears that threatened. What if Mitch got arrested?

"He didn't issue a counteroffer?" Raleigh sounded genuinely perplexed.

"Never mind the date. His half brother was there asking a lot of questions about something that happened years ago when Mitch lived in... I can hardly say it. Coot's Bayou. Did you know he was from a place called Coot's Bayou?"

"Seems I heard about it at some point."

"Did you know he stole a car?"

"He was a teenager at the time. The charges were dropped."

"So you did know. You should have told me."

"It's not like he's a criminal. He's a good person, Beth."

"Maybe." Deep down, Beth felt that Mitch was good, not that she could trust her own instincts where men were concerned. "But now he's being accused of murder. His own half brother seems to think he might have killed the guy—"

"Whoa, whoa. Murder? Start from the beginning."

Beth recounted the conversation between Mitch and his brother as best she could. Raleigh listened attentively, taking quick notes, firmly in lawyer mode.

When Beth was finished, Raleigh pulled off her

glasses and massaged her temples. "He needs to cooperate. He needs to clear this up."

"That's what I told him. But instead he got angry. I never saw Mitch get angry before."

"Everybody has buttons. Obviously Mitch and his brother have some issues."

"You have to talk to him, Raleigh. Convince him to hire himself a lawyer and go to Coot's Bayou and answer the questions."

"I can try. But honestly...you're the one who knows him better."

"And you're the lawyer. You know how to persuade juries and get witnesses to admit stuff."

"We'll talk to him together," Raleigh said decisively.

Beth nodded. "Okay. Let's do it now."

They exited the bathroom, but in the hallway Raleigh paused as if something just occurred to her. "Why do you think the half brother showed up with the news?"

"He said he thought it would go down easier if Mitch saw a friendly face. But that guy's face was far from friendly. He was loving every minute of the exchange. There is bad blood between those two."

MITCH WAS SO STEAMED about his brother's high-handed prank that he didn't return to the bull pen. He needed quiet, not the controlled chaos of the large, open area, where the Project Justice junior investigators and interns worked. He headed upstairs to his private office, shut the door and collapsed into the leather chair behind his desk.

He didn't want to see or talk to anyone.

He was supposed to be searching for a missing witness pertaining to another investigator's case, but not even the prospect of losing himself in online research could distract him from his irritation.

Dwayne could have called. He could have emailed him or texted. He could have showed up at Mitch's house. Walking into Mitch's place of business and announcing to everyone within earshot that he was a murder suspect was the kind of cruelty Dwayne had always gone for.

He'd done it on purpose, of course—to humiliate Mitch as thoroughly as possible.

Mitch slammed his fist into his left palm. Hell, why was this happening now? He had a fight scheduled for Friday night, and he couldn't afford to lose focus, not if he wanted to continue his winning streak.

He needed to sweat, to work out the anger and frustration. Beating the crap out of a punching bag, pushing his body until every muscle burned, was the only sane way he knew how to deal with stress. It sure as hell beat joyriding in stolen cars, or downing a case of beer.

After a futile hour, he decided concentrating was impossible. He closed his laptop and loaded it into his backpack. No one would notice if he cut out a couple of hours early, and he could put in a few more hours of research tonight at home. Right now, he had to get out of here.

He was heading for the door when someone knocked. Damn, no clean getaway. He yanked the door open.

Beth and Raleigh. Neither of them was smiling.

"Hey. I was just on my way out—"

"This will only take a few moments." Raleigh pushed her way inside his office without invitation. Beth followed, and Mitch inhaled deeply as she brushed past him. Today's scent was green-apple. She liked to wear all different kinds of perfumes, mostly botanical scents like kiwi and watermelon and vanilla. He'd made a game out of trying to guess the scent of the day.

But the stubborn expression on her pretty, feminine face told him this was not the time for games. He knew that expression. He was in for a fight.

Mitch smiled his best good-ol'-boy smile. "Ladies, I have a dentist appointment—"

"So you'll be five minutes late," Raleigh said. "As chief legal counsel for Project Justice, I have something to say. Now, you might not care if a posse of Louisiana cops shows up tomorrow with sirens and bullhorns and guns flashing, but I do. If you get arrested for so much as littering, it reflects badly on the foundation, and I can't let that happen."

"That won't happen," he assured her. At least, he didn't think so. "My brother was just trying to piss me off. They don't have any evidence."

"They *do* have evidence," Beth nearly exploded. "If you were the last person known to see the victim alive, that's plenty of evidence to bring you in for questioning. You're only making things worse. If you keep sticking your head in the sand—"

He held up one hand to stop the tirade. "I've got this

under control, okay? I know how the local cops oper-
ate in Coot's Bayou. I worked for them for a few years.
They're just shaking the bushes, hoping something will
fall out.

"I'm not falling out. I'll see you tomorrow." He
turned his back on them, daring them to try and stop
him from exiting his own office. If he didn't find a
punching bag soon, he was going to lose it. But he
heard no steps behind him, no clatter of high heels on
the polished wood floor.

It was a fine spring day, cool and crisp in a way per-
petually muggy Houston seldom saw. He'd ridden the
Harley to work, and as he settled into his eight-mile
commute home, he hoped the wind in his face would
clear his mind. But when he pulled into his driveway,
he was every bit as tense and angry as when he'd left
work.

He didn't bother putting his bike in the garage. He
stepped inside his small ranch house long enough to
shed his jeans and golf shirt and throw on shorts and a
T-shirt with the arms ripped out. Barefoot, he headed
outside again, straight through the backyard to the gate
that led to the adjacent property.

Mitch lived next to a played-out oil field. He'd
bought the little house out near Hobby Airport for a
song because most people didn't care for the sound of
pumps and the occasional smell of raw petroleum. That
was three years ago, and now the pumps were silent
and still. The oil reserves were empty.

The quiet wouldn't last forever. Even now, the oil
company that owned the mineral rights to this two-

hundred-acre chunk of land was in the process of ac-
quiring more sophisticated drills and pumps that could
go deeper into the ground. But for now the field was
still and peaceful except for the breeze rustling through
weeds that had reclaimed the ground and the occasional
bird chirp.

Most of the old machinery had been removed, but
one rusted grasshopper pump was left, abandoned, and
Mitch had turned it into his private gym. It had just the
ambiance he needed to train for a cage fight.

Mitch normally started his workout with some general fitness training—push-ups, jumping rope or agility
drills with resistance bands wrapped around his thighs.
But today he skipped all that. He tugged on a pair of
four-ounce gloves, which offered minimal protection
for his hand but left his fingers free, then went to work
on the heavy punching bag he'd suspended from the
pump.

Jab. Jab. Left hook. Right uppercut. Knee to the
solar plexus. Head shot. Body shot. Like always, he
imagined an opponent. Usually, he visualized the guy
he was scheduled to fight. He would study any videos
he could find of the guy, imprint his fighting style into
his brain, then picture all the various ways he could
beat him.

Today, his opponent was not Ricky "Quick Death"
Marquita. Today, the face he saw was his brother's.

Dwayne was the one who'd motivated him to learn
to fight—not by encouraging him, but by beating him
up a few times when they were kids. Bigger, older,
Dwayne had had no trouble besting his little brother.

Mitch continued to rain punches and kicks onto the hapless bag filled with sand and gel, pausing only long enough to whip off his T-shirt after he'd gotten good and warmed up. Roundhouse kick to the head. Elbow to the chin. Inside crescent kick to the knee. He kept going long past exhaustion. Sometimes, the winner of a cage fight was simply the one who could stay upright the longest. Fighting through exhaustion was a key skill.

If he and Dwayne fought today, things would be different. Dwayne still outweighed Mitch by a good thirty pounds. But Mitch was sure that if they ever met in a chain-link cage—or in a back alley—he could smear the mat with his brother.

CHAPTER TWO

BETH TRIED TO TELL HERSELF she'd done what she could. If Mitch was determined to be an idiot about this situation, how could she talk him out of it? Arguing wasn't her best skill; she left that for the lawyers.

Turned out Daniel didn't agree. He shared Raleigh's concern about a scandal being detrimental to Project Justice, and he didn't allow anything to get in the way of the foundation's efforts to free wrongly convicted men and women from prison. But he also cared about Mitch, who had been one of the first people Daniel had hired when he and his father had started the foundation.

After Mitch had stormed down the hall toward the elevator, Beth had returned to her little laboratory, the place where she felt most comfortable. Fingerprints, fibers and blood didn't argue. They spoke only the truth. They weren't all that complicated.

Men—Mitch, in particular—were.

But she hadn't been in the lab ten minutes before Daniel called her.

"You want me to try again to convince Mitch to co-operate?" Beth asked, almost before Daniel had said two words.

"You're the one who knows him the best, Beth," Daniel said. "I'm in the middle of a Logan Oil board meeting, or I would track him down myself and talk some sense into him."

Those were pretty strong words, coming from Daniel, who seldom left his estate unless it was for something really important. His new wife, Jamie, was in the process of pulling him out of his shell, but old habits died hard.

"Apparently I don't know him as well as I thought," Beth huffed. "Coot's Bayou? He's never said a word to me about his hometown. Or his half brother. Or his arrest record."

"He had good reasons for wanting to put that part of his life behind him, Beth. He wasn't trying to hide anything. He grew up under pretty harsh conditions and it's not something he wants to think about."

"He's sure trying to run from it now."

"He can be convinced to do the right thing, I know he can. He's smart, just bullheaded sometimes. Mitch cares about you and respects you. He'll listen to you if you try one more time."

Beth wasn't so sure. But despite his reclusive ways, her billionaire boss understood human nature better than most anyone Beth knew.

"If you really think it will help, I'll try." She would simply have to put her disastrous attempt at dating Mitch out of her mind. He was, first and foremost, her friend. He needed her, even if he didn't know it.

"Do it now. Because frankly, if you don't convince

him, I'm going to have to tell him to take a leave of absence from work."

Beth stifled a gasp. "Daniel, he didn't—"

"I know he didn't kill anyone," Daniel said impatiently. "But we have lots of innocent people depending on us. Having one of our key employees accused of murder, no matter how ridiculous the charge, could damage us beyond repair. I will stand behind Mitch a hundred percent. But I won't have him dragged off in cuffs from our offices, in front of TV cameras. Which is exactly what could happen if Mitch doesn't cooperate."

Beth swallowed, her mouth going dry. She'd known things could get bad for Mitch, and for everyone who worked at Project Justice as well as their clients. Why didn't Mitch see it?

"I'll go right now, Daniel. I'll find him. I'll convince him."

She tried calling Mitch's cell, then his home, but got voice mail both times. He was very good at ignoring a ringing phone when he didn't want to talk. "You can run, but you can't hide," Beth murmured as she grabbed her purse and headed out the door, putting her assistant, Cassie, in charge for the rest of the afternoon.

Mitch's house was less than ten miles from downtown and close to the I-610 loop, but it had kind of a rural feel, with a cow pasture across the street and an oil field next door.

Rush hour hadn't gotten a good grip on the city at three in the afternoon, so the trip to his home only took a few minutes. She pulled into the driveway and saw that his Harley was there. Good. But she didn't get out right away. She sat in the car, composing in her mind exactly what she would say to him.

By following him home, she was pushing the bounds of their friendship. But she couldn't sit back and allow him to be railroaded right into prison. Her job had presented her with too many examples of innocent men and women, accused of crimes, who had made their situations so much worse by going into denial.

Mitch's house was cute, Beth had to admit, even if the locale wasn't ideal. The white brick house had red shutters and a trellis shading the front porch, on which grew trumpet vine and morning glories poised to burst into bloom. Mitch kept everything in good repair, but Beth couldn't help thinking, as she mounted the front steps, that the place could use a woman's touch.

She rang the bell. When he didn't answer after a few moments, she rang again and knocked. "Mitch? I know you're in there. You better just come to the door, because I'm not leaving. We have to talk."

Still nothing. No sound.

Determined, she walked around the house and let herself into the backyard through the gate in the honeysuckle-choked chain-link fence. The patio and yard were empty, but she found the sliding glass door unlocked.

Nervous sweat broke out on her upper lip as she opened it. "Mitch?"

She was about to go inside when she heard something, a strange noise punctuating the silence.

Smack, smack, smack. And the unmistakable sound

of a human male exerting himself. The noise was not coming from inside the house, but behind her. From the yard...no, beyond the yard. Beyond the fence, into the otherwise still oil field.

What the hell?

Curiosity killed the cat, she reminded herself as she abandoned the sliding glass door and went in search of the source of the sound.

The back gate had been left ajar. As a trained crime scene investigator, she should have noticed that before. Mindful of her heels on the uneven ground, she crept through the gate and followed the strange sounds to another fence, a beat-up chain-link enclosure surrounding an old grasshopper pump.

She could see no way in, so she cleared away some of the tall weeds and peered through the gap she'd created.

Her breath caught in her throat. Finally she'd found Mitch, and he appeared to be beating the crap out of a punching bag, pounding it with his fists, bare feet, elbows and knees.

She was at once fascinated and horrified. Here was a male in the prime of his health and vitality, shirtless, muscles rippling and sheened with sweat. He was beautiful...and terrifying.

Her jaw throbbed and she rubbed it, trying hard not to think about the damage Mitch's fists could do to a human being.

Suddenly he growled like a wild animal and rushed at the punching bag headfirst, hitting it so hard that it disconnected from the chain and crashed to the broken concrete at the base of the pump. The chain that had held it suspended whipped around and struck Mitch in the shoulder, but he seemed to not notice. He was intent on doing more damage to the bag, kicking it savagely with his heel. Then he jumped on top of it and beat it a few more times with his fists.

She must have made some kind of noise, because he slowly stilled his fists, then turned his head and looked right at her.

Embarrassed to have been caught staring at what should have been a private moment for Mitch, she wanted to shrink back behind the weeds and creep away. But it was too late.

"Beth?" He looked both surprised and…yes, apprehensive.

"I c-couldn't find you and I heard something strange," she stammered out. "I didn't mean to spy but, Mitch…" She gained a bit of confidence when he didn't aim his obvious anger at her. "What the hell is all this?"

Gasping for air, he slowly rose from straddling the bag and regained his feet. "This is where I work out."

"Here?"

"Why not here? There's plenty of space for my gear, and no one else is using it. And it's private. Or it's supposed to be," he said pointedly. He grabbed a towel to wipe the sweat off his face, neck and shoulders, then picked up a water bottle, tipped back his head and took a long draw.

Beth watched, fascinated, as his Adam's apple

bobbed up and down and the cords of his neck flexed and relaxed.

She shook her head to clear it, ordering her runaway libido into line. Mitch's body wasn't hers to ogle. She was here on a mission.

"What kind of workout is this?" she asked, stalling. "Are you some kind of black belt killing machine?" She said it with a nervous laugh. She'd known Mitch was fit. No one who filled out a pair of jeans and a T-shirt like he did sat in front of a computer *all* the time.

"I'm not a black belt anything." He sounded defensive. "It's just a good way to stay in shape and work off stress."

"Is it working?"

He peeled off his gloves, which were not like any boxing gloves Beth had ever seen, not that she ever paid much attention. They were small, and didn't cover his fingers. She'd seen bruises and cuts on Mitch's hands before, but he claimed to have gotten them doing yard work or fixing his bike.

"I'm not bouncing off the walls anymore, so, yeah, I guess it helps. Beth, what are you doing here?"

"Come out of that cage and let's talk. Please," she added, since he was under no obligation to speak to her after she'd followed him uninvited and spied on his workout.

He scooped up his discarded T-shirt and threw it on. Beth mourned the loss as he covered up those beautiful pecs and the washboard abs, but it was better this way. Mitch was distracting enough even when he wasn't the next closest thing to completely naked.

Mitch gathered up his gloves, towel and water bottle. But rather than exiting through a gate, he peeled back a section of fencing that had been snipped open with bolt cutters and levered himself through, managing not to catch anything on the raggedly cut chain links.

But he was bleeding, where that punching bag chain had caught him on the shoulder. "You're injured."

"Hmm?"

She pointed to his shoulder and he looked, disinterested. "Oh." He swiped at the blood with his towel, then seemed to forget about it.

"Doesn't it hurt? And look at your knuckles." They were red and swollen, and one of them had a small cut. More blood. Beth was torn between the desire to nurse him with antiseptic and bandages and an even stronger need to turn away in revulsion.

Revulsion won. Blood in a lab she could deal with— nice, clean blood in a test tube or on a cotton swab. But live, bleeding flesh and blood was not her thing. She'd discovered that at the police academy before she'd been booted out.

He shrugged, then stopped to hold the back gate open for her. No matter what, Mitch had the manners of a Southern gentleman, one of the things that drew her to him. Along with his calm, easygoing personality.

Which apparently had been nothing but a facade.

THAT WAS CLOSE. Panic had coursed through Mitch's veins right along with the rush of his blood when he'd spotted Beth peering at him through the fence, a colorful tropical flower completely out of context in his personal gym of rust, metal, leather, concrete and sweat.

He'd thought for sure she would recognize the discipline suggested by his workout. The abbreviated gloves, the combination of punching, kicking and wrestling on the ground screamed mixed martial arts. But though the sport had gained popularity and respectability in recent years, not everyone was into it.

Sweet Beth apparently had no knowledge or interest in his particular fighting style, because she let his weak explanation ride. That was a good thing; he'd gone to a lot of trouble to keep his sporting life separate from his professional work because neither would enhance the other. What fighter would be intimidated by a computer geek who worked for a charitable foundation? And he didn't even want to think about the negative fallout should the press get hold of the connection. What if it came out while he was testifying in court?

Not even Daniel knew about the UFC matches he'd been fighting over the past few years, and it looked as if he could keep it that way awhile longer.

But that didn't mean he was home free. He knew why Beth was here, what she wanted him to do.

He tromped through his backyard and across the brick patio, wishing she was here for some other reason. Like maybe she'd decided his brush with the law turned her on and she wanted some hot, sweaty sex.

Yeah, he'd thought about it. Plenty of times. Every time he saw her, in fact. But she'd been giving him Do Not Touch signals for so long, he'd given up on that idea.

He entered his stuffy house through the sliding glass door, knowing she would follow.

"Mitch, are you going to sit down and listen to me?" she asked as he cruised into the kitchen, ignoring her presence, and grabbed himself the remains of a high-protein energy shake he'd mixed up that morning. What he really wanted was a cold beer, but he never drank the week before a match.

"I already know what you're going to say," he replied wearily. "You want something to drink?"

"No, thank you," she said primly. "If you're so smart, what do you think I'm going to say?"

He turned to face her in the small galley kitchen, still decorated in all its 1970s glory of red and harvest-gold. Beth's hot-pink flowered dress made the decor look old and tired. "The same thing you already said. That I should indulge those backwoods cops from back home to answer stupid questions about a crime I know nothing about. Only you'll probably throw in something about how I should patch things up with my brother. Because he's family, and family is important." Beth enjoyed a warm, loving relationship with her parents, two sisters, brothers-in-law, nieces and nephews. "Does that about sum things up?"

She seemed to shrink a little in the face of his displeasure, and he made a mental note to dial it down a notch. This was Beth, who wouldn't hurt a fly, and she was here only because she thought she was being helpful. She was his friend. Still, that didn't mean he wanted her meddling in his überdysfunctional family.

Usually it took very little to deflect Beth from any

line of conversation he didn't want to pursue. That was one of the reasons he liked hanging with her; she could take a hint when he didn't want to talk about personal stuff.

Now, apparently, she wasn't going to cooperate. She didn't look as though she was about to back down from this fight. He tried to think of some way to change the stubborn thrust of her chin. His gaze focused briefly on her plump, pink lips.

A kiss would give her something else to think about.

"Yes, of course I'm here about your brother's visit," she said, bumping his attention back to the matter at hand. "Can we sit down? Will you at least hear me out?"

"Fine," he mumbled. He suddenly became aware of his sweaty, bedraggled state. Beth was her usual fresh-as-a-daisy self in her sleeveless, summery dress, and he probably looked awful and smelled worse. "Can I take a shower first?"

"If you want, but I don't mind you this way."

For half an instant, Mitch read innuendo into her words. His traitorous mind visualized her leaning in and licking the sweat off his neck, like the fight groupies, who hung out at the gym, sometimes offered.

Then he gave himself a mental smack to the head. This was Beth, his friend, his work buddy, who liked sharing a pizza and watching true crime shows with him so they could make bets on who the real culprit would turn out to be. She was just being considerate. How many times did he have to remind himself she was Off-Limits, in capital letters?

"I'll be out in five minutes. Go sit down." He grabbed himself a protein bar on his way out of the kitchen. He was famished. Burning five hundred calories in one forty-five-minute workout could do that to a guy, and he didn't want to drop any more weight. He was already lighter than most of his light-heavyweight-class opponents.

When he returned to the living room a few minutes later in jeans and a clean T-shirt, he found Beth sitting stiff-backed on the edge of a chair, looking anything but comfortable.

Man, this thing with Dwayne and Robby had gotten her all tied into knots. She must be convinced it was some kind of big deal. His heart felt a small twinge for causing her to worry. She didn't deserve that.

Mitch sprawled onto the sofa, feeling a little better after his brutal workout, a stinging shower and ingesting a few calories. "All right, Bethy, lay it on me. Say what you have to say."

"First, Mitch, Daniel wants you to know that he doesn't—that no one at work thinks you killed anyone. The notion is preposterous."

As hard as he was trying to remain detached, his coworkers' faith in him touched something soft inside him. "Thank you. That means a lot."

"That said, are you out of your mind?"

Mitch sat up, startled by her vehemence. "Excuse me?" He'd been expecting a much gentler approach from Beth. Some sympathy, maybe.

"You practically told a law enforcement officer to go

to hell. I don't care if he's related to you. He was acting in his official capacity."

Mitch shook his head. "It might have looked that way to you, but it was personal. He was doing his level best to embarrass me."

"Why?" Beth asked. "Why would he do that?"

He looked at her, an angry retort on the tip of his tongue, then squelched whatever he'd been about to say. She was asking out of genuine concern, not prurient interest.

"A long and ugly family history," he finally said. "Dwayne doesn't have my best interest at heart."

"So why don't you stand up to him? Accept his challenge, prove him wrong."

"Look, I appreciate your concern. But the police couldn't possibly have any evidence against me. I didn't kill Robby, and I don't know anything about how he died. He was my buddy."

"Mitch." Beth stood and began pacing. "Who do you work for?"

"Is this a trick question?"

"You work for Project Justice," she said, in a hurry to make her point. "And what is Project Justice's mission statement?"

His gaze lingered on her trim calves and thighs. "To free those unjustly imprisoned for crimes they did not commit." Every employee was required to memorize that statement and be able to quote it backward and forward.

"And how many people in this country are sitting in prison, right now, for crimes they didn't commit?"

"You're sounding a lot like Raleigh." And he didn't mean that as a compliment.

"Just answer."

"The answer is unknown."

"True. But it's in the hundreds, possibly the thousands. How many people has Project Justice exonerated?"

The total was always posted in the lobby, but he hadn't looked at it lately. "Sixty-three?"

"Seventy-two," she corrected him.

"Look," he said sensibly. "The police are on a fishing expedition. They couldn't possibly have any evidence against me."

Suddenly Beth sat down next to him, her face inches from his. "Mitch, listen to yourself. Do you have any idea how many of our clients were convicted on really bad evidence? Circumstantial evidence? Or *no* evidence? I'll answer for you. A lot. And do you know what a lot of them say?"

Mitch could only shake his head. He'd never seen Beth grandstand like this. She could speak eloquently when called for, if it was about DNA or fibers or soil samples. But she never made impassioned speeches. Not around him, anyway.

Impatient, she answered the question for him. "They say, 'If I'd known this could happen, I would have taken it more seriously.'" She skewered him so effectively with those big baby-blue eyes that he was afraid she'd soon push him out onto the patio and pop him onto his gas grill. "They say, 'I would have hired a lawyer from the very beginning.' Do you want to be one of those people? Do you want to hide your head in the sand until the cops show up with a warrant and handcuffs?"

The room went deathly quiet. Not even the air-conditioning fan whirred to break the silence. He couldn't hear a bird outside or a passing car. Just the sound of his heart pounding in his ears.

Beth, all rosy-cheeked with her passion, was the sexiest thing he'd ever seen.

Clearly she was waiting for him to say something.

"You think I should go to Coot's Bayou and answer their questions?"

Beth seemed to remember herself. She scooted a few inches away from him, looked down and cleared her throat. "Yes."

"And you think I need to hire a lawyer?"

Beth, looking a bit shell-shocked by her own outburst, squeaked out an answer. "Don't you dare let the police question you without one. Raleigh will go. Eventually you might have to hire someone from the area who knows the local justice system, but she said she can handle the preliminary questioning."

"Won't hiring a lawyer just make it look like I have something to hide?" He couldn't believe he was actually considering taking Beth's advice. But she had made several good points.

"You know what cops do when a suspect agrees to be questioned without a lawyer, right? They stand up and cheer. You used to work for a police department."

"Just computer stuff," he said with a shrug. "I wasn't anywhere near where they questioned suspects."

"Well, know this. A good interrogator can trip you up six ways to Sunday, and every word you say can come back to haunt you during a trial. Let Raleigh be there for you."

"Raleigh has her own cases to manage," he argued, even though arguing was the first step toward defeat. He should have refused to even discuss this with Beth. But he couldn't bring himself to fling any more harsh words at her. "Traveling to Louisiana to answer ridiculous accusations flung at a coworker falls way outside her job description."

"Daniel made it clear," Beth said quietly. "You are his—everyone's—priority right now."

"I appreciate this unnecessary outpouring of concern," he tried again. "But as I've said before—"

"He's going to fire you, Mitch!" Beth said suddenly.

"What?"

"Or suspend you or put you on paid leave or something," she amended. "But he said he can't have a murder suspect working at Project Justice. It could jeopardize everything he's worked for."

"Ah. So the concern isn't really for me."

"You're being deliberately obtuse. Would you please just get your ass over to Louisiana to answer the damn charges?"

"Do I have a choice?" He was getting pissed off all over again, though he knew Beth was only the messenger. A suddenly sexy messenger. Every time her passion rose, so did his. Sure, he'd thought about what it would be like to go to bed with her. She was more than average pretty with a curvy little body that begged for a man's most lavish attention. But he'd always dismissed the notion as ridiculous—first because they were co-workers, second because they were friends, and third… well, third, she needed a *nice* boyfriend. She'd gone to a private Catholic girls' school, for cryin' out loud. And he was a Cajun street punk. He didn't know the first thing about how to treat a sweet, classy woman like Beth.

"Just give the word," she said, unaware of where his thoughts had skipped, "and Raleigh will arrange for a meeting tomorrow morning. The two of you will drive down first thing."

Dammit all to hell. This wasn't going to go away. "Fine. I'll go. But I want you there, too."

"M-me? Why?"

"Because you know physical evidence better than anybody. If they have anything—anything at all—I want your take on it. Because if they claim they found something, it's bogus." He didn't add that he wanted a friendly face in the room while those asses in Coot's Bayou grilled him. Raleigh was a formidable ally, but she was not exactly warm and fuzzy.

"I'll clear it with Daniel," Beth said.

"Then I'll go. But only so I can prove y'all wrong." It galled Mitch to give in to his brother's manipulations. But if that was what it took to make this problem go away, he'd do it.

"And ditch the attitude."

"Yes, ma'am."

"This isn't funny!"

He actually smiled. "I'm not used to seeing you all bossy. It's kind of a turn-on."

She didn't respond to his flirting. Not at all. Instead she stood stiffly and grabbed her purse. "We'll meet at the office at eight tomorrow morning. And would it hurt you to maybe wear something besides holey jeans and a T-shirt?" With that parting shot, she whooshed out of his living room, out the front door, leaving Mitch to stare at the little hitch in her hips, completely flummoxed.

He'd thought he had a pretty good handle on Beth McClelland, but her behavior was odd to say the least. Well, what could he expect? Before today, she hadn't known anything of his sordid past. Now she knew he'd been a car thief. And that he had a half brother he'd never mentioned.

He was afraid she would know a whole lot more about him that he didn't want her to know before this ordeal was finished. And their easy friendship might be over.

CHAPTER THREE

THE COOT'S BAYOU police headquarters hadn't changed a bit in the past ten years. Oh, the interrogation room where they brought Mitch might have received a fresh coat of paint to cover graffiti left there by suspects, going from gray to a sickly green, but new graffiti had replaced the old. Likewise, the furniture was new, but the table's veneer was already peeling up, and the cheap metal chairs were bent out of shape, wobbling uncomfortably.

But the smell—a nauseating mixture of burned coffee, stale cigarettes, sweat and fear—was exactly the same.

Sitting here made Mitch feel seventeen years old again. But this time, they weren't questioning him about a missing car.

At least they hadn't let his brother interrogate him. Mitch never would have been able to hold on to his temper if he'd had to answer to that smug bastard.

Instead, the cop questioning him—Lieutenant Gary Addlestein—was a fortyish man with the shape and overall charm of a fire hydrant, and he clearly thought Mitch was guilty. Every question he shot Mitch's way dripped with skepticism. Every answer Mitch gave resulted in the guy raising a suspicious eyebrow and staring, saying nothing, waiting for Mitch to fill the silence with some incriminating additions to his story.

Raleigh had warned him about that. She'd counseled Mitch to answer as briefly as possible, then resist adding or clarifying anything unless asked specifically.

Although Mitch had been the one to insist, he had second thoughts about the wisdom of including Beth. It wasn't that he doubted her abilities. She definitely knew her stuff. The very first thing she'd done was request to see the security video from the grocery store where he and Robby had stolen the Monte Carlo.

Not that Mitch would attempt to deny it was him and Robby on the tape, and that they had, indeed, stolen a car. But she made note of the date and time on the video, the license plate of the car, the clothing each of them was wearing—any of which might become crucial when it came down to establishing a time line for the evening's events.

"So, let me get this straight," Raleigh said. "This video footage is the sum total of the evidence you have against my client?"

"That, and his admission of guilt in the car theft."

"The car theft has nothing to do with the murder. And I will move to bar any mention of that alleged crime during a trial, if it comes to that. The charges were dropped. Mitch's arrest record was expunged."

"Yeah, that was a sweet little deal you worked out, courtesy of your billionaire boss," Detective Addlestein drawled. "But the cops in this department have long memories."

"Robby and Mitch spent lots of evenings together. They were friends," Raleigh continued. "The fact they happened to be together the night Robby may have disappeared doesn't say much. You have no motive. You have no murder weapon, no trace evidence, no witnesses. My client has no history of violence."

"No history of violence?" Addlestein hooted. "The kid was in a fight every other weekend."

Mitch tried not to cringe. This was exactly the subject he didn't want to discuss. He glanced over at Beth. Her face revealed nothing.

"I don't see that any assault charges were ever filed."

"No one bothers to file charges over street fighting, long as both parties are still breathing when it's over. Doesn't mean your client wasn't prone to violence."

"Throwing a punch now and then isn't the same as shooting someone with a gun. It's well established my client never owned a gun and didn't even like guns. Have you even talked to Mitch's mother?"

Mitch nudged Raleigh with his foot. He did not want his mother dragged into this.

Raleigh ignored his hint. "Mr. Delacroix maintains he was home in bed less than an hour after the surveillance video was taken, because he had to work the next day. His mother could corroborate this."

Or she could throw him to the wolves. Mitch wasn't close to his mom and had no way of knowing whether she would try to help him, or hammer nails into his coffin by making him look like a liar.

"An hour isn't much time to joyride," Raleigh continued, "have an argument, shoot someone, dispose of the body and the car, and arrive home to kiss your mother good-night."

The cop leaned back in his chair, as if bored by Raleigh's arguments. "Well, now, she was probably questioned after the car theft, if sonny-boy here tried to use her as an alibi. At the time, she might have said what time he came home. But all of that information is gone now. Expunged. Destroyed."

"You and I both know you never really throw that stuff away," Raleigh argued.

Addlestein shrugged helplessly.

Great. Getting his arrest record expunged was supposed to help Mitch. Now it was biting him in the butt.

"What about Larry?" Mitch asked suddenly.

"Who?" Raleigh and the detective asked at the same time.

"Crazy Larry. He was with us that night."

The cop suddenly looked more alert. "First I've heard of it."

"I never mentioned it before because I didn't want to drag him into the car theft thing. And, let's face it, being a known associate of Crazy Larry wasn't likely to help me twelve years ago. But now it could."

"You're talking about Larry Montague."

"Yeah, that's him. You should talk to him. He was with Robby after I went home. And if he knew something, even if he just saw something, it's not likely he would have gone voluntarily to the police."

Addlestein scribbled something on his pad. "Last I knew, Larry Montague was homeless. He floats in and out of the area. I'll talk to him—if I can find him."

"I can locate him," Mitch said. "It's what I'm good at." Addlestein knew that. He'd been a young detective on the force when Mitch had worked for the CBPD. "Give me his full name and his social and I'll find him."

"I can do that, but I doubt you'll have any luck tracing him by computer. I'm betting the guy flies under the wire. Off the grid."

As most homeless people did. But it was worth a try. Even homeless people left traces in cyberspace from time to time—arrest records, usually, but sometimes admissions information in hospitals or homeless shelters.

"Is there anything else?" Raleigh asked. "Because if not, we have things to do."

Addlestein pursed his lips and ran his palm over his silver crew cut. He didn't want to let Mitch go, but it seemed pretty obvious he didn't have enough to hold him. Score one for the good guys. Mitch couldn't wait to get out of this place and breathe some fresh air.

He would take Raleigh and Beth out for a late lunch, and they could be home by nightfall. It was nice of them to work so hard to exonerate him. He was lucky to work for a company that appreciated not just the contributions he made to the bottom line, but valued him as a person.

If the Conch & Crab was still open, he'd take them there. Freshest seafood in all of South Louisiana and a jukebox filled with 1970s—

"Excuse me, Lieutenant Addlestein?" A young

female uniformed cop was at the door. "Could you step out here a moment?"

Looking impatient, Addlestein did as the woman asked. He was gone several minutes.

"I don't like this," Raleigh said after a long, uncomfortable silence among the three of them. "He was about to cut you loose."

Mitch didn't like it, either. A persistent itch had started at the base of his spine, a visceral, instinctual cue that told him something wasn't right.

When the door opened and Addlestein returned, he wore a smug grin. Bad news was coming.

"Seems that stolen Monte Carlo was located. Sunk in the bayou about a hunnert yards from where Robby's body was buried. And guess what was found in the glove box?"

"We're not here to play guessing games," Raleigh said tartly. "What?"

"A .22 handgun."

"What caliber bullet killed Robby?" Beth immediately asked.

"That's unknown. Cause of death couldn't be determined. But a hole in the skull suggested a gunshot wound. A jury won't care about that. The gun was rusted to hell, but they got a serial number off it and ran it through the database. Guess whose name came up?"

Mitch shrugged. "I never owned a gun in my life, so it can't be mine."

"Not yours. It belonged to Willard C. Bell."

It took a moment for the shock to sink in. Oh, Lord,

he was so screwed. He could hear the prison doors clanging shut and the key tinkling as it fell down a gutter.

"Who's that?" Beth asked.

"You want to tell them," Addlestein said, "or should I?"

"Willard C. Bell was my father."

BETH FELT HELPLESS and clueless as she watched two police officers put handcuffs on Mitch and take him away. If this was a nightmare for her, how must he be feeling?

He hadn't been able to offer any explanation for his father's gun ending up in the stolen car's glove box. He recalled that his dad had owned a couple of handguns along with a selection of shotguns and rifles for hunting, but he claimed not to have seen or even thought about his dad's guns in years.

"I never touched my dad's guns," Mitch had insisted. "Talk to my mom. She might know what happened to the guns. But my dad sure as hell never gave me a firearm. He always said I didn't have the temperament to own a gun."

Mitch's denial didn't hold much weight with the cops. They typed up a warrant immediately, and in a matter of minutes Mitch had been in custody.

"What now?" Beth had almost wailed when she and Raleigh had been left alone in the room. "Daniel will get him out, right? He can't stay in jail, he used to work for the police. It might not be safe—"

Raleigh cut her off with a glare, and Beth clamped

her mouth closed. They were still in an interrogation room; anyone could be listening, and probably was.

"Let's go," Raleigh said. "We have work to do."

She said nothing more until they were in the car. She started the engine and rolled down the windows of her Volvo. Though it was still early spring, the weather was already warm and muggy, the air fragrant with a mixture of magnolia, ocean and oil refinery like nowhere else in the world.

"Beth, how well do you really know Mitch?"

That was a very good question. "Until yesterday, I'd have said I knew him pretty well. I mean, we've worked together for five or six years, and the past few months we've even hung out after hours a few times. But I didn't know he had a half brother or an arrest record. I didn't know his parents were never married, which I guess they weren't if Mitch and his dad have different last names. I didn't know about the history of f-fighting."

"What do you talk about?" Raleigh asked.

"Well…nothing very personal, I guess. We talk shop. Computers and science and evidence, and true-crime books and TV shows. And pizza—we both have a thing for pizza. I knew he had family in Louisiana, but he never got specific."

Raleigh put the car in Reverse, but she didn't back out of the parking place. Beth could see the gears in her brain were turning.

"What are you getting at?" But Beth had an uncomfortable feeling she already knew.

"People can compartmentalize their lives. A guy can

be funny and kind at work, then go home and beat the crap out of his wife and kids every night. I've seen it."

"Oh, Raleigh." Beth was horrified at the direction of Raleigh's conversation. "You think he did it."

"I don't know what to think, except the evidence suddenly got pretty compelling. Think about it. Who had reason to sink that car in the bayou?"

"Someone who thought he could be tied to the car."

"Mitch might have known, or suspected, he'd been caught on video in the parking lot."

"But *anyone* trying to cover up the murder would have sunk the car, hoping everyone would believe Robby had left town," Beth pointed out, trying not to sound pathetically desperate. Just because she'd been crushing on Mitch for months, was she grasping at straws? Failing to see the obvious?

"I'm just trying to think like a prosecutor," Raleigh said. "I haven't written him off yet."

"But you think it's possible he did it."

"You don't?"

She took a deep breath. "No, Raleigh. Call it women's intuition or gut instinct—"

"—or wishful thinking?"

"No. At least, I don't think so. He rejected me. If anybody has an ax to grind, it's me. Whether Mitch is guilty or innocent, in jail or out, we'll never be together in…in that way. But I don't think he did it. I don't."

"Okay. Just checking. His arraignment and bail hearing are tomorrow morning. I'm sure Daniel will post the bond."

"Even when he hears about the gun?"

"Yes. Remember, Daniel is the man arrested for a murder he didn't commit, with his fingerprints all over the murder weapon. He knows physical evidence isn't the end of the story."

"I sure hope it isn't. What if they won't let him out on bond? Sometimes they don't, for a serious crime."

"We'll get him out somehow. Meanwhile, how do you feel about returning tomorrow with me to lovely Coot's Bayou?"

"I've got nothing pressing," Beth said. Cassie could cover the bases tomorrow. "But why do you need me?"

"Frankly...I need you to deal with Mitch. You have a way of getting through to him, and he seems to be on his best behavior when you're around."

"If you think so."

"Good, it's settled. Meanwhile, I'll need to find Mitch another lawyer. While I'm flattered by his faith in me, and I'm licensed to practice in Louisiana, I think he needs someone local who knows which cops and judges are corrupt."

"You're thinking of bribing someone?" Beth asked, only half kidding.

"Beth, of course not. I want to know which might have already been bribed, who owes favors to whom, that sort of thing. This whole affair smells like something is going on behind the scenes. Grudges, revenge, you know."

"Agreed. First place we should look for a grudge is Mitch's half brother. He seemed way too complacent about his brother's arrest." Sergeant Dwayne Bell hadn't been involved directly in Mitch's interrogation—that wouldn't be kosher even in a backwater town like Coot's Bayou. But he'd been hanging around, lurking.

"You know who would give some background on that situation? Mitch's mother. Let's go pay her a friendly visit. She might want to know her son is in jail."

"MYRA? SOMEONE HERE to see you."

The man who answered the door was neatly dressed in pressed khakis and a plaid shirt, and he looked mildly annoyed to be bothered by strangers in the middle of the afternoon. A black Labrador retriever mix hid behind his master's leg, peeking out and looking worried.

Mitch's mother lived on the outskirts of town on a little piece of land that backed up to a creek. It was kind of pretty, especially this time of year when everything was green and blooming.

The small house was run-down. It had once been painted white with brown trim, but it desperately needed a new coat of paint. The roof appeared to be patched and repatched, and several boards on the creaky front porch were rotted.

But someone had tried to make the place homey. A huge pot of blooming geraniums sat near the front steps, and a morning glory vine added a note of cheerfulness to the sagging porch railing. The front door sported a straw wreath festooned with small wooden ducks and bunnies peeking out from silk flowers.

From the little Beth had gathered during Mitch's interrogation, she knew he'd grown up pretty poor.

The woman who appeared at the door looked too old to be Mitch's mother. Her shoulder-length hair had been dyed reddish-gold, but a good inch of brown and gray roots had grown out. She wore a garish shade of orange lipstick, and her low-cut blouse and tight jeans were less than flattering.

Her shoulders slumped in that peculiar way of people who had lost any enthusiasm they once had for living.

The man lingered nearby. Mitch had made no mention of a stepfather in the picture, but these two appeared to be a couple.

"I'm Myra LeBeau. Can I help you with something?"

LeBeau, not Delacroix. This man probably was her husband, then. Beth and Raleigh introduced themselves and explained that they worked with Mitch at Project Justice.

Myra, no idiot, immediately guessed there was a problem. Her hand fluttered at her breast. "Has something happened to Mitch?"

"I'm sorry to have to tell you this, but he's in jail."

Myra actually looked relieved. "In jail. Oh, thank goodness. I thought you were going to tell me he was dead. I mean, jail's not good, of course… Won't you come in? It's warm for this time of year. I'll get you some iced tea."

They stepped into the creaky little house, and Myra showed them into her small kitchen and asked them to sit down. "So what trouble has Mitch gotten himself into this time? I thought we were past all that, but some boys never grow up. His daddy sure didn't." A surliness entered her voice at the mention of Willard Bell, but by the time she brought glasses of tall, sweetened tea to the table, her smile was firmly in place.

The husband, who hadn't bothered to introduce himself, had returned to the living room, where he was watching a game show on TV. Apparently a grown stepson in jail wasn't his concern.

"So what'd he do?" she asked again.

"He didn't do anything," Beth said, a note of challenge creeping into her voice, but Raleigh shot her a warning look and she clamped her mouth closed.

"There's no easy way to say this, Mrs. LeBeau. He's been arrested for murder. They think he killed Robby Racine."

Myra, halfway to joining them at the table, fell the rest of the way into her chair, a hand to her mouth stifling a gasp. A genuine reaction, Beth thought, though she was no body language expert.

"I heard about the body they found on my land…it was Robby?"

Raleigh nodded. "He was killed soon after he and Mitch stole a car together. Probably that same night."

"Why do they think it was Mitch? He and Robby were friends! There's no way—*no way* my baby would do something like that. And, anyway, all those years ago, I didn't own that land. It belonged to my great-aunt, Robby's grandmother. Robby and Mitch were second cousins."

"So the land was connected to Robby, not Mitch." Raleigh pulled her phone out of her pocket and made a few quick notes. "That's one damning piece of evidence we can easily discount."

Beth couldn't stand it anymore. "Mrs. LeBeau, Mitch's father owned some guns. Do you know what happened to them?"

At the mention of guns, Myra's demeanor changed dramatically. She sat up straighter and started fidgeting with a paper napkin. "I don't know. I'm sure I don't know. I never touched his guns." She looked over her shoulder at her husband, still watching TV. "Davy! Do you know what happened to Willard's guns?"

"I have no clue," he answered in a deadpan. "Never saw 'em."

"Do you own any firearms yourself, Mrs. LeBeau?" Raleigh asked casually.

"No, ma'am. No guns."

"If you don't remember what happened to Willard's guns, how can you be so sure you don't still have them around somewhere?" Beth asked.

Myra's eyes narrowed. "After Willard died, I cleaned this house top to bottom. I'm sure if there'd been any guns, I'd have noticed them. Are you here to help Mitch? 'Cause you don't sound that helpful."

"We're on his side, I promise," Beth said. "The police are going to want to know about the guns."

Myra settled back into her chair. "I wish I could help, but I just have no idea."

"Did Mitch know how to use a gun?"

"His daddy tried to teach him to shoot. You grow

up around here, you learn how to hunt and that's that. Every boy does. That doesn't mean anything. Mitch never took to it and Willard gave up."

"Okay." Raleigh set her iced tea to the side and blotted her mouth with the paper napkin she'd been using as a coaster. "We appreciate your time, Mrs. LeBeau."

"Thank you for telling me about Mitch," she said a little stiffly. "Lord knows he wouldn't go out of his way to tell me anything. Have they set his bail?"

"The hearing is tomorrow morning at nine. It would be good if you could be there. They might deny bail, given the seriousness of the crime. But if we show the judge he has a supportive family, that he's not a flight risk, it might help."

Myra cast a worried glance toward her husband. "I'll try to come."

They said their goodbyes and returned to Raleigh's car.

"What did you think?" Beth asked. "I mean, that was weird, huh? Your wife is being questioned by a couple of strangers, one of them a lawyer, and you just sit in the living room watching TV?"

"And did you see the way she got all nervous when I brought up the guns? She knows something."

"Maybe her husband did it. He was trying to move in on Myra, and he wanted the stepson out of the way, so he framed Mitch for murder."

Raleigh thought about that, then shook her head. "If someone had been trying to frame Mitch, they wouldn't have worked so hard to hide the body. Still, we'll have to find out how long Davy's been in the picture."

"She's not going to be a big help," Beth said with a sigh.

"No. She's not happy her son is in jail, but there's something just a little off about her reaction."

"She didn't ask enough questions," Beth pointed out. "If I had a son, and I found out he was in jail, I'd be bouncing off the walls trying to find out details and figuring out how to get him released. She didn't even ask how Robby died."

"She'd already heard about the body," Raleigh reasoned. "She might have known it was a suspected gunshot. As for her reaction to Mitch's arrest...it's possible she doesn't care."

"How could she not care about her own son?"

"We know nothing about their relationship," Raleigh said. "Maybe Mitch can shed some light on things."

CHAPTER FOUR

THE COOT'S BAYOU courthouse wasn't much to look at outside—a cinder-block building covered in coat after coat of beige paint. Apparently it was a popular target for graffiti, because a fresh set of gang tags had eluded the paint roller on this muggy Wednesday morning.

The inside was even less judicial—a room reminiscent of a church basement with metal chairs and folding tables. The magistrate, a jowly man with a bright red comb-over, wore a scuffed black leather jacket instead of robes.

The prosecutor had already said his piece, arguing that bail should be denied.

"Your Honor." Mitch's newly hired defense lawyer, a young, earnest man named Buck Michoux, cleared his throat. Raleigh had put him in charge of speaking at the hearing because judges were sometimes more favorably inclined to a hometown boy than they were some strange woman lawyer from the big city. "My client is a law-abiding citizen with a good job and family in the area. We request that he be released on his own recognizance."

The judge rolled his eyes. "If I had a sense of humor, I'd laugh. Mr. Delacroix was booked for murder, son.

Bail is hereby set at two million dollars. An additional condition of bail is that Mr. Delacroix cannot travel outside of Bernadette Parish." He pounded his gavel.

Mitch breathed a sigh of relief. At least they were willing to let him out. Two million dollars was an appalling bail, but Raleigh had assured him Daniel would cover it no matter how ridiculous. It was hard to feel lucky in his situation, but he sure was lucky to have a boss who had faith in him despite the evidence.

Mitch still wore yesterday's clothes. The Coot's Bayou Jail wasn't exactly the Ritz. He hadn't been allowed to shower or shave or brush his teeth, and the meals they'd served had as much appeal as warmed-over roadkill.

The bailiff handcuffed him and prepared to escort him back to his cell, across the street.

"Is that necessary?"

Mitch groaned inwardly. Beth. She'd proved herself useful during the interrogation, speaking with confidence and authority to Lieutenant Addlestein when it came to matters of evidence. But why was she still here?

He'd rather spend another week in jail than have her see him like this.

"Standard procedure with any felony suspect," the bailiff said, unconcerned as he gave the handcuffs an extra twist. Mitch winced.

"Beth, what are you doing here?"

"Working on getting you out of jail. Permanently."

The bailiff made a noise that sounded suspiciously like a snicker.

"Don't you have other work? Other innocent people you can save with your microscope and test tubes?"

Beth shrank back a bit. She looked hurt by his dismissive words, and he felt a pang of guilt. "Daniel says you're a priority." Her voice was so soft he could barely hear it, reflecting nothing of yesterday's confidence. "If our positions were reversed, you'd be working just as hard to get me free, wouldn't you?"

"No one would ever accuse you of murder. The whole idea is ludicrous."

"I suppose I should take that as a compliment." She appeared anything but flattered.

"Time to go." The bailiff grabbed his arm and dragged him toward the exit. Physically, the guy was no match for Mitch. Mitch found himself imagining how he'd take the guy out. A simple ducking maneuver, an elbow to the gut, a knee to the face and he'd be down for the count.

"You'll be free soon," Beth called after him. "Try not to worry."

Yeah. Right. Louisiana was a death penalty state, and the judicial system in Bernadette Parish was so crooked, he couldn't count on an acquittal no matter what kind of evidence Project Justice came up with.

But Beth was good. She and Raleigh would give these good ol' boys a run for their money. And when it was all over, if by chance he was a free man, he'd be lucky if Daniel let him keep his job after the trouble he'd caused for Project Justice. He was pretty sure Beth would never look at him the same way again.

He'd started to really enjoy their time together, to

count on it, even. But after this was over, she would probably cross the street to avoid speaking to him. He was in for a long and ugly fight, one that was likely to consume him. One that he might not win. He might go to hell for a lot of reasons, but involving sweet Beth in this mess wasn't one of them.

The bailiff put Mitch back into the same stinking holding cell in which he'd spent the night, and he sat there for another hideous three hours. What the hell was taking so long? Though coming up with two million dollars wasn't something that happened in ten minutes, if Daniel had made the decision to bail an employee out of jail, he would make things happen quickly. So either Mitch should get out, or they should take him to Bernadette Parish lockup, where prisoners awaiting trial were kept.

At least there he would get a shower and a clean jumpsuit.

His cell mate, with the unlikely name of Canthus, had been affable last night when they'd thrown him in here because he'd been drunk. Now he was good and sober…and mean. He'd already taken a swing at Mitch, and the only thing that had prevented Mitch from flattening the guy like a roach was a reluctance to add more charges to his record.

Canthus was currently crouched in a corner, twisting a dreadlock. "You gonna make bail?" he asked, apparently having forgotten their argument of ten minutes ago over who got to sit on what bench.

"I don't know yet. You?" He didn't even know what Canthus was in for.

"Naw, no one'll bail me out. A few days would be okay, if they feed me. But I'd seriously rather sleep under a bridge."

Mitch hadn't seen any signs of food this morning, and he was getting pretty hungry. Didn't prisoners have rights? Then something Canthus had said sank in. "You homeless, man?"

Canthus straightened his spine and stared at Mitch with dead, obsidian eyes. "You want to make something of it? I suppose you live in a mansion on the shores of Lake Pontchartrain."

"I didn't mean anything," Mitch said affably. He had no desire to duck any more punches by the increasingly sober man. "I was just wondering if you might know a guy used to be a friend of mine. Larry."

"Just Larry?"

That's all Mitch had ever called him. But Addlestein had mentioned Larry's last name...Montford? No, Montague. "Larry Montague. I used to hang with him. Back then we called him Crazy Larry 'cause he'd do anything for a laugh. Scrawny guy, long blond, curly hair, real pale skin. He has a tat on his upper arm of a snake and a heart."

Mitch remembered the night Larry had gotten the tattoo, on his twenty-first birthday. Mitch, only sixteen, had watched in fascination as the needle had puckered Larry's skin, and marveled at how Larry hadn't even winced.

Suddenly the light of recognition dawned in Canthus's eyes. "That Larry! He is crazy. Saw that guy jump off a railroad trestle once when we was running from the cops."

That sounded like Larry. "You happen to know where he is?"

Canthus shook his head. "No, man, ain't seen him for months. He might've said he was going to New Orleans for the winter. Huh, kinda stupid. It's not much warmer there than here in the winter."

If Larry had gone away for the winter, that meant he might be returning soon. "If you see him, do you think you could let me know? I really need to talk to the dude." Mitch pulled a card out of his pocket. He always kept a few there, though he seldom needed them since his work usually kept him at the office, behind a computer.

"You work for Project Justice? I've seen those dudes on TV, man. At Brewskies, they're always watching those crime shows on the TV over the bar. You got it made, man. Hey, think they could get me off? I'm looking at sixty days."

"I can't make any promises, but if you find Larry for me, I'll see what we can do."

"That'd be cool, man." Canthus started cleaning his nails with the corner of Mitch's business card.

Mitch didn't hold out much hope. How would Canthus locate Larry from jail?

Finally, the bailiff returned. "Looks like you got some friends in high places."

"I made bail?" Praise be.

"Yeah, but there's a small complication. Remember, the judge said you had to stay in Bernadette Parish?"

"Sure, no problem." Once he was out of this place, he would worry about how to get around that rule. He'd get Raleigh to talk to the judge again. Maybe the judge would remand him into Raleigh's custody. Or Beth's.

No, not Beth's. He gave himself a swift mental kick, but that didn't stop a forbidden fantasy from popping to mind involving handcuffs and a riding crop. He ruthlessly squelched it. Beth wasn't that kind of girl.

"See, the thing is, the judge won't just take your word for it. So you have to be fitted with a monitor." The bailiff got the cell door unlocked, but Mitch just stood there.

"You gotta be kidding me. Where am I going to stay? I don't live here anymore."

"You got kin here, right?"

"I'm sure as hell not staying at my brother's house." He'd rather be thrown into a cold dungeon and starved than endure living under the same roof as Dwayne and Linda. Dwayne was bad enough, but Linda—she had obsessive-compulsive disorder. Dwayne's high school sweetheart freaked out if she couldn't count her French fries before eating them. Mitch could remember her making Dwayne clean her hubcaps with a toothbrush.

The bailiff shrugged. "All I know is they got something worked out."

Ten minutes later, Mitch was the proud wearer of a black cuff around his ankle that appeared to be made of Kryptonite—indestructible and designed to rat him out if he tried to tamper with it.

"The cuff is equipped with a GPS signal that will report your exact location to a monitoring center," Raleigh explained. Beth, who for unknown reasons was still hanging out in Coot's Bayou, sat nearby watching somberly. They were in a small conference room at police headquarters, where they had cuffed him to a chair while the technician from the monitoring company did his thing.

"If you set foot outside Bernadette Parish," Raleigh continued to explain, "the police have the right to arrest you and return you to jail to await trial."

"This completely sucks," Mitch objected. "I have to be able to move around. I have things to do. Obligations."

"If you're worried about work, don't be. Daniel is having your entire computer system moved down here so you can telecommute."

"From where? Where exactly is it that I'm supposed to stay? Do I rent an apartment? Stay in a motel? And who's paying for that?" He had a sinking feeling Raleigh hadn't told him the worst news. "What?"

"You'll stay at your mother's house, of course. It looks good, shows you've got support, and it'll save you some money."

Horrified, Mitch shook his head. "There's no way. We don't get along, and anyway, she'd never agree."

Beth picked that moment to speak up. "She already has."

This just got worse and worse. "Aw, now, why did you have to go and get her involved?"

"Did you want her to hear about your arrest on the news?" Beth asked. "We talked to her. She's anxious to help any way she can."

"Yeah? I didn't see her at the bail hearing. And what about Davy? Was he anxious?"

"He was agreeable to the arrangement," Beth said. "They both want to help."

The technician checked that the cuff was working, and left. Raleigh left, too, mumbling something about signing out with the bailiff. Finally it was just Mitch and Beth in the room, staring at each other.

"Beth, what are you still doing here?"

"You were the one who wanted me here," she said coolly.

"Yeah, when I thought I was just going to answer a few questions. Don't you have work to do?"

"This *is* my work. I need to be there while they're processing the car, the gun—"

"Good luck with that." The Bernadette Parish crime lab wouldn't let her within five hundred feet of their precious evidence, not until they were good and done with it—which meant making anything that didn't support their case disappear. Then, if she wanted to run her own tests, Raleigh would have to file requests with the court, a process that could take weeks.

"You don't want me hanging around." She studied her fingernails with great interest. "That's obvious. But you're not going to scare me away by acting like a jerk. This is work. It has nothing to do with…with our personal relationship. Which we don't have anyway."

Beth's face flushed to a lovely shell-pink as her argument wound down.

What the hell was she talking about? "So you're no

longer my friend?" he asked, just to be sure he understood. "We're just associates now?"

"I'm not sure we *can* be friends," she said glumly. "When a line is crossed…well, I could have just left things alone, but I didn't and I ruined everything."

"*You* ruined it?" What the *hell* was she talking about? "Sorry, I'm confused."

"Can we not talk about this?" she pleaded.

"Talk about what?" Why were women so confusing? Why didn't she just spit out what was bothering her?

"I just want to make sure you understand that I'm here only because Daniel asked me to stay on top of things. I'm not trying to…change your mind."

He gave up demanding that she clarify; his questions were getting monotonous. When faced with an unreasonable female, his strategy was to agree. Saved a lot of unproductive arguing.

"Okay," he said, offering up a smile.

With a frustrated sigh, she turned and exited the room, and Mitch couldn't help appreciating the way her sassy little butt twitched back and forth with each tap of her heel on the hard vinyl floor.

He racked his brain to figure out what was stuck in her craw. Maybe she was so repulsed by the things she'd learned about him recently that she really didn't want to be friends.

That was a depressing thought.

But she said it was a line *she'd* crossed, not him. What had she done recently regarding… Wait a minute. The zydeco concert. She'd offered him her extra ticket, and she'd acted kind of strange when she did it, standing in the doorway whispering with Raleigh.

Was it possible she had asked him out on a *date?* And he'd just blown her off like it was no big deal. He'd even suggested Billy Cantu could take the extra ticket. As if he was trying to fix her up or something.

Beth had made it pretty clear she wasn't interested in dating at this point in her life. She'd even told him outright that she liked having male companionship without the drama of romance and sex.

Had she changed her mind?

For a few moments, he let himself fantasize about what it would be like to not just sleep with Beth, but to date her, to have the new dimension of romance and sex added to their budding friendship.

He'd never had a girlfriend like her. The girls he dated tended to be rough around the edges and interested more in "hooking up" than having a real relationship. They weren't easily offended or shocked, and they didn't expect to be wooed with flowers and sweet words. Not that Beth hadn't seen and heard her share of harsh things, given that she'd worked CSI at the Houston P.D. But she had an air of vulnerability about her, especially since her problem with Vince.

Beth was someone who needed to be treated gently. Could he do that?

Then he snapped back to reality. It wasn't a possibility. Maybe she had taken that first step of asking him out, but that was before the manure hit the fan. Now, she wouldn't touch him wearing plastic gloves and a gas mask. She was just getting over that macho jerk who'd beat her up. A computer geek probably sounded like a nice, safe companion. But a car thief/murder suspect whom she witnessed beating the crap out of his punching bag to the point of injuring himself?

Not likely.

He'd seen the look on her face when Dwayne had all but accused him of murder. She wouldn't date someone she thought was a violent criminal. He'd lost any chance with Beth, and maybe that was for the best. For her, anyway. She deserved better than a former hell-raiser-turned-computer-geek with a pedigree as refined as that of a mongrel dog.

Depressing as that reality was, he had another problem to deal with. How was he going to get to his cage fight in Houston Friday night without getting himself thrown back in jail?

CHAPTER FIVE

"YOU'RE PROBABLY USED to something a little nicer, but you spent a lot of years sleeping in this room." Mitch's mom stood aside to allow Mitch into his childhood bedroom.

Memories flooded back as he took in the music posters, everything from Bon Jovi to Eminem to—yes, that was Britney Spears. At sixteen, he'd thought she was pretty hot.

His gaze bounced from the faded rag rug to the blue corduroy bedspread adorning his old twin bed. Memories surged, making his skin prickle. He'd been sixteen and desperate to be free of this place where his father had treated him with less consideration than he'd given his hunting dogs. Mitch's gut churned, and he struggled a moment to control his feelings.

Beth and Raleigh had given him a ride from the police station to his mother's house and were sipping iced tea in the living room. He had to hold on to his civilized facade at least a while longer.

He opened a dresser drawer and saw that some of his old clothes were still there. "Mom, why didn't you get rid of all this stuff?"

She shrugged. "I guess I always figured you'd come

to visit. If I threw all your stuff out…you might have thought I didn't care about you."

His stomach clenched again. He felt lower than a crawdad's toe. His mom had a knack for making him feel guilty. He hadn't felt he owed her anything after he moved out. She'd never once taken his side against his dad. But apparently his lengthy absences from her life had caused her pain.

"I guess I should have come back to see you more, especially after Dad died."

"I don't blame you, Mitchell," she said softly, then suddenly became brisk. "I can clear out all this old stuff. I imagine you have your own new clothes you'd like to wear. Did you bring them with you? What about your toothbrush and such?"

"My boss is having my car driven down here, and a suitcase full of clothes." Daniel's new assistant, Elena, was packing up a few things for him. "Then if I need anything I can go out and buy it. Don't worry about the room," he added. "I'll sort through all this stuff while I'm here."

He would probably have plenty of time. It might be weeks before the district attorney filed formal charges against him, then more weeks, maybe months, before a trial, if it came to that.

"I'll get you towels and a fresh bar of soap, at least." His mom turned and bustled down the hall, seeming happy for an excuse to do something for him.

Mitch sat on the bed and, taking advantage of some rare solitude, took stock of his situation.

He hadn't felt this helpless since he was a kid. From

the first time he left home, he'd arranged his life with freedom in mind. He'd never had a serious girlfriend because that meant obligations, and having to take someone else's wants and needs into consideration. His house, his job and his fighting were the only real commitments he had. He could walk away from any of those, if he wanted to. Even the fighting, he could quit once he'd honored the short-term contracts he'd signed.

Now, here he was living at home again, and he couldn't set foot outside the parish. He couldn't even call Robby and go joyriding to burn off his energy. Robby was dead.

That fact was one of the hardest to escape. He'd always pictured Robby down in Mexico, maybe working on a boat or selling souvenirs on the beach and flirting with tourists, when all this time he'd been dead.

Mitch might end up that way, too—a lot sooner than expected—if he didn't figure a way out of this murder charge. Raleigh and Beth wanted to have a strategy session before they headed back home.

He supposed he better get to it.

He found the two women downstairs in the living room making small talk with Davy. Davy was an okay guy, Mitch supposed. He treated Mitch's mother a lot better than Willard had. Willard hadn't even bothered to marry Myra. But Davy didn't take to strangers very quickly and preferred his own company to anyone else's. When they'd arrived a few minutes ago he'd been in the backyard nailing up some new siding, and he probably was ready to get back to it.

Mitch was surprised that Davy was making the effort, but maybe he was doing it for Myra.

When Beth caught sight of Mitch, she hopped to her feet. "All set?" She didn't seem angry anymore, just a little nervous.

"I'm good. Let's sit outside at the picnic table," he suggested, both for privacy's sake, and because the air would be fresher. His mom didn't have air-conditioning, and the temperature was climbing outside.

A few minutes later the three of them—Beth, Raleigh and Mitch—were seated at the worn redwood picnic table shaded by an ancient pecan tree. Myra had brought them a plate of store-bought sandwich cookies, which Mitch thought was kind of funny. His mom had never been much of a hostess, but he supposed every good Southern woman felt obligated to feed and water visitors, even if this wasn't a social occasion.

"So, here's the deal, Mitch," Raleigh said, getting down to business. "Right now, we don't know where to focus this investigation. We can try to find Larry Montague—he seems our best lead. But the chances of finding him seem slim."

"Soon as I have my computer, I'm all over that," Mitch said. "I'll find him. A guy I talked to in the jail knows him and thinks he might be in New Orleans." There was an online message board dedicated to homeless people, where they could check in so their friends and loved ones wouldn't worry. He could post a message there, and someone who'd seen Larry might reply or pass word to him.

"Meanwhile," Raleigh continued, "we should pursue other leads. We need to come up with a theory as to what really happened to Robby. Mitch, you knew him better than anyone. Who might have wanted him dead?"

Mitch blew out a breath. "I've been thinking about that. Robby tended to piss off a lot of people."

"I need names," Raleigh said.

"He had a girlfriend, Amanda Ludlow. She was always jealous, thinking he was flirting with other girls—and he was. Maybe she shot him in a jealous rage."

Raleigh wrote furiously. "Age?"

"She'd be late twenties by now. Then there was a guy who used to fence stuff for Robby. He got himself arrested, and the cops questioned Robby. Maybe the fence thought Robby was going to testify against him."

"Name?" Raleigh asked.

"We called him Studs. But I can locate him, don't worry. I'll find all these people, and you can talk to them."

"Did Robby know the owner of the stolen car?" Beth asked suddenly.

Interesting question. No one had thought about that before. Mitch tried to remember what had led him and Robby to boost that particular car. "I think he did know who it belonged to." A vague memory stirred. "A neighbor, or a friend of his mother's. Robby knew somehow they kept the spare key under the mat. If you'll get me the car's license plate, I'll add that to my list of stuff to check out."

An angry crime victim could have taken matters into his own hands. It was a long shot, but worth at least checking in to.

"We're looking not just for a murder motive," Beth said, "but a motive for framing you, Mitch. So who, twelve years ago, had a grudge against *you?* And who could have gotten hold of your father's gun and planted it?"

"It doesn't make sense, someone trying to frame me," Mitch said. "Why would they have hidden the evidence so thoroughly that it wouldn't be found for twelve years?"

"Maybe the murderer thought the crime would come to light long before it did," Beth said. "Humor me, just in case. Who didn't like you?"

Did he even want to go there? He shrugged one shoulder. "Half the people in town."

"Think you could narrow it down to the top ten or twenty?" Beth sounded more than exasperated, but he was only telling the truth.

"I was a punk kid, angry at the world. I treated everyone like hell—kids at school, girlfriends, people at work. But I think we're on the wrong track here. My dad could have given that gun to anyone. He had a lot of gun-totin' buddies. Or it could have been stolen. Or someone could have been trying to frame *him,* for all we know."

"Don't forget," Beth said, lowering her voice, "that Myra acted a little strange when we asked her about Willard's guns."

He lifted his knee and placed his foot on the picnic

bench so he could examine the monitoring cuff. It was made of what looked like black, waterproof Gore-Tex. It housed a GPS locator chip and a radio transmitter, which communicated Mitch's location every five minutes or so to a monitoring center. If he strayed beyond the limits of Bernadette Parish, it would set off an alarm at the monitoring center, someone would call the cops, and he would be in deeper trouble than he already was.

The bracelet also had a body-mass indicator, so that if it were removed, the monitoring center would be notified.

But this wasn't the latest, greatest model. It was worn and frayed, as if many a prisoner or parolee had worn it. The bracelet was connected to his leg via two industrial-strength rivets.

If Mitch could get those rivets detached and remove the bracelet without disconnecting any wires... But he would have to get another person about his size to wear it while he was gone. And he somehow doubted his mom or Davy would line up to try it. Hell, even if they would, he wasn't enough of a jerk to ask them to commit a crime and go to jail for him.

"But there must be some standouts," Raleigh insisted, pulling Mitch back into the conversation. "I hate to bring this up, but what about your half brother? He certainly would have had access to your father's guns."

"Mr. Law-and-Order?" Mitch laughed at the very idea. "He's not a rule breaker. True, we aren't all warm and fuzzy. But I can't see him launching some elaborate plot to frame me for murder. He doesn't have the brains or the guts. Or the patience to wait twelve years for the payoff."

"Was there a falling-out between you two?" Beth asked.

Mitch didn't want to talk about this. It wasn't pertinent.

"It might be important," Beth said, obviously sensing his reluctance. "Raleigh and I can be objective where you can't."

He sighed. "No, there wasn't a falling-out. Dwayne and I just never got along. Our dad left Dwayne and his mother to be with me and my mom when I was born, and Dwayne always resented me for it. Like it was my fault. Hell, I'd have been happy to give him back."

"So Dwayne never had much of a relationship with your father?"

"He had a better relationship than I did, for sure," Mitch said. "Dad spent more time with Dwayne. Every weekend, practically, they would go hunting or camping, or Dad would go teach him how to throw a ball or fix a car."

"And he didn't teach you those things?"

"What I learned of fixing stuff, I picked up on my own. And I never could throw a ball or shoot worth a damn. I was into computers, which my dad thought was sissy crap."

"Could your dad have killed Robby?" Raleigh asked suddenly.

Wouldn't that be ironic, one last way the old man could get to Mitch. Kill his best friend, then let him take the fall. Was that why his mom had been so nervous? Did she know something?

"I wouldn't put it past him. He was a mean son of a bitch." When Willard died suddenly a few years ago, Mitch hadn't even attended the funeral. He couldn't force himself to grieve for the man. His mom had said it would "look bad" if he didn't show up, but Mitch was long past caring about appearances.

"Mitch, stop fussing with that ankle cuff," Raleigh said. "They're impossible to cheat."

Hah. Impossible for most people. But how hard could it be to hack into the monitoring center's computers and set up some kind of false signal?

He lowered his foot back to the ground, then stood and stretched. "All this talk is getting us nowhere. We need to be out doing something."

"Like what?" Beth asked. "To investigate, we have to follow leads. We need to locate these people you've given us first."

"Why don't we try to find the murder scene?" Mitch asked. "I know something the cops don't. I know where Robby might have headed that night, if he'd chickened out about going to Mexico."

"Where?" Raleigh asked, pen poised to take notes.

"I can't tell you. I'll have to show you. The place doesn't exactly have a street address."

"Let's go, then." Beth was on her feet, apparently as anxious to do something proactive as he was. But all three of them froze in their tracks as a Coot's Bayou squad car pulled into the driveway. What now? Had the cops found even more trumped-up evidence? Were they going to change their minds and drag him to jail after all?

BETH HELD HER BREATH as the squad car came to a stop. Why couldn't the police leave Mitch alone? How was he supposed to prove his innocence if they harassed him like this?

When the car's engine stilled and the door opened, it turned out to be Dwayne Bell, Mitch's half brother, and every muscle in Beth's body tensed.

Dwayne and Mitch didn't look much alike. They were both tall, around six feet or so, but where Mitch was lean and mean, Dwayne could only be described as beefy. He had a good thirty pounds on his brother.

His hair was darker than Mitch's, too, and cut military short. His hairline receded slightly, but he was still the sort of guy some women swooned over—G.I. Joe-handsome, straight backed, dark, penetrating eyes, serious expression.

"Oh, shit," Mitch muttered. "What the hell is he doing here?"

"Sergeant Bell," Raleigh said in her reserved, lawyer voice. "If you want to speak to my client, we'd be happy to come to the police station for another formal interview."

"This isn't an official visit," Dwayne said, his gaze flickering toward Mitch, then back to Raleigh as he approached. "I'm off duty, and I'm here as a family member, not a cop."

"Family, my ass," Mitch said, still speaking under his breath. Only Beth could hear.

She shot him a warning look. If he was going to fight with his brother, he could damn well do it some other time.

Louder, Mitch asked, "Why are you really here, Dwayne?"

"Look, Mitch, I know we've had our quarrels. We'll never be best friends. But Daddy would be real disappointed if I stood by and let my associates railroad you into jail."

"You didn't seem to mind when your friends were interrogating me. You were practically crowing."

"I admit it, I thought it was funny that you were being questioned about Robby's death. I wanted you to get hassled a bit. You always had a way of squirming out of trouble when you were a kid, and I figured this was payback for all the times you *should* have been arrested and you weren't.

"But, Mitch, I swear, I did not think they would arrest you. When that car and the gun turned up I 'bout fell out of my chair. I know you didn't kill Robby. You might have been a pain in the ass, and you might have punched in a face or two, but you never would have messed with Daddy's guns."

"Fine," Mitch said. "I appreciate the vote of confidence."

"I'm not just offering moral support. My colleagues rushed to arrest you pretty damn fast. We haven't even considered other suspects. I gather that's what your Project Justice buddies are here to do—investigate the crime as it should be investigated, turning over every rock, interviewing every potential witness or suspect, all things a small city police force can't do on its tiny budget."

"So you're offering..."

"I can at least verify that no evidence is mishandled and no witnesses are unduly influenced."

"Mighty friendly of you." Mitch's eyes glittered dangerously. "But we don't need a cop looking over our shoulder, trying to trip us up."

Dwayne shook his head. "You are one bullheaded idiot, you know that?"

"Now if we're gonna get into name-calling—"

"Wait a minute, Mitch," Raleigh interrupted. "Dwayne has a point. One of the hurdles Project Justice often faces is the accusation of evidence tampering."

"That's right," Beth chimed in. "No matter how careful we are about maintaining chain of custody, there's always the suspicion that we planted or otherwise messed with physical evidence. If we have a police representative with us, he can verify that everything is on the up-and-up."

"And he could just as easily argue the opposite. He could claim he witnessed one of us tampering with a blood sample or coaching a witness."

A pained expression came over Dwayne's face. "Mitch, I would never do that. Come on."

Beth exchanged a look with Raleigh, who dealt on a daily basis with liars. Did she actually think Dwayne was sincere?

Raleigh gave a small nod. "Sorry, Mitch, but it's not up to you. I'm the lead on this investigation—you're the client. And I say we accept your brother's generous offer of help."

Mitch looked as if he wanted to spit bullets at

Dwayne, but he clamped his mouth shut, folded his arms and said nothing.

"Thanks, Ms. Shinn. Let me know what I can do to help. For starters, maybe I can look through the car theft file—if it's still around—and see if any other witnesses were questioned. I was just a green rookie on the force back then, but I remember the case."

"That would be helpful," Raleigh said. "But right now, we were headed to a location where Robby might have gone that night after he and Mitch parted ways. Mitch was going to take us there."

Dwayne raised a questioning eyebrow. "That old shack near Simmons Slough?"

"That's what I was thinking," Mitch said, loosening up a fraction. "That's where he'd go when he couldn't go home."

"Surely that place isn't even standing anymore," Dwayne said. "It was practically falling down twelve years ago when you kids used to have your drinking parties there."

"There must be something left of it," Beth said. "A foundation, a few bricks or timbers."

"It's worth a look." Raleigh gathered up her things.

"Mind if I ride with you?" Beth asked Dwayne. "Raleigh's backseat is a little cramped."

"Sure, no problem."

Mitch looked horrified. Probably didn't want her cozying up with the enemy. Maybe he thought Dwayne would poison Beth's mind against Mitch. But Beth wanted a few minutes alone with the stiff-backed cop.

She felt as though she was missing something; maybe Dwayne could fill in the gaps.

"So," she began pleasantly once she was in the front seat of the squad car, her portable evidence collection kit, which she brought with her everywhere she went, resting between her feet. "What was Mitch like as a kid?"

Dwayne didn't crack a smile. "Wild as they come. Hell-raiser, always in trouble at school, at home. He had a chip on his shoulder. I understand it better now than I did back then. He was trying to prove something, just like I was. We went about it in different ways, though."

Beth was a little surprised Dwayne had opened up so easily to her. But she often had that effect on some people. She was so utterly unintimidating, she supposed, that people felt safe with her.

"If he was such a hell-raiser, how did he end up working for the police department? Seems kind of a strange choice."

"Oh, it wasn't his choice. You obviously haven't heard the whole story." Dwayne let Raleigh's car take the lead, following her down the narrow, rutted lane where Myra lived. "After he got arrested for stealing the car, he managed to gain access to the police department computer and erase all evidence of the crime. One thing Mitch knows, and that's computers."

"He hacked into a police computer?" That took guts.

"Yeah. If computers ran our criminal justice system, he would have gotten away with it. Instead he just caused a huge headache for our IT people. They couldn't figure out how he got in. So he cut a deal—

the auto theft charges were put on hold, and in return he showed them his hacker secrets. He was so good, they ended up offering him a job in cyber security, and doing skip-tracing. He didn't really want to work for the police department, but with that felony charge hanging over his head, he couldn't say no."

Interesting. Daniel must have spotted Mitch's talent and buried those charges for good, gaining Mitch his freedom.

"Now it's my turn to ask questions. Why are you personally involved in trying to help Mitch? I understand you run the lab at Project Justice. You're not an investigator."

"I used to be CSI for the Houston P.D. My boss wants me to personally evaluate any physical evidence. Which reminds me—when will your lab finish with the car and the gun? And the body—we'd like our own forensic expert to examine Robby's remains."

"I'm not officially part of this case," Dwayne answered. "You'll have to ask Lieutenant Addlestein."

"Is there any possibility your presence during our investigation will be a detriment?" Beth asked. "Will they accuse you of planting evidence to exonerate your brother?"

Dwayne's mouth hitched up in a half smile. "I don't think so. Aside from the fact that I'm known as the only cop in town who won't take a bribe, everybody knows Mitch and I don't get along."

"So why go out of your way to help?"

"Honestly? Mitch and I might not be best friends, but he is my flesh and blood, and I feel a little guilty for pointing the investigation right at him. I never thought he'd actually get arrested, and I know—I mean, I know in my gut he didn't do it. I couldn't live with myself if he ended up convicted of a crime he didn't commit, when I was the one who put the wheels in motion."

"How did you—"

"I was the one who remembered the car theft, and the circumstances of Robby's disappearance. The records were buried, but I remembered it all too well. I'm the one who told them Mitch was the last one to see Robby alive, and I really wish I hadn't."

Dwayne was either genuinely regretful, or he was a helluva good actor.

"Where is this place we're going?" Beth asked.

"Not far."

They'd followed a main road for maybe half a mile, then turned off onto a winding dirt road that gradually narrowed until it was more of a goat path. Eventually it became impassable, at least without four-wheel drive. Raleigh stopped her Volvo and Dwayne parked right behind her. They were blocking the road, but it didn't look like any cars had come this way in quite some time.

"What kind of shoes are you wearing?" Dwayne asked.

Beth glanced down at her wedge sandals and bare legs, then out at the oak and cypress dripping with Spanish moss towering all around them.

"Not hiking shoes."

"This might be a little dicey then." He reached into the glove box and procured a can of bug repellant, then sprayed it liberally on his face, neck and hands before passing it to her. "You'll need this."

If there was a mosquito anywhere within five miles it would find Beth, so she doused herself with the bug spray, grimacing at the smell. When she exited the car, she noted the mushy texture of the ground. And they were still on the road.

Wordlessly she handed the can of Off! to Raleigh, who frowned and sprayed a tiny amount on her hands and neck. At least she was wearing sensible shoes and long pants.

Mitch declined the bug repellant. "Mosquitoes steer clear of me. I think it's all the hot sauce I eat."

Beth didn't doubt it. He loved spicy food, the hotter the better.

"So how far do we have to walk to get to this place?" Beth asked.

"'Bout a quarter mile," Mitch answered. "Not far."

She looked down again at her impractical sandals. "Depends on what kind of shoes you're wearing."

Dwayne had put on knee-high galoshes, and he had a machete in hand and a metal detector slung over one shoulder. He was quite the Boy Scout.

"Let's go." Dwayne and his machete took the lead, hacking away at clinging vines, branches and tall weeds that blocked their path. Beth couldn't see any discernible path, but Dwayne didn't hesitate and seemed to know right where he was going.

Mitch brought up the rear. And Beth just tried not to slow everyone down—or break an ankle—as she squish-squished through the dense bayou vegetation that blotted out the heat and light of the sun. Not a breath of breeze stirred the leaves and the draping Spanish moss.

"Perfect setting for a slasher movie," she couldn't help saying, then wished she hadn't. They were looking for a murder scene, after all, and what better place than a swamp? It was beautiful in its own way, so lush and vibrant with life. Yet she couldn't deny an air of menace, so it wasn't someplace she wanted to spend a lot of time.

She was thankful to be here on a bright, sunny afternoon, rather than at night.

The spongy ground abruptly turned muddy, sucking at one of her shoes so that she almost tripped. Mitch was right there, a hand to her elbow.

"You okay? You're not exactly dressed for a hike through the swamp."

"No kidding. I'm okay for now."

"Here, you can hang on to my arm if you want."

It was a friendly offer, but she wasn't sure if she could handle touching him, not when she was trying to stop fantasizing about him. "I'm okay."

"Want me to carry your bag?"

She hitched her evidence kit higher on her shoulder. "Really, I'm fine."

A loud splash off to her right caught her attention, and she looked just in time to see a scaly tail disappear beneath the murky water.

"Holy crap, that was an alligator!" She realized she was hanging on to Mitch's arm despite her best intentions. She must have instinctively reached for him. She quickly let go. "Sorry. I've just never been that close to one in the wild before."

"They won't bother us," Dwayne said casually. "I worry more about the copperheads and water moccasins."

"Snakes?" Raleigh's shriek set off a hundred bird calls.

Beth wasn't thrilled by the idea of poisonous snakes, either, but she'd tromped around enough isolated crime scenes to know that reptiles usually did their best to steer clear of humans.

"Just don't put your hands and feet anywhere you can't see," Mitch warned. "This time of day, they like dark, cool places. They're more afraid of you than you are of them."

"That is highly doubtful," Raleigh said, and Beth felt a rush of affection for her friend, braving this hostile environment for Mitch's sake.

By the time they reached a small clearing, Beth's sandals were utterly ruined.

Dwayne came to a halt. "There it is."

Beth had to squint and do a thorough visual search before she saw anything. Then she wondered how she could have missed it, a falling-down wood structure almost entirely covered with vines. It had once been a house on stilts, but half of it was completely collapsed. The other half was missing most of the roof and at least one wall.

A flock of crows had gathered to caw in a nearby skeletal tree, adding to the horror-movie ambiance.

"Can't believe it's still standing," Mitch said.

"How far is this from where the victim's body was found?" Beth asked.

"Not far," Mitch answered. "Where Simmons Slough empties into the bayou, about a quarter to a half mile from here."

"Long way to carry a body," Dwayne commented.

"If the body was dumped in the slough, it could have washed downstream. We need to check what kind of weather was happening around that time."

"Let's do what we came here to do, then get the hell out of this place," Raleigh said. "It gives me the creeps."

Beth shook off her own sense of dread. Examining a crime scene was her area of expertise, and she should take charge.

"Dwayne, since you're the one with the metal detector and the boots, why don't you start a grid search here in this front yard area. Stands to reason if there was an altercation, Robby might have come out of the house first. The rest of us can—"

Her words were cut off by a loud crack that sent the flock of crows flying, and something whizzed past Beth's head.

"Everybody down!" Dwayne shouted, but Mitch was already ahead of him. He'd taken a flying leap at Beth and tackled her to the muddy ground.

CHAPTER SIX

ANOTHER SHOT RANG OUT, and Mitch felt way too exposed lying flat on the ground, his body nestled over Beth's intriguingly soft curves. They needed cover and he needed to get his mind out of the gutter. What kind of idiot thinks about how good a woman feels when he's getting shot at?

An ancient fallen oak tree lay just to the edge of the clearing, and he aimed to get Beth and Raleigh safely behind it.

"We're gonna move," he said, scrambling to his feet and dragging Beth with him, shielding her with his body as best he could.

She stumbled along with him as he half dragged her to the fallen tree and shoved her down behind it. Dwayne, he saw, had Raleigh with him behind the cover of a tall group of cypress knees. They were ankle deep in mud. Dwayne had his gun out, but the shooter wasn't visible. He was hiding inside the shack.

Although the structure was in worse shape than Mitch remembered it, he still knew every tree, stump and vine that grew here.

"Stay here and don't move," he whispered to Beth.

"Trust me, I'm not moving." She crouched next to

him, her eyes wide with fear and her whole body trembling as she clutched her canvas bag to her chest. One of her shoulders was covered in mud and a trickle of blood ran down from her skinned knee. "Wait, where are you going?" she asked when he moved away from her.

"I'm fine, don't worry."

"Don't worry?"

"Dwayne, cover me," Mitch said just loud enough for his brother to hear. "I'm gonna circle around to the back."

Mitch expected his brother to argue, but he didn't. He fired a shot over the roof of the shack to distract their assailant, who maybe wouldn't notice where Mitch was moving.

Mitch delved deeper into the cover of the woods, making his way swift and silent as he harkened back to all the hours he'd spent in the swamp as a kid. Although Mitch had never taken to hunting, his father had taught him how to track and move without detection in the wild.

Darting from tree to shrub, he made his way around the shack to the back. From this side, Mitch could see that someone had made some amateur repairs, cobbling a makeshift shelter inside with a tar-paper roof, maybe a place to at least keep the rain off. The rickety stairs had been repaired, too, and looked like they might hold Mitch's weight.

The shooter fired again. Mitch expected Dwayne to return fire, but he didn't. Maybe he didn't subscribe to the Coot's Bayou police motto of Shoot First, Explain Later.

"Police!" Dwayne bellowed. "Come out with your hands up."

Like that was gonna happen. They'd stumbled upon some river rat's crib, and he seemed set on defending it.

There wasn't much cover between Mitch and the staircase, so he got across it as quickly as he could. No bullets slammed into him; the shooter was focused on the threat from the front of the house and obviously hadn't seen Mitch on the move.

As quietly as he could, Mitch climbed the stairs in a crouch. When his head reached floor level of the shack he squinted against the late afternoon sun and peered into the shady interior. A scrawny man in filthy, baggy jeans and a green hoodie crouched just below a window that had only two of its six panes remaining.

If Mitch could get to him, he'd have the guy stripped of his gun and disabled in a flash. But those few feet between the top of the stairs and his target...Mitch just hoped the guy would be slow to react. Judging from the number of empty beer cans littering the warped wood floor, that might be the case.

Mitch had to go for it. Any more delay might mean the shooter would get lucky and actually hit someone.

He waited until the shooter took aim again, then launched himself across the floor and tackled the man, making sure he got control of the gun hand. Sprawling on top of him, using his chin and knees and elbows to make sure he couldn't move, Mitch grabbed the guy's arm and beat it against the floor until he dropped the weapon.

The man squealed in protest. "You broke my nose!"

"I'm gonna break your neck if you don't stop wiggling."

"Awright, awright, lemme go!"

"I got him!" Mitch yelled to Dwayne. "Need cuffs!"

Seconds later, Dwayne appeared at what was once the front door, weapon drawn and cuffs in hand.

"Damn, good job, Mitch." His voice held a tinge of awe as he holstered his weapon and knelt to cuff the shooter. "That took some *cojones.*"

"*Cojones* I got," he said grimly. "Good sense, not so much." Between them they flipped their shooter onto his back.

"Holy smokes," Dwayne said. "I don't believe this."

Beth and Raleigh had joined them, and they stared at the bloody-faced man who now cowered in terror.

"What happened to him?" Beth asked. "Did he shoot himself?"

"He broke my nose," the man whined.

The guy did look a bit worse for wear. His nose was bent and swelling, and blood covered his face and dripped into his greasy hair. But despite the disfigurement, and the years that had passed, Mitch instantly recognized him.

"Crazy Larry. You stupid son of a bitch, why were you shooting at us?"

BETH SHUT HER EYES, but not before she'd gotten a good look at that poor man's bloody face. Granted, just moments earlier he'd been trying to kill them, but that didn't stop her from reacting to the blood. Her head swam and she grabbed on to Raleigh's sleeve for support.

"Hey, you okay?" Raleigh whispered.

"I'm good, I'm fine," she lied, unwilling to admit she had a weak stomach.

"You don't look fine. Here, sit down." But there was nowhere to sit in the disgusting remains.

"I'm okay. What about him?" She couldn't believe the damage Mitch had done to the guy's face. Her Mitch, her sweet computer geek, had just broken a man's nose.

And possibly saved all of their lives, she reminded herself. His actions were entirely justified. But that fact didn't stop her stomach from roiling. She was supposed to be a professional; working static crime scenes, even bloody murder scenes, didn't bother her the way a living, breathing, bleeding person did.

"Son-of-a-friggin'-gun," Larry said, actually smiling as Dwayne hoisted him to his feet. "Mitch Delacroix, is that you?"

"Sure is. How you been?" Mitch sounded as friendly as if they'd just met in a bar.

"Oh, you know, up and down. Little bit down right now."

"I'll say," Dwayne muttered. "You're about to be charged with attempted murder."

"Aw, hell, I wasn't aiming to hit anybody. Just didn't want anybody pokin' around. If people'd just leave me alone when I want 'em to, I'd be fine."

Maybe Larry hadn't meant to kill somebody, but Beth remembered hearing that bullet whiz right past her head.

Dwayne patted Larry down, then searched his pockets. "I won't find any needles, will I, Larry?"

"Naw, I don't do that stuff. Just booze, mostly, when my pain pills run out. Hurt my back a few years ago."

"You have the right to remain silent," Dwayne began, but Larry interrupted.

"Yeah, yeah, whatever. Just take me to jail. Maybe I'll luck out and they'll actually feed me."

Dwayne escorted Larry outside and cuffed him to the stair railing. "Just sit here for a bit."

"Okay." Larry sat on the rickety steps, meek as a milk cow. He didn't seem overly bothered about being arrested.

Dwayne returned and, having put on a pair of blue gloves, collected Larry's gun and put it in a plastic bag. "Crazy as a bedbug," he muttered. "Lucky I didn't blow his head off."

Once that chore was taken care of, Beth did what she came to do—search for any signs of a murder scene. There wasn't much to search; just one room of the shack remained intact. The collapsed portion of the house wasn't safe, but she could bring out a specialized team with the right equipment and safety gear, and they could take down the shack timber by timber.

But that decision would be up to Raleigh, and Daniel, since the cost to Project Justice would be high. Daniel never scrimped, so if Raleigh thought it was important, she would make it happen. But only if they found some evidence that this location was important to their case.

Beth handed each person a garbage bag from her kit, then assigned each of them one quarter of the room to examine. They searched first with only their eyes, then began removing trash and debris, most of which looked far more recent than twelve years old.

"I remember this table," Mitch said, referring to a wobbly, three-legged table that had long ago lost any semblance of form or finish. "And this rag-and-rope rug. I think it used to be in the other room, when there was another room."

That was encouraging news. If furnishings had survived, so might evidence.

"Let's move the rug," Beth said.

"You can if you want," Dwayne said with a snort. "God knows what's living under there."

Beth wasn't afraid of creepy crawlers so long as they weren't the lethally poisonous variety. She grabbed one end of the rug and folded it in half. Mitch helped her pick it up and heave it off to the side. The rug could be a gold mine of physical evidence, since it obviously hadn't been cleaned in twenty years. But she wouldn't devote her resources to it yet; just getting it out of this swamp and back to Houston would be a logistical challenge.

The wood planks on which the rug had lain were less worn than the rest of the floor, but mottled with all kinds of stains. Beth squatted down to have a closer look.

Her heart beat a bit faster. "This could be blood," she announced.

"Where? Lemme see." Dwayne dropped to his hands and knees, getting almost nose to nose with the stains in question. "Hard to tell. Looks like leftover wood stain to me."

"If Beth says it's blood, it's blood." Mitch sounded upbeat for the first time that day.

Beth produced an X-Acto knife from her kit and started chipping up bits of the wood floor.

"Ah, maybe you should leave the evidence collecting for the police," Dwayne said.

"Since this isn't an official crime scene," Beth said carefully, "it should be okay for me to take a few samples. I'll give some to you, and you can take it to your crime lab. But our lab is accredited, and we have some of the best, most modern equipment in the country. Plus, we can move faster."

"The parish lab does get backed up." But Dwayne did accept her offer to collect evidence for both of them. She quickly labeled two plastic bags, put splinters in each of them, and handed one to Dwayne.

"Hold your horses, I found something," Raleigh announced. She was peering at a window frame that was half-rotted and riddled with holes. Beth came closer. One of those holes had a bullet in it.

"This isn't your bullet, is it, Dwayne?" Beth asked.

"Can't be. I only fired one round, and I made sure I aimed well over the roof."

"Here's another one," Mitch said excitedly, pointing to a spot a few inches away.

Beth scanned the wall, feeling like she was on a macabre Easter egg hunt. "There's a hole near the roofline. Is that one?"

Dwayne dragged over a milk crate and stood on it. "Sure is. Good eyes. Now there's nothin' that says these bullets have anything to do with Robby Racine. Hell, for all we know, Crazy Larry's been shooting the walls. But I think, given what we've found, I should call in an evidence team to do a proper search."

"Agreed." Beth hated to give up the scene just when good stuff was turning up, but Dwayne was right. An official team should examine the area, take measurements and photos in case what they found turned out to be relevant.

"I don't trust the locals," Mitch said flatly.

Dwayne punched his brother on the arm. "Don't be paranoid. We got good evidence people. Most of 'em don't know you, never heard of you, and they aren't going to manufacture evidence or perjure themselves. And if you want, you can send one of your people to observe."

Beth had taken out her camera and was snapping pictures of the bullets they'd found. "There are lots of projectiles here," she observed. "I'm going to remove a couple, but I'll tag where I took them from."

"No, Beth," Dwayne said. "If this is a crime scene, we need to let it alone."

Damn. "Get your people out here tomorrow morning, then. I'll be here to observe."

"That settles that." Dwayne headed for the stairs.

"Meanwhile, I have a suspect I have to transport back to—" He went suddenly silent, then swore viciously.

Soon they all saw what had caused the reaction. Crazy Larry had broken the stair railing he'd been cuffed to. He was nowhere to be seen.

Frustration welled up in Beth's chest. Larry could be the key to everything. He might even be the real murderer, trying to scare them away from the scene of the crime. They'd had him, and now he was gone, and he wouldn't be easy to find again.

"Got a present for you," Mitch whispered in her ear. His warm breath tickled her hair.

"What?"

He took her hand and pressed something small. When she examined his gift, she realized it was a bullet.

THERE'S NO NEED FOR YOU to stay in a hotel," Myra said to Beth. On the way back from the swamp, Beth had decided she would spend the night in Coot's Bayou, since the evidence team would gather at the shack early tomorrow morning. But when Myra overheard her plans to rent a room, she wouldn't hear of it.

"The closest motel is the Sleepy Time, next town over, and I hear they have bedbugs. Lake Charles has all the chain motels, but that's miles away and you don't even have a car."

"I was planning to rent one."

"Nearest rental car place is at the Lake Charles airport. No reason for you to go to all that trouble when I have a perfectly good guest room here. You're in the country, now, not some big city. You can even borrow my car tomorrow if you need to."

"That's awful nice of you, Mrs. LeBeau—"

"Please, call me Myra. And I'd be pleased to have you as a guest. You're trying to help Mitch and I would be one ungrateful witch if I didn't do everything possible to help you out."

"Where is Mitch, anyway?" Raleigh asked.

"I imagine he's out back tending the livestock. That was always his chore when he was a boy, and old habits die hard."

"Livestock?"

"Just a few chickens and a couple of goats."

The sound of tires crunching in the gravel driveway caught their attention. Beth and Raleigh stepped out onto the porch as two vehicles pulled up. One of them Beth recognized as Mitch's classic metallic gold El Camino, which he'd restored to pristine condition. The other was a red BMW. The Beamer's door opened and a long, tanned leg emerged.

"Daniel's new administrative assistant, Elena," Raleigh whispered as the statuesque blonde emerged. The driver's door of Mitch's car opened and out hopped Celeste, spry as a twenty-year-old.

"Yee-hah, that El Camino has some get-up-and-go!" Celeste's costume today was relatively tame—a pair of striped capri pants and an aqua cardigan cinched with a black patent-leather belt. Aqua wedge sandals completed the outfit.

The black dog, which Beth had learned was named Poppy, bounded off the porch to bark at the new visitors, wagging her tail to show she wanted to make friends.

"Do you know how hard it was for me to keep up with you?" Elena grinned at Celeste, clearly enjoying herself. "It's a miracle neither of us got a ticket."

Though she looked like a model, Elena was ultraprofessionally dressed in a suit and pumps. She mounted the porch, hand outstretched.

"Hello, Raleigh, nice to see you again." She shook hands with Raleigh. "And you must be Beth. Daniel sent some clothes and things for you and Mitch, along with all of Mitch's computer toys."

Celeste didn't bother with any niceties. She had her gun out and was stalking the driveway. "Hey," she called over one shoulder. "What's hunting season for 'gators, anyway? I'm about due for a new pair of boots."

Beth shared a look with Raleigh. "How did Daniel know I was going to stay overnight, when I didn't know myself until an hour ago?"

Elena shrugged. "Sometimes he just knows." She glanced at Beth's mud-stained dress and bare feet, then at Raleigh, who was in a similar state of dishabille. "Apparently I arrived in the nick of time."

Raleigh made quick introductions, but Elena and Celeste didn't stick around. After a brief argument over who would drive, Celeste claimed the keys and slid behind the wheel of Elena's car, which was out of earshot by the time Mitch reappeared.

Seeing his car filled with computer equipment, his eyes brightened. "Finally. I can make myself useful."

"And I need to get on the road," Raleigh announced.

She gave Mitch a careful hug, mindful of the fact he'd showered and changed his clothes while she remained a mess. "Hang in there. And call me if you need anything at all." She hugged Beth, too. "Are you okay with this?" she whispered. "I can drop you at a hotel on my way home."

Beth *wasn't* okay with sleeping under the same roof as Mitch. Knowing he was so close, in bed, possibly naked, would make sleep impossible. She would have much preferred a private hotel room and a long hot soak in a tub. But to make a fuss seemed rude and ungrateful when Myra was going out of her way to be accommodating. Plus, Beth sensed Mitch needed someone there to quell the tension that filled the air between him and his mother.

"I'm good. If you could drop these samples from the shack by the lab tomorrow morning and let Cassie get started on them, that would be great." She'd already handed off the splinters and the illegally obtained slug to Raleigh.

"I will. Call if you need anything."

Mitch was unloading his computer from the back of the El Camino even before the dust from Raleigh's departure settled. He did tend to get twitchy if he was away from his bits and bytes for too long. Checking email on his iPhone only went so far.

"Need a hand?" she asked.

"I got it. But you can grab one of those little suitcases if you want."

Fresh clothes. Yes, she would. "Are you okay with

me staying here?" She probably should have asked him before she accepted Myra's invitation.

"Beth, I've pretty much quit trying to bend events the way I want them. No, I'm not really okay with any of this. Bad enough I have to stay here, and now you're stuck here, too."

"You'll only have to put up with me for one night." She tried not to sound as offended as she felt. He didn't want to date her, she got that, but she'd hoped they could somehow remain friends.

"It's not me who has to worry. It's you."

"I'm not worried."

"You haven't spent enough time with Myra and Davy yet."

Beth supposed everyone was a little embarrassed by their parents. She could remember cringe-worthy times when her father interrogated boyfriends she and her sisters brought home, or when her mother brought out the photo albums or force-fed her friends her awful broccoli casserole.

Mitch flashed her a sad half smile. "You've been warned."

While Mitch set up his computer, she took the opportunity to freshen up. Inside the small rolling bag Elena had packed she found two changes of clothes. Not her clothes, but they were exactly her size and taste. How Elena accomplished this feat was amazing. She'd even provided Beth with toiletries and a blow-dryer.

Myra's house had only one bathroom, with no tub, but it was clean and functional. Beth figured her little floral dress was probably ruined. That was what she got for wearing such girlie clothes. On some subconscious level she was probably trying to impress Mitch. She folded the ruined garment and set it on the vanity, then scrubbed herself in the shower until she was sure no mud remained on her skin, and no bugs in her hair.

A few minutes later she was reasonably well-groomed. As she exited the bathroom, she could smell dinner cooking.

"Corn bread," she murmured, realizing she was starving. Since both of Beth's parents had held down full-time jobs, their family dinners had mostly been takeout or convenience foods, but her grandmother had occasionally stayed with them and cooked meals from scratch. The memory of fried shrimp and hush puppies flooded her brain and gave her a warm feeling. Maybe staying with Mitch and his family wouldn't be so bad after all.

ONCE MITCH GOT HIS COMPUTER set up, he quickly lost himself in cyberspace.

Finding Crazy Larry on the web was a low priority now that he knew his old friend was somewhere in town. Mitch intended to search—in person—all the places he knew of where homeless people hung out. But first he had lots of other tasks to accomplish online.

Robby's old girlfriend, Amanda, was easy to find. She was married to a long-haul trucker and still living in town. He made a note of her address.

He was about to move on to the next task when he heard a noise behind him and turned. Beth stood in the doorway, fresh from her shower and wearing tight jeans and a tailored shirt that accentuated her full breasts, and Mitch instantly salivated.

They locked gazes for a couple of seconds before he dredged up a smile that would hopefully erase the naked lust that must have shown on his face.

"I'm done with the bathroom if you need it," she said. "Are you finding anything?"

"Got Robby's girlfriend's current address."

"Wow, that was fast."

"I was just about to see if I could locate the owner of the stolen car."

"How are you gonna do that?"

"Ah…you don't really want to know."

"Mitch, you aren't going to hack into a police department computer, are you? Aren't you in enough trouble? Dwayne was going to get the name for you."

"They'll never know I was there. When I was at the cop shop earlier, I noticed they were still using the same computer system as when I worked there. Amazing they haven't updated in six years."

"But surely they've upgraded their security. Changed passwords and all that."

"Maybe. Sure, but no good hacker works on any system without leaving himself a back door."

"A secret way into the system?" She came closer, peering at the computer screen as if intrigued despite her disapproval.

Oh, God, she smelled great. Like…like chocolate and raspberry.

This scent had to be his favorite so far.

He forced himself to focus on the keyboard and screen. "Let's just see." He knew the website address from memory and called it up, then converted it to code and added his secret phrase, which brought him to another web page—one no one but him would ever find. It asked for a password, and he entered it.

And just like that, he was in.

"Oh, my God. Mitch. Is that what I think it is? You're actually in their computer system?"

"Moving through like a ghost. Let's just hope that when my arrest record was expunged, they didn't actually obliterate the file." He sifted through the archives, and within five minutes he'd found it. He read through the initial incident report and made note of the complainant's name—Harvey Clayton.

How could he have forgotten that name?

"You got it? Just like that?"

"What can I say? I'm good, baby."

The report didn't mention any witnesses, only the name of the grocery store manager who provided the police with the surveillance video.

"Is your arrest record there?" Beth asked, so close he could feel her hair tickling his.

"Can't find it. Maybe they really did delete it."

Before he pulled out of the police computer, he did a quick search on Harvey's name. "Whew, look at this. Guy's got a criminal record. Violent crime. Assault and battery. Armed robbery." Whether Harvey had anything to do with Robby's death or not, he made a dandy suspect.

Using a plain old search engine, he soon had Harvey's address. "We can only hope the guy's not in prison. Sounds like he stays in trouble."

"So, Harvey Clayton. And Robby's girlfriend... Amanda?"

"Amanda Laurent is her name now. Two good leads to pursue tomorrow."

"And...don't forget Larry. Hey, you don't suppose... No, never mind."

"What? You think Dwayne *let* him escape?"

Beth inhaled sharply. "That is exactly what I was going to say. But I don't really believe it."

Mitch frowned. "I don't really believe that, either. Don't worry, Larry will turn up again. He's not the brightest bulb in the marquee. But until he does, I bet my brother is gonna take a lot of crap from his colleagues." Mitch didn't feel quite as happy about that as he would have even a day ago.

"Say what you will about Dwayne, but he was very accommodating today. He seems like he genuinely wants to help."

"Yeah. He wants to help put me in the ground." The quip was automatic; he'd spent so many years despising his half brother, it was hard to switch gears. He wasn't certain he could do it. Maybe Dwayne was genuinely sorry for the way he'd treated Mitch when they were kids, but he couldn't undo what he'd done.

"Why do you say that? Maybe he's grown up and put the past behind him."

"Meaning I haven't?"

"I didn't mean...well, maybe I did mean that. Have you thought about maybe letting go of a few grudges?"

"Forgiveness is for wussies. Have you forgiven Vince for breaking your jaw?"

She blinked a couple of times, and he realized bringing up her abusive ex-boyfriend was a stupid and mean thing to do.

"I don't know." Abruptly she turned and mumbled something about helping his mom with dinner.

"Way to go, jerk," he grumbled to himself. He had every right to hold a grudge if he wanted to. Beth had no idea what his childhood and teen years had been like. Living in constant fear of getting beat up by your father at home and tormented by your half brother anywhere else in town...then again, maybe she did know something about fear.

Maybe he had a right to his grudge, but he didn't have a right to lash out at Beth. Beth, who'd actually asked him out on a date. He'd already hurt her with his ignorant, cavalier reaction to her invitation. But that didn't mean he should go on hurting her.

He would have to make things right, but without encouraging her to revisit the idea of a romance between them. He could do her that favor, at least.

Mitch followed Beth downstairs, intending to get her alone and apologize, but as he passed the dining room he noticed the table was set. For six.

His mother was in the kitchen, bustling around to get everything ready. She probably didn't have company very often, so he didn't begrudge her making the most of it. But he had to ask.

"Mom? Who else is eating dinner with us? Did you invite Aunt Trudy?"

His mother stilled. "Mitchell, Trudy passed two years ago."

"She—aw, hell, I didn't know."

"If you ever listened to the messages I leave on your answering machine, you'd know. I did call you."

"I'm sorry. I'd have come to her funeral." At his mother's dubious look he added, "I would have. I liked Trudy." His mother's older sister had been a merry soul, as plump and full of laughter as Myra was gaunt and dour. "So who's coming to dinner?"

"Now don't be angry with me, Mitchell, but I invited Dwayne and Linda."

Mitch groaned. "Why did you do that? Bad enough I had to spend half the day with him."

"He's family." And that seemed to be a good enough explanation for her.

"He's not *your* family."

"But he's your half brother. Since Trudy passed, I've come to realize how important family is. You two shouldn't dislike each other simply because of some unfortunate...parentage."

"Are they actually coming?"

"Dwayne called a while ago and said they would be here. So please, for me, try to get along. I know he was a bit of a bully when you were kids, but he's grown up into a fine man, and Linda is always volunteering at the church. She keeps the graveyard so neat and attractive, always brings cut flowers."

Mitch sighed. He'd rather eat his dinner with the goats.

CHAPTER SEVEN

DINNER WAS A MIXED BAG. The meal was actually delicious, if a bit unhealthy—fried shrimp, hush puppies, and collard greens dripping in butter and salt, followed by bread pudding.

But the conversation had been strained. Davy said almost nothing, shoveling down his food as if it were a race. Myra made polite inquiries about Beth's job, but, like most people, her eyes glazed over when Beth tried to explain what she actually did in the lab. Dwayne limited his comments to praising Myra's cooking.

Most of the conversation was taken up by Linda, Dwayne's wife, who chattered cheerfully about her volunteer work, her garden and activities at the church that she and Myra both attended. She was pretty, in a delicate, china-doll way, with black hair in a sleek bob and heavy lipstick that left dark pinky-orange prints on her water glass. Her shallow chitchat was a blessing: it prevented those awful, awkward silences.

Mitch and his mother cast wary glances at each other throughout the meal. She kept offering him seconds, which he repeatedly declined.

"I thought you loved fried shrimp," she said. "You used to eat it by the boatload."

"I do love it, Mom. I just can't eat like I did when I was a kid."

Beth had seen Mitch polish off whole pizzas, and he claimed to have a cast-iron stomach, but she didn't argue the point.

After dinner, Davy announced he intended to watch a baseball game on TV. "You boys are welcome to join me," he offered in his quiet voice.

"I'll watch an inning or two," Dwayne said.

But predictably, Mitch didn't jump at the invitation. "I'll go see to the critters."

"Which of course leaves the womenfolk to the dishes," Linda said good-naturedly, as if she was used to it. She rose and bussed her own dishes to the sink.

"Now, Linda, put that down," Myra admonished. "You're a guest."

"And if we all work together we can get this kitchen cleaned up in a snap. Then we can all relax."

It was hard to dissuade her. Linda was a cleaning tornado, and Myra, too mild-mannered to argue further, went with the flow. Beth jumped in, too. There were plenty of dishes to wash and food to put away, and Myra didn't have an automatic dishwasher.

"It was nice of you to invite us," Linda was saying. "I've often told Dwayne he should invite Mitch to visit. I think their daddy would be happy to see them gettin' along."

"Oh, I agree," Myra said. "I'll be the first to admit their daddy was no prize, but those boys do share his blood."

"I tell Dwayne all the time, Mitch is the only brother

he's got. I don't have any siblings—always wished I did. Beth, do you have brothers and sisters?"

"Two older sisters." Beth found some aluminum foil to cover the bread pudding dish. "We're very close."

Myra sighed. "If Dwayne and Mitch would just get over themselves, they have more in common than they think. If they would just share…there's healing to be done."

Healing? Beth wanted to ask for clarification, but to question Myra's meaning would just be plain nosy.

"You mean 'cause of what their daddy did." Linda's voice turned hard.

Beth's heart tried to come up into her throat. Was Linda talking about abuse? Beth never would have imagined Mitch to be an abuse victim. He seemed so relaxed and easy-going, like nothing bothered him.

Of course, she'd seen through that facade the past couple of days. Mitch obviously did have issues, something dark simmering just below the surface.

Abuse was something she understood.

Granted, she'd been a grown woman, not a helpless child, when she'd been victimized. But she'd put up with far more than she should have. Vince had verbally abused her long before he'd physically struck her. He had hurled words at her as hurtful as any fists, and he'd thrown things, broken things.

She'd been afraid to stay with him but even more frightened of breaking up with him. It wasn't until he escalated to actually striking her that she'd found the courage to get him out of her life, and even then it hadn't been easy.

How much harder was it for a child who couldn't simply walk away from an abusive parent? Beth could think of no greater crime than for a parent to pervert the responsibility he had to love and nurture his child.

Myra, who'd been at the sink drying a platter, grew still and looked out the kitchen window into the darkness, likely seeing something years in the past. "I never knew for sure if Dwayne suffered as Mitch and I did, but I suspected."

As Mitch and I. Which meant Myra had probably been abused, as well. Beth felt an urge to reach out to the woman, who carried such an air of sadness about her.

Suddenly Myra looked over at Beth, contrite. "Beth, honey, I'm sorry. I'm sure you don't want to hear all this awful family history."

"I don't mind," she said easily. "Mitch has said little about his childhood to me."

"And now you know why," Myra said. "Forgive me for being blunt, but are you and Mitch...do you—"

"We're just friends and coworkers," Beth said firmly.

"Now, that's a shame." Linda dried her hands on an ancient calendar dishcloth. "Going through this mess, he'd be better off with a good woman at his side. I understand juries are highly influenced by a show of familial support."

Which brought Beth squarely back to the reason she was here in Coot's Bayou: to prove Mitch's innocence. Not to heal his psychological wounds or mend his family rifts. "I'm doing my best to make sure it never gets to a jury."

Once the kitchen was clean, Dwayne and Linda got ready to go home—and Mitch was nowhere to be found.

"Well, tell him we said good-night," Linda said. "I'm sure we'll see him again soon."

Beth thought it was unspeakably rude for Mitch to disappear like that and not even say goodbye. She had to remind herself, once again, that she might not know the whole story.

MITCH WAITED IN THE SHADOWS for Dwayne to leave. He had a few words to say to his half brother that he didn't want Beth or his mother to hear. He didn't want Linda there, either, but she was a little harder to get rid of.

"Dwayne," he said as soon as the front door had closed.

Dwayne whirled around, his hand going automatically to a weapon he wasn't currently wearing as he squinted into the darkness. "Mitch?"

"Right here." Mitch stepped out of the shadows. "I just want a word with you. In private."

Dwayne handed his car keys to Linda. "Wait for me in the car." He never took his eyes off Mitch.

"Do you think that's a good idea?" Linda asked.

"Just do it."

Linda took the keys and skulked away, shooting one last worried look over her shoulder before unlocking the car door and scooting inside.

"Now, what is it you have to say to me that can't be said in front of anyone else? You don't want witnesses?" Dwayne took a few steps forward, his hands bunched into fists.

"I want you to stay away from my family. If you want to flash your badge and spy on me and meddle in my business as a cop, fine, whatever. I can't stop you. But I draw the line with you trying to get all cozy with my mother. Or with Beth, for that matter."

"What the hell are you so afraid of?"

"I'm not afraid of anything!" Mitch automatically countered. But there was something he feared, he realized. Right now, the only thing he had going for him was the loyalty of his Project Justice colleagues and his mother.

"You think I'll turn them against you? Is that it?" Dwayne asked. "You must have an inflated view of your importance in my life. I don't sit around plotting how I can get the better of you. Your mother invited me to dinner and I accepted. What's so wrong with that?"

"Because you never could stand it if I had something you didn't. Now that you see I have friends, a good job, a place I belong, you'd like to take it away from me. Remember that girl in junior high, Sandy?"

"What the hell are you talking about?"

"You caught us making out under the bleachers. You humiliated me in front of her 'cause you just couldn't stand it that I might have a girlfriend. She wouldn't even talk to me after that."

"You're still mad at me for that?"

"That was just one way out of a hundred you made my life miserable as a kid."

"It was a two-way street, you little bastard. You once filled my car's exhaust pipe with potatoes."

Mitch smiled. "I'd forgotten about that."

"Yeah, well, that's one I haven't forgotten. I should have pounded your face for that."

"Why didn't you, huh? Maybe because I'd grown enough that I wasn't so easy to beat up anymore?"

"Don't kid yourself. I was still twice as big as you, and I could have turned you into a grease spot on the pavement if I'd wanted to. But I'd have gotten thrown off the football team if I'd beat you up."

"You're not twice as big as me now."

"You want to take a punch at me, huh? That's what you always wanted to do. Well, go ahead. Beat me up. Then maybe you'd get this stupid grudge out of your system."

It was so, so tempting. But Mitch wasn't going to fall into any traps. "Yeah, so you can arrest me for assaulting a police officer?"

"I'm not wearing a badge or a uniform or a gun. I'm off duty. This is between you and me. C'mon, weenie-boy, put your money where your mouth is."

"I'm not gonna hit you."

Dwayne grinned, and suddenly his fist was making contact with Mitch's jaw. It was just a little tap, not enough to leave a bruise or loosen teeth, but it was enough.

"Okay, that did it." Mitch reared back and punched Dwayne right in the solar plexus.

Damn. The guy's gut was made of cast iron. Mitch

drew back his hand and shook it, wondering if he'd broken a bone.

Dwayne barely reacted. "Is that all you got?"

Mitch snapped to attention. Clearly his brother was not the easy opponent Mitch had thought he would be. He yanked off his shoes and crouched, arms extended and slightly bent. Dwayne took off his shirt and assumed his own fighting stance. Now they circled each other, wary.

"Weenie-boy, huh?" Mitch said. "I'd forgotten about that nickname."

"What'd you used to call me? Dork-head?"

"And Fat-neck."

"Boney-ass wimp."

"Shit-for-brains."

Mitch wasn't dumb enough to use his fists again. He moved in close and attempted to sweep Dwayne's right leg out from under him, but Dwayne deflected the move with enough skill that Mitch could tell he'd had martial arts training.

He never would have pictured his brother having the discipline to study martial arts.

Dwayne moved in for a punch. Mitch turned and let it glide off his body, then grabbed his brother's arm and got him in an elbow lock. In moments Dwayne was on his knees, but with his free hand he managed to grab one of Mitch's legs and throw off his balance.

Moments later they were both in the grass, rolling around and punching and yelling. All fighting finesse had gone straight out the window. Mitch grabbed

Dwayne's ear and yanked; Dwayne managed a palm to Mitch's nose, which started bleeding.

It wasn't until a cold blast of water hit them that they came to their senses. Sputtering their objections, they sprang apart to see Beth standing near the front porch, holding a garden hose and spraying them down like a couple of dogs.

Mitch looked at Dwayne, and all of a sudden the whole thing became hilarious. He started laughing, and soon Dwayne joined in.

"Would you look at us?" Dwayne said.

"I could have sworn I was twelve years old again."

"Your nose is bleedin', dude."

Mitch tipped his head back and pinched his nostrils closed. "It'll stop in a minute."

"Feel any better?"

"No, I still hate your guts, Pig-breath."

It was then that Mitch became aware of the hard stares he was getting from Beth and his mother. Linda stood with them, arms folded, glaring at her husband.

"Guess I better get going," Dwayne said. "And try to mend some fences so I don't have to sleep on the couch." He stood and offered a hand to Mitch. Mitch almost took it. Almost. But one fight wasn't going to undo years of animosity.

He pushed himself to his feet.

"Of all the ridiculous behavior," Linda said as she hustled Dwayne to the car. "Two grown men scuffling like children."

Beth and Myra didn't bother scolding. They just

shook their heads and walked back into the house, leaving him to bleed in solitude.

An hour later, Mitch still had not returned to the house. "I should go look for him," Beth said to Myra. "What if he was hurt worse than just a nosebleed?" Her head swam, just thinking about the blood dripping down his face.

"I expect he's off somewhere, licking his wounds."

Beth was horrified by what she'd seen when she'd heard some strange noises and walked outside. Mitch had lost it. Lost his temper and resorted to violence. This was different from what she'd seen when he worked out. This was violence and anger aimed at another human being.

It scared her. Yet she felt compelled to seek him out.

"I'm going to check on him, make sure he's okay."

"And I'm going to bed," Myra said, as if she'd seen this before and it didn't alarm her.

Beth exited through the back door, Poppy following at her heels. Once the dog had figured out Beth was no threat, she'd become a devoted fan.

Mitch wasn't too hard to find; he was with the goats in the tiny barn behind the house.

The barn looked authentic, with its double doors and hayloft, except it was in miniature, reminding Beth of the incredibly detailed playhouse her dad had built for her and her sisters. Inside the barn were three stalls, and each of them held one goat. Beth didn't know beans about goats, but she could at least recognize that the white one in the front stall was a billy. He had big horns and a beard, and he was lying in some hay contentedly chewing his cud.

The second stall held a large brown goat, no beard, smaller horns. She appeared to be asleep.

And in the third stall—oh, my. Another brown goat, and a tiny baby. And Mitch, sitting on a milking stool and rubbing the mother between her horns as the baby, no bigger than a cocker spaniel, nursed.

"Mitch."

He looked up, not with any degree of surprise, so he must have heard her approach. He'd cleaned up the blood from his nosebleed and, other than some slight swelling around his nose and a small cut on his chin, he didn't look like he'd suffered any serious injuries.

"Are you okay?"

"I'm fine. Are you?"

She sighed. How could she answer that? "What happened?" she finally asked. "How did you end up in a fight with Dwayne? What did he say to set you off?"

"We said a lot of things to each other. That fight was a long time coming."

"I can understand your being angry but does the word *self-control* mean anything to you?"

"He told me to hit him."

"That doesn't mean you had to do it."

"We didn't hurt each other. Not really."

She leaned her elbows on top of the stall door. "That wasn't what it looked like to me. Violence is not the answer. It's never the right answer, especially toward people who are trying to help you."

"I don't care what it looks like, Dwayne isn't trying

to help. He has an angle. My guess is, he's a spy for the police. He wants to keep an eye on us, so if we do uncover any exculpatory evidence, they can jump on it."

"And your mom? You haven't been very nice to her, either, and she definitely doesn't have an angle. She just wants to keep you out of prison."

Mitch blew out a long breath. "I don't know what she's doing. Keeping my room like some kind of shrine. Making me fried shrimp, like that's going to fix everything."

The mother goat, perhaps sensing Mitch's roiling emotions, backed up and put herself between him and the baby.

"Did you ever think it's because she loves you?"

"Not in a healthy way." He stood up, knocking over the milking stool, which he didn't bother to right. He let himself out the door of the stall, then latched it and headed for the exit.

"Why do you say that?"

"It's not important."

"I think it is."

He left the barn and stalked to the back porch, but he didn't enter the house. He went to an old refrigerator that stood in the corner and pulled out a cold bottle of beer, then twisted off the top and took a long draw.

"If my mother loves me, it's a new development," he finally said. On the move again, he stepped off the porch and walked around to the front of the house, to the picnic table they'd all shared earlier. There were no lights in the front yard, and this far from any big town, it was dark. At least Beth had on a pair of running shoes now instead of the ridiculously high heels, so she wasn't as likely to break her ankle by stepping in a hole.

"Why do you think she didn't love you?" Beth pushed, following him despite the fact he was obviously trying to get away from her. It was probably none of her business, but she'd been told often enough that curiosity killed the cat. She was nothing if not insanely curious about what made Mitch Delacroix tick.

"She sure never gave any indication she cared whether I lived or died."

Beth had a hard time reconciling that picture with the woman she'd just washed dishes with. Yes, Myra had behaved a bit oddly at first, but...then a thought occurred to her.

"Because she didn't protect you." She'd said the words out loud without meaning to.

She felt, rather than saw, Mitch turn his attention toward her. His breathing accelerated. "What the hell did you women talk about while you cleaned the kitchen? My whole life story?"

"It just...came out. Linda and your mother sort of forgot I was there," she rushed to explain. "They were both saying how they wished you and your brother were closer because...because you shared..." She couldn't quite bring herself to say the words.

"We share bad blood, that's all."

"You shared an abusive father," Beth insisted, forcing the truth out in the open.

Mitch barked out a pain-filled laugh. "Willard C.

Bell, lifting a hand to his favorite son, his golden boy?
Not likely."

"It's not only likely, it's a sure thing. According to
Linda, anyway. Parents don't normally single out one
child for abuse—"

"I wasn't abused. Don't label me. My daddy had a
temper and a drinking problem, and sometimes I just
didn't get out of the way fast enough."

She understood why he would bristle. She'd done
the same thing when someone in her counseling group
had referred to her as an "abuse victim." She hated that
word, *victim*. Everybody had their hot buttons.

"So you don't think it's possible sometimes Dwayne
didn't move fast enough?"

"He was the perfect one. I was the one who always
came up short. I didn't make the football team. I didn't
want to go out and kill small furry things. My grades
sucked. I didn't date cheerleaders."

"So, the bastard made constant comparisons. But
did it ever occur to you he might have done exactly the
same thing to Dwayne? If he wanted to find flaws in
Dwayne, he no doubt could find them."

He studied her, looking supremely uncomfortable.

"It makes sense, Mitch. A bully is a bully. And the
fact that Dwayne bullied you only makes me believe
he was continuing a cycle of abuse—"

"Dammit, Beth, stop using that word!"

The anger, hurled through the darkness at Beth, had
the desired effect. She clammed up in a hurry as her
chest constricted and her eyes burned.

Poppy whined and took off.

Mitch might have a temper—he'd certainly proved that tonight—but he'd never raised his voice at Beth.

"I'm sorry, Mitch." Her apology came out as a whisper as she struggled to control her trembling. "I didn't mean to..." She couldn't continue. Sucking in an uneven gulp of air, she tried her best to hold in the sobs that wanted to escape.

She wanted to flee like the dog had, but she also didn't feel right leaving him out here alone when he was in such a black mood.

He would never hurt me. Not Mitch. No way.

What the hell was she doing, trying to drag painful admissions out of him? She knew that keeping dark secrets inside wasn't healthy, but neither was rubbing someone's nose in traumatic memories when they weren't ready. Talking about her trauma in a safe place had helped her tremendously, but that didn't qualify her to attempt do-it-yourself therapy on Mitch.

He had every right to tell her to go straight to hell.

Her eyes brimmed, and she sniffed, trying to suck the tears back, but it didn't work.

"Are you crying?"

"No," she lied.

"You sound like you're crying."

"Allergies."

"Uh-huh." His voice wasn't raised anymore. In fact, it was velvety quiet, all the anger drained out of it. "Great. On top of everything else, I made you cry."

"I overstepped." She silently cursed her stupid, quavery voice. "You had every right to—"

"The hell I did. I shouldn't have yelled at you."

"I always do this. I don't recognize the signs that I've pissed someone off until—"

"So it's your fault I lost my temper?"

"You never lost your temper with me before," she pointed out. "You're already stressed out and I'm just adding to it, prodding you about something that's none of my business. I'll go away now." She stood up, but he grabbed her hand, preventing her departure. She was surprised how close he was, how quickly he moved.

Just for a moment, an image of Vince shattered the barriers she'd built against the painful memories—of how impossibly fast he'd moved, how he'd caught her when she'd tried to leave, how she'd struggled to escape as he'd smashed his fist into her face. This was Mitch, not Vince—but she'd become increasingly aware of how little she knew Mitch, and how physically powerful her supposed computer geek really was.

"Sit down," he said. "I'm the one who's sorry. I know you don't like raised voices."

"Then I shouldn't bait you." She tried to tug her hand away, but he pulled her down next to him on the bench. She landed half in his lap and quickly scooted off. "Let go, please." Her heart raced as she flashed back to how Vince used to use his superior strength to manipulate her—not by striking her or causing pain, but by simply forcing her to stay in one place or move to another at his whim.

Mitch immediately released her hand. "Whoa."

"We all have baggage, Mitch. Mine doesn't make me special. Yours doesn't make you special, either. We just have to find ways to move on. My promise to myself is that, no matter what, I won't contribute to someone else's baggage. I won't let my pain become another person's. For a minute there, I thought I might have some special insight into your pain. But that's a dangerous supposition. People seeking out other people, trying to make pain a common denominator—it's no good. Never works.

"Forgive me. Please forgive me for intruding where I don't belong. Please tell me I haven't destroyed our friendship."

"And here I was worried I'd already done that."

She detected a bit of her old, familiar Mitch in the teasing line, and she couldn't help smiling through the last of her tears. "You haven't done anything."

"The local cops think differently, and they're the ones with the handcuffs and a nice cozy jail cell waiting for me. The one thing that's gotten me through so far is that you still believe in me. Well, you and everybody at work, but mostly you."

"That won't change. And, you know what? If you need to vent, if you want to yell and scream and throw things, don't be afraid to do it in front of me. I won't enjoy it, but I'll still be there when you're done."

"I don't deserve a friend like you." She heard the rustle of his clothing, felt the warmth of his hand as he extended it, but he didn't touch her. His hand hovered just inches from the skin of her arm.

He shouldn't have lost his temper with her, but she'd overreacted, too. She'd made him afraid to touch her.

Their hands collided as she reached out to meet him halfway. They clasped hands, but suddenly that didn't seem strong enough. The touch seemed too faint and impersonal to seal the verbal bargain they'd just made.

She felt his breath ruffling her hair, then the warmth of it on her neck near her ear.

"I don't want to scare you like I did before." He sounded unsure of himself. It wasn't an attitude she was accustomed to getting from Mitch.

"I'm not scared. Not now. Sometimes...it's just a reflex. Not logical. Comes straight up from my reptilian brain."

Oh, God, why was she talking about her lizard brain?

His mouth was near her cheek, now. All she had to do was turn her head. Blood pounded in her ears. This was something she'd wanted for a long time...but with her old Mitch, the gentle, easy-going computer nerd with the lazy drawl.

Did she want it with the real man she was coming to know?

The answer was an immediate yes. If anything, the layers she had started to uncover, the depths that made him more complex and fascinating, also drew her to him.

Like a moth to a flame...

She turned her head one inch, two. They were sharing one breath, then one desperate gasp as their lips touched. He pulled her hand he was holding closer to his chest, then buried his other hand in her hair as he crushed his mouth against hers.

Oh, Lord in heaven. How many times had she dreamed about this moment? How many times, when they were watching a true-crime show or a dorky comedy movie, had she yearned for him to move closer, to touch her, take her hand, kiss her?

She'd never thought it would happen like this, and she'd never imagined how really, really good it would feel to be kissed so roughly—and so soon after she'd had that mild freak-out over him grabbing her hand.

She'd always been drawn to the wrong sort of man—macho tough guys who made Rambo look like a milquetoast. Mitch had been her exception. But was he really? Had she sensed that darkness in him all along?

Was she making another error in judgment, worse than all the others combined?

CHAPTER EIGHT

MITCH KNEW, IN SOME DEEP, dark recess of his mind, that kissing Beth senseless was a mistake. But he could no more stop kissing her than he could stop breathing.

Somehow, comforting her and reassuring her had turned into something he'd never intended. If she would just give him the slightest indication that his advance was unwelcome, he would back off. But how was he supposed to show good sense when she was kissing him back like a greedy kitten lapping milk?

She was all softness and sweet, feminine smells, and her mouth tasted like honey with a hint of rum from the bread pudding and her hair smelled like raspberries. She was like the prettiest, most delectable cupcake in the bakery window.

That's how he'd always thought of her—pretty to look at, like a candy confection, but off-limits, the way candy was when he was training.

He'd just broken training.

Beth was already half in his lap, and suddenly she rose up and swung one leg over his, straddling him. Never breaking the kiss.

Good Lord.

Her hands were everywhere, in his hair, on his back,

on his chest, and her touch was not tentative. She even took his hands and put them where she wanted them, and where she wanted them was over her breasts.

He was feeling Beth McClelland's breasts. He'd dived into the icing headfirst and had smeared it all over his body. He wanted to taste her all over and find out if she was as sweet as she smelled.

He inhaled sharply, intoxicated by the unique combination of scents and the heady night air. He'd forgotten how Louisiana nights smelled, heavy and damp, laced with night-blooming flowers that lurked in nearby swamps and creek beds.

His blood roared in his ears, drowning out the drone of crickets as the universe shrank to him and Beth. While he was kissing her, with her hips pressed snugly against his sex and his hands filled with her cushiony breasts, the ugliness from his life, past and present, receded to nothing more threatening than the buzz of a mosquito.

She slid back and dipped her head, kissing his neck, squiggling her tongue into the hollow at his throat. For some reason that was the sexiest thing anyone had ever done to him. Her clever hands worked at the buttons of his denim shirt. He leaned back, the edge of the picnic table cutting into his vertebrae. Balanced precariously on his knees, she leaned down farther still and kissed his chest, her tongue whirling around one of his nipples until he groaned with unspeakable pleasure and the pain of wanting more.

"Beth, honey..." he croaked, not exactly the strong

objection that was called for. But she was rapidly driving him past the point of any reasoning power.

She slid off his lap, and for a minute he thought she'd heeded his warning, but no, she was going for the button of his jeans.

"You're kidding me."

"I'll stop if you want me to." Her words were rough with desire, not the sweet, honey-glazed voice he was used to.

She *was* kidding if she thought he was strong enough to put a stop to this, although he should. It was wrong, one-sided. He should make love to Beth on a feather bed amidst rose petals, not have her blow him on a rough picnic table in his mother's front yard. She'd seen enough roughness in her life.

Three more buttons undone. Then she was reaching her hand inside his fly, almost there.

He groaned at the first silky touch of her questing fingers. "Beth, no..." he managed.

She went still. "You're saying no?" She sounded hurt.

"No. I mean, yes." Oh, God, what did he mean?

Beth cleared her throat. "I thought you...when you kissed me..."

"I do want it. Just not like this..."

"What's wrong with this?" she almost wailed. "It's dark, it's a beautiful, warm night. I have no expectations. I just want to do something for you. I can't change your past and I can't make the murder charge go away, but I could help you forget for a little while."

No expectations? He wished he could see her face,

but there was no moon tonight, no stars. "Beth, honey, I don't want sex with you to be an escape from something. I want it to be a journey *to* something. You deserve better than this."

"Nothing could be better than this."

"How about a four-star hotel with a hot tub?"

"Nothing could be better than this, right here, right now," she insisted. "And we aren't going to get a four-star hotel. In fact, I suspect if it doesn't happen in the next ten minutes it won't happen at all."

She thought he would regain his senses and reject her. And, dammit, maybe she was right. Gently, he pulled her up until she was sitting on his lap again, but not straddling him. He put his arms around her and just held her for a few seconds.

"You're too good for me. You're too nice. I'm a poor Cajun boy with a criminal record and one thing I do well." One thing he would tell her about, anyway. "I hack into computers. You're a brilliant scientist—"

She made a strangled note in the back of her throat. "Save it, okay? I guess I should appreciate that you didn't let me go on when you really aren't interested—"

"What?"

She struggled off of his lap, and he didn't try to hold her there, but only because the last time he'd tried to hold her where she didn't want to be, he'd scared her. "It's okay, Mitch. Let's just move forward. I guess I caught you in a weak moment, and that's not really fair, is it?"

She turned and headed for the house.

Mitch opened his mouth twice to say something,

then clamped it shut. How could he explain how he felt when he didn't know? She thought he didn't want her, that he wasn't attracted, and that was about as far from the truth as she could get. But overriding his raging hard-on was the fact that he truly didn't want to hurt her. And falling for a guy who beats people up for fun when she abhors violence—a guy who might be sentenced to death row in the next few weeks—didn't sound like the shortest path to happiness and fulfillment.

There was one thing he could do, though, to at least prove to her that he'd listened.

After giving Beth time to get upstairs, he straightened his clothes and followed her inside. The kitchen was dark, but a glow from the TV drew him to the living room. His mother was slumped in her Barcalounger, a glass of red wine at her elbow. He'd wondered if she still drank wine. She obviously hadn't felt comfortable enough to imbibe when they had guests.

"Hey, Mom," he said softly from the doorway, not wanting to startle her.

He did anyway. She turned suddenly. "Oh, Mitch. I guess I thought you'd gone to bed."

"I was out with the goats. You know you have a new kid, right?"

She flashed a little smile. "It came a couple of nights ago. I wanted to name it Snowball, but Davy tells me not to name the babies. It hurts too much when we sell them."

Mitch remembered now how his mother doted over

the baby goats, and baby chicks when they had them. And how cruel his father had been when it came time to sell the babies, or the old hens that had stopped laying eggs.

"I suspect it still hurts. You always were partial to those little goats."

"We can't keep all the babies. But I keep the old chickens now. It costs so little to feed them, and it doesn't seem fair to send them off to be soup when they've given me years of loyal service. Davy doesn't mind. He's kind to the animals. He talks to them and gives them treats. He makes sure they're warm enough in the winter. And if the goats or the dog gets sick, he calls the vet."

Instead of using his shotgun to deal with the problem.

"Are you happy with Davy?"

"He's a good man. But he's shy, doesn't show much of himself to you until he knows you and trusts you."

"He obviously doesn't trust me." Mitch sat in the chair next to his mom's, the one Davy usually claimed. The dog, asleep by the chair, roused herself enough to settle her head on Mitch's foot.

"Give him time."

"For what it's worth, I'm glad you're happy."

"We do a lot of give and take. I compromise here, he does there, and we pick our battles. So, yeah, I'm happy. Well, not about everything."

Mitch knew what that meant. "I guess I haven't been a very good son to you."

"Why should you be?" She studied one of her ragged

fingernails, then picked up a nail file from the small table next to her and went to work. "I was no prize as a mother."

He wanted to deny her assessment, but the words wouldn't come. In his mind, she hadn't done the most basic thing a mother should do. Beth had guessed right; he resented that his mother hadn't done a better job protecting him from his brute of a father. Mitch had always thought that meant she didn't love him.

But surely that was a child's simplistic conclusion. If she didn't feel something for him, she would have turned her back on him when he'd been charged with murder. It would have been easy enough to just write him off as a bad seed.

Instead, she was trying to bridge the chasm between them.

He'd spent a lot of years consumed with hate for his father, but he'd also devoted no small amount of energy blaming his mother.

A few generations ago, women had no recourse against violent husbands and boyfriends. But even when he'd been a kid, surely his mother could have done something. Right?

One way to find out. "Mom, why didn't you leave him?"

Pain registered on her face before she quickly shuttered her expression. "Because he wouldn't let me. It's as simple as that."

Mitch was at a crossroads. He could argue that her maternal instincts should have been stronger than that, but he remembered the fear—no, the terror—of saying the wrong thing at the wrong time, making the wrong decision. She couldn't have simply packed up her bags and left if Willard didn't want her to.

"I tried once, you know," she said quietly. "You were a baby, and I feared for your life, truly I did. I didn't even pack a bag. I just showed up at your aunt Trudy's house. She'd told me often enough that she would help me get away from him. We were packing to move to Baton Rouge, getting some cash together. It lasted two whole days."

"What happened?"

"He showed up. And he told me if I didn't come home with him he would...he would..."

"He threatened to kill you?"

"No, baby, he threatened to kill *you.* Said he would smother you when my back was turned."

Jesus.

"The more I loved you, the more dangerous it was for you. You were his weapon against me. When he wanted to hurt me, he hurt you instead."

"You never told the police?"

"Oh, yes, I did. Three times. The first time he broke a rib, the second time he broke my arm. The third time, he broke *your* arm. I stopped after that."

A doctor had told him once that he had an old fracture, probably sustained before he could remember. In very cold weather, it ached.

"So why didn't he go to jail?"

"Because the chief of police was his hunting buddy, that's why."

Mitch just shook his head. "I don't know what to

say. I had everything so wrong. I was mad because you didn't protect me from him, but I should have done something, too."

"You were just a child—"

"Later, I mean. He left me alone once I got big enough to fight back. But did he leave you alone?" Willard Bell had been a big man, six foot two and 250 pounds. His mother was small, physically weak even for a woman. The thought of the damage he could have done to her... It made him shudder with revulsion.

Myra sat up straighter, and a fierceness entered her eyes. "You did nothing wrong, Mitchell. Once he couldn't bully you any longer, he lost interest. Found another woman. One who already had a child."

That horrific possibility had never even occurred to him. Yeah, he knew his dad ran around. In a town as small as Coot's Bayou, people talked. But people had known not to bring it up around him, so he hadn't ever heard any details. "How many lives did that one sick bastard ruin?"

"Mitch, listen to me. He didn't ruin our lives. Not if we don't let him. Don't give him that power. Yes, he caused us both pain. But it's far in the past now. We can't touch him, he can't touch us. The best revenge you can take on Willard Bell is to live a good life. Put your anger aside, and don't continue the cycle."

"I don't know how to put it aside, Mom," he confessed. "I was doing fine until I came back here." Now it was a festering, open wound.

"There's only one antidote to hate and fear."

"Yeah, beating the crap out of someone who deserves it."

"No," she said firmly. "The only cure is love, and more love. You have to let yourself feel love, and you have to give it back. You can do that, Mitch."

He wasn't so sure.

"Start small," she said, obviously sensing his doubts. "Build your life one small, loving act at a time."

"I'll try."

"You could start with a hug for your old ma."

His heart jumped with some unnamed emotion, but he went through with it. They both stood, and he wrapped his arms around her. She tentatively squeezed back.

He honestly couldn't remember ever hugging his mother. It wasn't so bad. He could almost feel her love radiating through him.

After a few self-conscious seconds, they pulled apart. "Thank you, Mom. For letting me stay here, for believing in me." And for protecting him the only way she knew how.

"You're welcome, son."

He wanted to tell her he loved her, but he wasn't there yet. His brain cells needed to process this new reality for a while before he could accept it as true. So before he said or did anything that would open a new can of worms, he turned and headed for the stairs.

Beth's bedroom door was closed, but a light shined from under the door, so she was still up. He stood in front of the door, his heart thumping like a rubber hammer on his ribs as he debated whether to knock.

Finally, he did. Just a soft tap, in case she'd gone to sleep with a lamp on. Some people didn't like the dark.

He heard rustling from inside the room, then the creak of floorboards. The door opened and Beth stood there framed by the soft glow of a bedside lamp behind her, creating a halo around her chocolate-brown hair. She wore a distinctly unsexy baby-blue nightshirt that reached almost to her knees, but it turned him on anyway. He thought he could see the outline of her nipples, and the memory of holding her breasts sprang instantly to mind. He forced his eyes down, but the sight of her bare legs and cute, pink-polished toenails was damn near as sexy.

"Mitch?" The one syllable was filled with questions.

He tore his gaze away from her trim calves and ankles to focus on her face. Hard to tell whether she was pleased to see him. She seemed to be keeping her voice and expression carefully neutral.

"I just wanted to tell you—you were right."

She opened the door wider and stepped back, allowing him inside, though she left it standing wide-open. Definitely not an invitation to anything but conversation.

She'd clearly been in bed, working on her laptop, which she'd set aside on the bed, along with her reading glasses.

"Right about what?"

"My mother. I just spent the last few minutes talking to her. Seems there's a lot I don't understand about what went on when I was a kid. Probably I'll never know everything. But I do think she cared for me in her own way."

Beth smiled as if he'd just handed her a dozen roses. "That's wonderful. I'm so glad you talked to her. It couldn't have been easy."

"No, it's a lot easier just to assume you know what's going on in someone's head." He waited to see if she would take the bait. She had to know he was talking about her, now, not his mother.

But she didn't respond as he'd hoped. "Right. Well, I better get some sleep. Long day tomorrow. I'll have to get up early if I want to observe the crime scene guys doing their thing."

He wanted to tell her she was wrong about him— that he did want her, that she hadn't merely caught him in a weak moment. Maybe she deserved better than him, but he could try to live up to what she deserved, couldn't he? He wanted to tell her that this was the wrong time and place, but that after all this was over— after he'd been proven innocent—he wanted to revisit the idea of him and Beth as more than friends.

But that was the crux of the issue. He might not be proven innocent. And until he was, he couldn't start anything. Or even talk about starting anything. It wouldn't be fair to Beth.

"Okay, then. Sleep well." He forced himself to turn and walk out. She closed the door behind him, the click of the latch sounding way too final.

"RALEIGH'S TIED UP IN COURT," Daniel informed Beth the next morning. Her yellow Ford Escape was parked on the side of the road near the footpath that led to the crime scene, and she'd been about to get out when her cell phone had rung. "She probably can't get back to Louisiana for a couple of days but she says the local attorney can handle anything minor that comes up. What's your status?"

"Been at the crime scene all morning, not that the CSIs let me anywhere close to the action." She'd been relegated to sitting on a log outside the yellow tape, watching as the investigators dismantled the shack and toted just about everything to a flatbed truck parked on the road.

One man with a metal detector had turned up a half-dozen bullets on the grounds—all different sizes and conditions, which didn't bode well for Mitch. A case could be made that any bullets found in the shack that didn't support him as the killer were unconnected to the murder, since apparently lots of guns were fired in this vicinity.

"Looks like we won't have access to the car for a while, and when we get it, it'll be swept cleaner than a quarter that's gone through the washing machine."

"The car's a dead end," Daniel said flatly. "The parish lab will find any evidence that's big enough to survive all those years underwater. We need to focus on people. Witnesses."

"Mitch and I are going to search for Crazy Larry as soon as I get back to his mom's house. Mitch knows all of the likely hangouts."

"Larry—the guy who almost killed you?"

"He said he was just trying to scare us off, not kill

anyone." Beth didn't mention how she'd felt one of the bullets pass only inches away from her head.

Daniel didn't respond immediately. She could tell he was thinking. "Is that the best use of your time? I can send someone else to scare up witnesses and interview them."

"If I'm needed back in Houston, I'll go right away. But meanwhile—" How could she explain that she didn't want to leave Mitch alone? He might start to feel as though he was at the bottom of the priority list if people at Project Justice kept passing around responsibility for his case.

"You want to stay with Mitch." Daniel sounded as if he didn't altogether approve.

"I can keep pressure on the locals as well as anyone. And I can interview witnesses. I might not have ever been a cop, but I did most of the training." She didn't add that she'd learned a great deal about interrogation from watching her true-crime shows and reading books and transcripts. "Hey, you've seen me face down the baddest of the badass lawyers in court."

"True. But working in the field, investigating—it's not really your job."

She might as well just spit it out. "I want to stay. Mitch doesn't just need competent investigators and legal help. He needs a friend. He can't face this alone."

"Beth, is there something I should know about you and Mitch?"

"No," she said, much too quickly and emphatically.

Daniel said nothing.

"We're not sleeping together, if that's what you

mean. I won't deny that I find him... What has Raleigh told you?"

He laughed. "Not a thing. I can hear it in your voice. And I just used the oldest interrogation trick in the book—going silent, forcing you to fill the gap."

"Dammit," she grumbled.

"This case is going to get ugly. The media haven't glommed on to it yet, but unfortunately, Project Justice has garnered enough national press lately that everything we do gets picked up sooner or later. You do understand that any hint of an affair between you and Mitch—"

"I get it. And I don't think you have to worry." Sad but true.

"Okay. I'm sending Billy down there to shake the bushes for witnesses, but I want you to stay, as well. Your job—besides evaluating physical evidence—is to keep Mitch on a leash. He's more of a loose cannon than I ever would have imagined. I understand he assaulted this Larry character."

Beth had been trying not to think about that. "He did it to get the gun away. And I think the floor did more of the assaulting than Mitch did."

"Very brave of him. And foolhardy. He needs to stay away from the investigation. The only good thing about Larry escaping custody is that no one took a picture of his broken nose. That's all a jury needs to see when we're trying to convince them Mitch isn't violent."

Daniel made a good argument. She wondered what he would think if he knew Mitch and Dwayne had scuffled, as well.

"Keep him at his computer. That's where he can do the most good."

"I'll do what I can, Daniel." But she suspected if Mitch didn't want to be kept someplace, he wouldn't be. He'd been paying far more attention to the black cuff around his ankle than she thought appropriate.

CHAPTER NINE

"BILLY WILL BE HERE this afternoon," Beth reported. She'd returned to Myra's house just in time for lunch—tuna salad sandwiches on soft white bread and fruit salad made from canned fruit and little marshmallows. It was another meal that reminded Beth of her grandmother.

They were seated at the picnic table again. Apparently this was where Myra served meals whenever the weather was at all hospitable. There was always a can of Off! around to discourage mosquitoes; Beth knew she would forever associate the scent of bug repellant with this episode in her life.

"So we're just supposed to sit on our hands and wait for him?" Mitch seemed antsy, and she supposed she couldn't blame him. He pulled a cherry out of the canned fruit cocktail and tossed it to Poppy, who waited patiently under the table.

"Daniel thinks your time is best spent doing what you do best."

"I've gone as far as I can in cyberspace." He crammed one of the neat triangles of sandwich into his mouth and chewed as if he couldn't taste anything.

"I have addresses for Amanda, for the Monte Carlo owner, and I even have a lead on Studs the Fence."

"We should let Billy question them," Beth insisted. "He's better at it than either of us."

"Why Billy?" Mitch asked suddenly. "Was that your idea?"

She thought the question odd. "No, it was Daniel's decision. We could wait for Raleigh to finish her court thing, but we might not have the luxury of time. Justice is pretty swift around these parts."

"About as swift and precise as a sledgehammer," Mitch agreed. "Still, there's one thing we can do. We can try to find Larry. And don't tell me Billy's more qualified to do that than me. I know all his favorite spots."

"It's not safe for us to be looking for Larry. He's dangerous."

"I'm not afraid of Larry. You don't have to come."

The hell she didn't. The mood Mitch was in today, no telling what trouble he might get into. He might hit the gas pedal on that El Camino and never stop.

Davy sat at one end of the picnic table, reading a newspaper and supposedly ignoring them, but Beth had figured Davy out. He was a listener. He might not appear to pay attention, but he took in everything.

Myra, meanwhile, was cutting into a pan of brownies that looked divine and smelled better. His mother had so far been content to let Mitch make his own decisions when it came to trying to clear his name, offering room and board and a safe haven, nothing more.

Now, though, she spoke up. "Beth is right, you know.

I never liked Larry when you used to hang out with him as a kid. He was a bad influence. What was a grown man like him doing hanging with teenagers?"

"He's mentally challenged, Mom," Mitch reminded her. "He had more in common with kids than adults."

"Still…he was a drunk and a thief."

"But essentially harmless."

"Are you sure? How do you know he didn't kill Robby, huh? If he's scared he'll get caught, he could do anything."

Mitch shrugged. "I'm going to look for him. Beth, you can come or stay behind, up to you."

No way was she letting him run around town unsupervised. What if one of the local cops hassled him? With his emotions running high, anything could happen.

Being Mitch's babysitter wasn't exactly her dream job, but someone had to do it. "I'll go with you."

"Have some brownies first, at least," Myra chided them as she served up a large square of the fudgy treat onto Mitch's plate.

Mitch's mouth twitched up on one side. "In case it's our last meal?"

"I wish you wouldn't joke about that." Myra's voice broke, and Mitch looked immediately contrite.

"Sorry, Mom."

Someday soon, Mitch might be requesting his real last meal. Now, that was a sobering thought.

As soon as the dishes were cleared, Mitch and Beth piled into the El Camino and set out on their quest to find Crazy Larry. Beth had ridden with Mitch a number of times in his truck, and she'd always considered him a safe, responsible driver. But sometime over the past couple of days, he'd developed a lead foot. He tore down the dirt road toward town way too fast for Beth's comfort.

She grabbed on to the door handle when he took a particularly sharp turn. "Can you slow down, please?"

"At this point, a speeding ticket is hardly a worry."

"It will be if it makes the news. Don't forget, the media could be around any corner. This case will turn into a circus, you can bet on it. No sense giving the reporters more grist for the mill than necessary."

He eased his foot off the gas. "Point taken. I guess when I lived here, I drove a lot faster than I do in Houston. I've been living in the past a lot the last few days."

"Yes, well, I'd prefer to live in the present. Rather than die."

He laughed. "I'll take that under consideration."

"Where are we going, anyway?"

"Larry's a drinker. If he has any money, he'll spend it at a bar. So we're gonna check every bar in town."

For a tiny town, Coot's Bayou had more than its share of bars. There were three smack in the middle of town, on Main Street, one bar and grill a few blocks off the main drag, and two more on the interstate.

They hit the highway bars first. One was a nasty, nameless spot in a corrugated tin building with a dirt parking lot filled with motorcycles and pickup trucks.

As they stepped through oil-slicked puddles, Beth had sudden doubts about her fitness as an investigator. Billy Cantu could walk into a place like this without a second thought, but no way she, or even Raleigh, could hope to blend in. Though Daniel had said to keep Mitch as far from the investigation as possible, she was glad to have him at her side. When she looked at him now, standing fierce and tall next to her, she did not see a mild-mannered computer geek. She saw a warrior on a mission.

And her heart skipped a beat.

Her insane, self-sabotaging heart.

"Stick close to me," he said. "Some pretty rough characters hang out here."

His warning was unnecessary. If she could connect the two of them at the hip with Velcro, she would. She was awfully glad to be dressed down in jeans and a plain beige cotton shirt. "So you're familiar with this establishment?"

"I tipped a few back here in my day." His face softened. "I'm just disappointing you right and left, aren't I."

"I'm getting to know a different side of you, that's all." She was surprised, true, but disappointed? Was that the right word?

Beth, come on. He beat up his own brother.

The memory of Mitch on top of Dwayne, pounding with his fists, made her shudder. Even if Dwayne had goaded Mitch into the fight, she disapproved. The man had a temper, and anyone who did not have control of his temper was dangerous.

Still, if Mitch wasn't so strong and physical, could he have subdued Larry? As Daniel had pointed out, Mitch had done a brave thing. Incredibly brave. An unarmed man facing an unbalanced person with a gun—Larry could have killed him. Or any of them.

She didn't know whether to be impressed with his physical prowess, repulsed or scared.

The inside of the no-name bar was dark and smoky. Business seemed brisk for one o'clock in the afternoon. A spirited pool game occupied one corner. Another table filled with men watched the sports channel featuring some replay of a hockey game. A couple more were bellied up to the bar, where a grizzled bartender washed glasses in a sink of gray water.

Beth was the only female in the place. And as she made her way toward the bar, hanging at Mitch's elbow, every eye in the place turned to look at them.

The bartender's face broke into a crooked smile featuring crooked teeth. "Mitch Delacroix! I'd have sworn you were dead!"

"Naw, I just went legit." He made it sound as if that was something to be ashamed of.

"Who's your lady?"

"Beth, this is Amos. Amos, Beth."

"Nice to meet you," Beth said politely.

"Oooowee, how'd you land a classy girl like her?"

"She's not mine, are you kidding? Like she'd have me. She's a coworker, trying to help me out of a jam. You heard about Robby?"

"They not tryin' to pin that on you, are they?"

"'Fraid so."

"That's just wrong." Amos shook his head sadly. "Can I get you somethin' to drink? On the house."

Mitch looked at Beth, and she shook her head. Even

if she drank at this hour of the day, Amos's cleanliness standards would have dissuaded her.

"We came looking for information," Beth said. "We're trying to find a possible witness. Larry Montague. Have you seen him?"

Amos immediately shook his head. "Ain't seen Larry for months."

"He's a fugitive," Beth added. "If you protect him, it's considered a crime."

She knew immediately it was the wrong thing to say. A hostile look came over Amos's face. "I told ya, ain't seen him."

"You'll have to excuse Beth," Mitch said. "She's a little gung ho about her job."

Beth shot him a look. *Thanks for backing me up.* She placed a card on the bar. "I'm sorry if I came off rude. Please call me if he shows up. I'll answer day or night."

Amos narrowed his eyes. "Are you a cop?"

"She's not a cop. She means well. We just want to talk to Larry, okay? No cops."

Beth was about to object, but Mitch shot her a look that quelled her urge to speak.

"Okay, dude." Amos extended his hand. "You take care. Come back some time when you can knock back a few. Catch me up." His message was clear: *next time, come without her.*

As soon as they were back in the parking lot, Mitch went on the offensive. "Beth, what in the hell were you thinking, going all tough-cop interrogator on him? You think that's how to get information from people like Amos? Threaten them with arrest?"

"I know, I know. You don't have to jump all over me. It was the wrong approach."

"No kidding."

"Daniel didn't think I was up to this job. You know, investigating. I guess I was just compensating."

Mitch opened her car door. "Daniel doesn't want you here?"

Maybe she shouldn't have told him that. He'd probably like an excuse to get rid of her; she was cramping his style. "He left it up to me. If I can be useful, he wants me to stay. You really are his top priority."

He didn't respond until he was behind the wheel. "Yeah, well, if you want to be helpful, maybe you better let me do the talking at the next bar."

"I'm sorry, okay?"

Gradually, his face relaxed. "Sorry I jumped all over you. I'm just a little on edge. Everything about being here reminds me of who I used to be. Something I tried to run from. But you can't run from who you are. It catches up with you eventually."

She wasn't sure what to say about that. She'd never tried to change herself. She was the same exact person she'd been in high school. At her ten-year high school reunion, she'd been voted "least changed."

"You made something of your life, Mitch. Every day, you do good. You help other people wrongly accused of crimes. You should be proud of that. Not everyone can make positive changes."

"Yeah, well, right now it sort of seems like I sold out."

"If selling out means you don't feel as if you belong in a bar like that, there's nothing wrong with it."

"Wait till you see the next place we're going. You'll think Amos's place is the Taj Mahal."

The next spot they hit was called Busties. It was a strip club.

Again, Beth was the only woman patron. But the smattering of customers didn't spare her much attention. Their gazes were locked on the anorexic stripper gyrating on stage, who was either bored or stoned out of her mind.

Beth averted her gaze—not because she was offended, but because the hopeless-looking girl made her sad.

No one recognized Mitch here, which was somewhat comforting.

The young bartender didn't know Larry, but one of the waitresses did. "Saw him a couple of weeks ago," she said. "He came in long enough to blow whatever cash he had in his pocket, then he left."

Beth's ears perked up. A couple of weeks ago? Funny that Dwayne hadn't seen him around. But maybe people like Larry Montague took pains not to be seen or noticed by cops.

Beth left her card, and she and Mitch headed to the next establishment.

The two bars on the town square were a little nicer, not quite so dark and smoky, and the clientele wasn't quite as scary. She and Mitch heard the same story they'd heard at Busties: Larry had been by and either got someone to buy him a drink or two, or he played pool and won money for drinking that way. Seemed he was usually out of money.

The last place they went, the Conch & Crab, was more of a sports bar with a kitschy down-on-the-bayou decor that included a six-foot stuffed alligator and a clam tank where you could select your own shellfish. It was the sort of place Beth wouldn't have minded spending time. The food smelled good, anyway.

No one in this place seemed to recognize Larry's picture. "I think I'd remember a face like that," said the bartender, who barely looked old enough to be serving liquor. Then he pointed at Mitch. "You, on the other hand, I've seen before."

"I used to live here years ago," Mitch said.

"No, it's more recent than that—wait a minute, I know. You're a martial artist. You were interviewed in *Fight Club Magazine.* Yeah, that's it! You're the Cagey Cajun!"

Beth burst out laughing. "Mitch, you didn't tell me you were a celebrity."

But Mitch violently shook his head. "No, that's not me, dude."

"Sure it is! Hey, Doug," the bartender called to a friend. "We got the Cagey Cajun right here. You want a beer? It's on the house."

"No, thanks. Let's go, Beth." He headed for the door.

"What's *Fight Club Magazine?*" Beth asked the bartender, wanting to smooth over Mitch's brusque behavior. "Is it local?"

"You're kidding, right? You don't watch MMA? Mixed Martial Arts? Cage fighting?"

She almost laughed at the absurdity of his question. "Is that like pro wrestling?"

"No, no, it's the real deal. The Cajun is lethal."

"Well, it's not Mitch." She placed her card on the bar.

The bartender looked supremely disappointed not to have been able to serve a beer to a celebrity. "It's cool. We have a UFC match on in here every Friday night. Draws a big crowd. You should come. You'll see for yourself how strong the resemblance is."

Beth felt herself blushing when she realized the guy was flirting with her. "I'm in town on business. I'll probably be working Friday night, but thanks for the invite." She didn't add that even the idea of guys beating up other guys for entertainment made her queasy. She'd rather peel off her own fingernails than actually watch men smash their fists into each other.

MITCH DIDN'T WAIT TO SEE if Beth was following him. He just got out of there as quick as he could. Damn, he'd known that MMA was becoming more popular, more mainstream, but he didn't expect to be recognized walking down the street.

Where was she, anyway? Maybe he should go in and make sure she was okay. He didn't like the way that baby-faced bartender was looking her over. Not that he could blame anyone with a Y chromosome for noticing Beth.

And that reminded him—Billy Cantu would be hitting town soon. He liked Billy, but he didn't like the idea of Beth and Billy together on a business trip. Billy would probably stay at the Sleepy Time Motel. Would Beth join him there? If she intended to stay in Coot's Bayou any length of time, she'd probably be more comfortable at a hotel, and the Sleepy Time didn't really have bedbugs, despite what his mother had claimed.

So, she'd be there with Billy in the room right next door, so they could work on his case together.

The pictures racing through his mind made his gut burn. He had no right to be jealous. He had no claim to Beth.

Finally Beth exited the bar and made her way to the El Camino.

"What was that all about?" he asked as he turned the ignition key.

"Our friend in there was *sure* you were this Cagey Cajun character. He was trying to get me to admit it." She laughed. "He even wanted me to come watch a fight on Friday night, so I could see for myself."

"I don't think that's why he invited you."

"I'm not sure if I should be flattered or horrified that a kid barely out of high school was flirting with me."

"You're not going, are you?" That would be very, very bad. He could *not* back out of this fight. He'd signed a contract, and nothing short of death or hospitalization would get him out of it.

"Yeah, I'm going to a bar to drink beer and watch cage fighting." She wrinkled her nose. "Gross."

"It's not *that* gross." He wanted to kick himself right

after the words were out. It was much better if Beth continued to hate his chosen avocation.

"Are you kidding? I can't imagine anything more disgusting."

Now that stung. "How can you say it's disgusting if you've never seen it?"

"So you're a fan of MM…whatever?"

"MMA. Not exactly."

"It's glorified violence." She shivered.

Mitch decided he better change the subject, even though part of him wanted her to understand that it was a sport, like any other, with rules and safeguards. Not like the bare-knuckle street-fighting he did when he was a kid. He still had scars from those days, when combatants threw more than punches. He'd been cut with broken bottles, chains, knives and two-by-fours. He was lucky he still had all his teeth.

He was lucky he hadn't been killed.

MMA was downright tame by comparison.

"We're out of bars," Beth said. "Shall we call it a day?"

"I thought we were just getting started. Larry's probably still in town, somewhere."

"Unless he fled because he's wanted by the police."

"It's more likely he's hanging out with other homeless people, bragging."

"You obviously have some idea of where to look."

"I know where homeless people used to hang. I bet it hasn't changed. But, hey, you've probably had enough of the seamier side of life for one day. Why don't I drop you back at my mom's. You can put your feet up, have a cup of tea—"

"Do I look like a tea drinker? Nothing doing. I know I can't stop you from nosing around, but I'm not going to let you do it alone."

He laughed. "You think you can keep me safe from trouble?"

"I've got a cell phone. I can call for help if I need to."

"You won't need to call anyone. We'll be fine."

"Just remember, if we find him, we back off and call the cops. No heroics."

"Only if you want him to run for the hills."

"You broke his nose! You don't think he'd run from you?"

"The floor broke his nose."

"After you slammed his face into it," she grumbled.

"You aren't seriously criticizing me for taking him down, are you?"

"I'm…" she paused "…okay, I guess I'm grateful. It was a brave thing to do. It was also stupid not to let Dwayne handle it. We could have hunkered down and waited for backup."

"Only if we'd wanted Larry dead. Louisiana cops shoot first and ask questions later."

"That's a gross generalization. Look, Mitch, I don't want to argue about this. It's done. Just promise me you won't go playing hero anymore. Because I assured Daniel I'd keep you out of trouble."

That stopped him. "Daniel thinks I'm going to get myself in trouble? In more trouble?" he amended.

"His words were, 'He's a bit of a loose cannon right now.' He doesn't blame you," she added hastily. "Anybody facing what you're facing would be a bit freaked out. But don't let it affect your judgment. That's all I'm asking. Please, Mitch. I would be devastated if anything happened to you."

Finally, she'd gotten through to him. She cared about him. And he was touched.

"I promise, Beth, that I won't do any more showboating. We'll look—cautiously—for Larry, and if we find him, or even get a whiff of him, we'll call Dwayne."

"Thank you."

"There used to be a homeless encampment near the bayou. We'll check that first."

The original town of Coot's Bayou had sprung up close to the meandering waterway it was named after. But numerous floods had forced the town to rebuild on higher ground. Still, remnants of the original settlement remained, including a bridge that went to nowhere. So long as it didn't rain too much, the area was kind of appealing, with mature cypress and live oak dripping with Spanish moss.

This time of year, it was awash with wildflowers and flitting birds—and a smattering of cardboard cartons, tin shacks, tents and old mattresses.

Mitch and Beth had to park on the dead-end road and walk down an incline to get to the encampment. It looked as though maybe a dozen people were living there, mostly men but a couple of women.

As Mitch and Beth drew closer, a dark-skinned man

in overalls and no shirt stepped in front of them like a brick wall blocking their path. A skinny, scarred bulldog hung at his heels, growling, and Mitch took an instinctive step in front of Beth.

"Who are you and what do you want?" the man asked suspiciously. Every community needed security, and Mitch guessed he'd just met it.

"I'm Mitch, this is Beth," Mitch said on an even keel. "We aren't cops. I've been accused of a crime, and I'm trying to find a guy who might be able to clear me. I'm not looking to cause trouble for anybody, including this guy."

"What guy would that be?"

"Larry. Sometimes they call him Crazy Larry."

"That's offensive. Larry's schizophrenic. He needs help, not labels."

"He calls *himself* that," Mitch explained. "So you know him? Is he around?" Mitch peered over the shoulder of Brick-wall Man to see most of the other transients staring at them with open curiosity. And hostility, from some.

Maybe he'd been wrong. Maybe he couldn't keep Beth safe. He should have insisted she not come with him.

Brick-wall Man loosened up. His dog relaxed, sitting on his haunches to scratch. "Larry has a crib here, but he ain't been around since yesterday evening. He said he was in trouble. Looked like someone had beat his face in. He washed up, put on some different clothes, then lit out of here like a chicken with a fox on its tail."

"Is that unusual?"

"Him getting beat up? No, happens pretty regular. Sometimes he stays out all night, too. But usually he comes back in the morning. So, yeah, a little strange."

"Can we see his place?" Beth asked. "We won't take anything."

Mitch stifled a groan. He wished she would let him handle this. She knew everything there was to know about evidence, but next to nothing about the segment of society they were dealing with.

To his surprise, though, Brick-wall Man agreed. "I guess if you want to just look, that's okay. But we don't put up with thieves around here. People look at us, think we're scum, but we got rules and we take care of our own. You sure you're not cops?"

Mitch extended his foot and pointed to the cuff on his leg. "I'm sure."

Brick-wall Man chuckled. "What they got you on?"

"Murder."

"Damn." The man stepped aside. Mitch wasn't sure if it was out of respect, fear or disgust. "Larry's tent is that red one right over there."

A dozen pairs of suspicious eyes watched them as they approached the red tent. Mitch squatted and lifted the flap. Inside was a filthy sleeping bag and a military-issue backpack stuffed to the gills. The pack sported strange, disturbing slogans scrawled in permanent marker, like Live to Die and Take No Prisoners. But inside, Mitch found only a few clothes, a disposable razor that had seen better days, some granola bars, a pack of cigarettes and a Bic lighter.

"No weapons," Beth observed.

"If he has weapons, he probably carries them on his person," Mitch said. "I can see him leaving clothes behind, but food? And cigarettes? Wherever he went, he planned on returning soon."

"So he's on the run," Beth concluded. "Came back only to change clothes—probably so he wouldn't be identified by that green hoodie."

"Why was he at the shack if he lives here?" Mitch wondered aloud.

"He liked to get off by himself, sometimes," the man answered. "Also, he might've had a girl."

Mitch swiveled around to find Brick-wall Man watching them closely, and listening, obviously.

"Larry had a girlfriend?" Mitch asked.

"I don't know if she was a girlfriend, but he was meeting someone yesterday. A woman. He put on his best camo pants and a clean T-shirt, and he even cleaned his nails. I'm just sayin'."

Beth stood and faced the giant. "Thank you. Your information could be very helpful." She handed him a card. "If you see him, can you let us know?"

He took the card and grinned. "Sure. I'll call you on my cell phone."

Beth either didn't get that he was joking, or chose to ignore the rib.

"If I find out you're out to hurt him," the big man said, "I'm not gonna be happy."

Even Mitch, with his fighting skills, didn't relish the thought of a showdown with this guy. "We just need his help, that's all," Mitch said.

"So," Beth said as they retreated, "is Larry a lady's man? Lots of girlfriends and such?"

"No. I mean, he liked to look, but I don't recall him ever having a girlfriend or even a date."

"He's kind of scary. Wouldn't be high on my list of—" She stopped abruptly.

"Beth? Something wrong?"

She tipped her head back and sniffed the air like a dog hoping to catch the scent of a rabbit. "Do you smell that?"

Mostly all he could smell was the slightly rank sent of the bayou, and the stench of nearby oil refineries. "Nothing out of the ordinary."

"It's unmistakable. Once you know it, you recognize it immediately."

Mitch sniffed the air again. "What?"

"Death. There's something dead nearby." She held her curly hair back from her face with one hand, sweeping her gaze slowly across the landscape as she spun around in a full circle. Finally she pointed to an area on the other side of the road from where they'd walked. It was overgrown with weeds and scrub, and it looked like someone had dumped their garbage. "There."

"How do you know?"

"I've worked enough death scenes that I know a good body dump area when I see one. Plus...I see flies headed that way."

"Oh, that's sick."

But she didn't seem put off by the thought of flies and a dead body. She headed straight across the road and forged her way through the weeds and nettles and thick mesquite shrubs that tore at their pant legs.

Then Mitch did smell something, and it turned his stomach. Surely it was just a dead animal.

Beth seemed to know exactly where she was headed. She paused once, read the signs like an expert tracker might, then changed direction.

The odor of death got really strong, and Mitch pulled the hem of his shirt across his nose and mouth as a makeshift mask.

When they found the body, they damn near tripped over it.

"Oh, shit," Mitch said. There was his old friend, Crazy Larry, with a big hole in the center of his forehead.

CHAPTER TEN

MITCH GRABBED BETH'S hand and tried to drag her away from the hideous scene. "Let's get out of here!"

"We can't just leave. We have to protect the crime scene until the police get here." She would have been faintly amused by Mitch's revulsion if she hadn't been so disturbed at finding their witness murdered. She took her cell phone out of her jeans pocket and dialed 9-1-1.

"This is Beth McClelland, and I've found a dead body. It's Larry Montague." She described their location with a bit of clarification from Mitch, then hung up.

"We should probably move away from the body," Mitch said sensibly. "We don't want to contaminate the crime scene."

Beth knew he was right. But she was in her element; that body could tell her so much, if only she had her plastic bags and a flashlight and tweezers. She could have sent Mitch back to the car for her evidence kit, but she had no legal authority to do anything except contact the police, and it was frustrating as hell.

"Beth, come on."

She whipped on a pair of plastic gloves, which she'd

stashed in her jeans pocket earlier. "I'm just looking. You can go stand by the road if you want, make sure the cops can find us."

"I'm not leaving you alone with a dead body. What if the murderer is still hanging around?"

"Judging from the insect activity, and the lividity I can see on his neck and his arms, he's been here for at least a few hours." She lifted one arm, testing for stiffness, then carefully placed it back exactly where it had been. "He's already been through rigor mortis. So he probably was killed last night some time. It looks like the gun used to kill him was a small caliber, probably a .22."

Beth's hands itched to string up some crime scene tape.

Her gaze traced a path of broken weeds and scrapes in the dry earth that lead away from Larry's feet. "See those marks? He was dragged here and dumped."

"So he wasn't killed here?" Mitch asked. He stood a few feet away, his back facing the body.

It occurred to Beth then that she was being rather callous. To Mitch this wasn't just a dead body, a pile of evidence. It was his old friend.

"Mitch, I'm sorry. I forgot for a minute that you and he were buddies. First you found out Robby's dead, and now you lose Larry."

"Yeah. My mom always said those two would come to bad ends, but I never thought she was right. When you're a kid, you think you're immortal."

He sounded so sad. Beth wanted nothing more than to put her arms around him, to lead him away from this tragic end of a sad life. But she had a duty to perform. The evidence collection guys from the parish lab hadn't impressed her much with their thoroughness or attention to detail; she might be able to spot something they would miss.

"Keep going, Beth. What else do you see?"

She cleared her throat and got back down to business. "When a body is dumped, it can mean that the actual crime scene was someplace that might incriminate the murderer, like in his house or car. Or, it might just mean he didn't want the body discovered for a while. But he wasn't *too* concerned about that, or he would have buried the body or thrown it into the bayou."

"So maybe he needed enough time to clean up, dispose of evidence, but he wanted the body found— because the police will naturally suspect me."

That thought had crossed Beth's mind. If Larry had witnessed Robby's murder, the murderer had a good reason to get rid of him. But the police still assumed Mitch was the actual killer.

"Fortunately, you're wearing that cuff. The GPS history will prove you were at your mom's house when the crime was most likely committed. Right?"

Mitch didn't answer.

"Right, Mitch?"

"I might have gone for a drive last night."

Beth closed her eyes. "Tell me you're kidding."

"I couldn't sleep. I was restless. I took my car and tore up some back roads."

"Great," she muttered, wishing that just once they

could catch a break. Not only was their best chance to clear Mitch lying dead, but the police could conceivably find a way to pin his death on Mitch.

"I didn't come anywhere near here."

"He wasn't killed here."

"But I would've had to move his body here."

"Your accomplice did that."

"What?"

"Just saying. When the police want to make a case, they sometimes invent a mysterious accomplice to explain a lack of evidence." She forced her attention back to the scene. "There's a lot of trash around the body. We might want to tell the crime scene folks to collect it, on the off-chance our murderer discarded a cigarette butt or a piece of gum. But we'll stand a better chance of finding the perp's DNA on the victim's clothes. He was probably nervous when he was moving the body, especially with the homeless camp so close by. He might have been sweating. Or bleeding, even, if there was a struggle. See, there's a red stain on the sleeve of the victim's shirt. That could be very significant."

"Blood?" Mitch asked.

She shook her head. "Dried blood would be more rusty colored. But it's something."

"I hear a siren," Mitch said. "Can we go back to the road now?"

They reached the road just as a Coot's Bayou squad car rounded the bend, then squealed its brakes to avoid hurtling past the dead end into a tree.

Dwayne Bell climbed out from behind the steering wheel, joined by another officer from the passenger seat.

He didn't look pleased.

"What the hell kind of trouble have you two gotten into now?" Dwayne demanded.

"It's Larry," Mitch said. "He's dead."

"The dispatcher told me that much. How is it that you two, of all people on God's green earth, are the ones to find the body?"

"Because we were the ones looking for him," Beth said, not liking Dwayne's tone. "Which is more than the Coot's Bayou police were doing, apparently. If you'd come to this homeless encampment searching for him like we did, you'd have found the body yourself." She was pretty sure the police hadn't been by looking for Larry, or the large man in overalls would have said something about it.

Dwayne glanced at the pathetic grouping of tents and boxes, where the ever-suspicious eyes continued to survey them. Probably ready to run if anybody with a uniform got any closer.

"The body's in there?" He jerked a thumb toward the makeshift town, not sounding pleased by the prospect.

"No, back in there." Beth pointed in the general direction of the untamed scrub. "About thirty or forty yards."

"Then how did you know it was there?"

"You mean you can't smell it?"

Dwayne and his partner, whose name tag identified him as Gomez, both sniffed the air. "No," Dwayne said. "That's a long way to smell a body."

She shrugged. "I have a good nose. It's this way."

Thirty minutes later, the area was crawling with

cops. Seemed every officer from the Coot's Bayou department and the parish force, too, even the ones not on duty, showed up to take a look at the body.

Beth tried to insinuate herself into the crime scene processing, but the CSIs didn't want her anywhere near it. She hadn't exactly endeared herself to them at the shack earlier that day, shouting out her suggestions from behind the crime scene tape and pointing out things they'd missed.

Now they asked Dwayne to remove her, and he made one of those impossible-to-ignore suggestions that she leave them to their jobs.

"They moved the body before they took pictures," she groused. "Who trains these guys? They suck."

"You've got bigger fish to fry," Dwayne reminded her. "Like, I'm still not clear how you so conveniently found the body. *Smelled* the body."

"Ask anyone I used to work with at the Houston P.D.," she said, tripping on a root and barely catching herself before she fell on her face. "I was always the first to smell death. Anyway, I keep telling you, we were *looking* for Larry. If I had a friend who was missing, and I went to her house looking for her and found her dead in the alley behind her house, that wouldn't be a coincidence would it?"

Dwayne sighed. "I suppose not. Lieutenant Addlestein wants to talk to you, though. He's not very happy you two are running around playing cops and robbers. You've been making the rounds, asking questions. You're perilously close to interfering with a police investigation."

KARA LENNOX 171

It wasn't the first time Project Justice personnel had been accused of that, and it wouldn't be the last. It didn't scare her.

"Maybe if you guys would do your job—"

"Whoa, whoa." It was Mitch, who had come out of nowhere when Dwayne and Beth reached the road. "It's my job to fight with my brother, not yours."

Mitch was right. She shouldn't be antagonizing the police, especially the only cop who at least pretended to be on their side.

Beth took a deep breath. "I'm sorry, Dwayne. I'm not trying to be troublesome. But I figured we had a better chance of catching up with Larry than you did. He was going to be avoiding the police."

Dwayne nodded, conceding the point.

"And now I've got a crime scene, my area of expertise, and I can't even watch it being processed and it's driving me crazy."

"It's better for everyone if you stay away from the evidence," Dwayne said. "You're hardly impartial."

Mitch took a step in front of his brother, blocking his way. "Are you insinuating Beth would tamper with evidence?"

"I'm saying she could be accused of that."

"Boys, boys, enough. Mitch, Dwayne is right. I'm not impartial, I'm not a cop. We have to leave this to the police and hope for the best. But, Dwayne, could you do me one teensy favor?"

"What?" he asked, suspicious.

"The victim has a reddish stain on the left shoulder of his shirt. Could you get me a sample? On a Q-tip?"

"I'm sure our lab will analyze it."

"In my lab I have the most advanced ultraviolet-visible spectroscopy. Does Bernadette Parish?"

Dwayne sighed. "I'll see what I can do, but don't hold your breath."

Mitch relaxed slightly and stepped out of Dwayne's way. "My mom called a few minutes ago," he said to Beth. "She wants to know what time we'll be home for dinner."

Such a mundane question. Beth wished with all her heart that she could sit down at Myra's table and enjoy another cholesterol-laden meal, drink a beer and forget about murder for an hour or two.

"Better tell her to start without you," Dwayne said. "Lieutenant Addlestein has lots of questions for you."

Just then a bright red pickup truck came roaring down the road, raising a cloud of dust and causing everyone who'd been milling around to freeze and look up. The vehicle screeched to a stop in the middle of the road. As the engine stilled, the driver's door opened and a powerfully built Hispanic man climbed out and surveyed the scene.

His eyes lit on Beth and a big smile split his face as he strode toward her, his ostrich-hide boots thunking on the blacktop with every step.

He scooped Beth into a bear hug. He was one of those people who hugged a lot, and Beth didn't mind. She was relieved to have reinforcements finally arrive.

"You just had to go and find a dead body without me?"

"I'm talented that way," Beth said.

"Who the hell are you?" Dwayne demanded.

The man turned toward Dwayne, friendly as an oversized puppy. One with teeth. "Howdy. I'm Billy Cantu, from Project Justice."

Dwayne shook Billy's outstretched hand only grudgingly. "It's getting so thick with you Project Justice people around here I can't spit without hitting one of you."

"That's 'cause Mitch is one of our own. We're pulling out all the stops." He nodded to Mitch. "*Amigo.* Daniel says to get your ass in front of the computer where it belongs."

"MITCH." DWAYNE NODDED toward his squad car. "I'll give you a ride to the station."

Right. Mitch had a date with Lieutenant Addlestein.

His first instinct was to tell his brother to forget it, he'd sooner walk all the way to the station, barefoot, on broken glass, than accept a ride. Back when they were kids and Dwayne had bought his first car, Mitch had secretly hoped his big brother would acknowledge him, maybe give him a ride now and then. But Dwayne had refused to let Mitch so much as touch his wheels— which had led to the potatoes-in-the-tailpipe incident.

Then Mitch saw the look Beth gave him, and he was forced to reconsider. She didn't have to say a word; he saw it all in her eyes. She wanted him to make nice.

He could feel the muscles in his jaw tensing, but he forced himself to slide into the passenger side of Dwayne's vehicle. He even fastened his seat belt without being prodded.

For a few minutes the two men rode in silence. Dwayne seemed to be trying to come up with something to say; he opened his mouth a couple of times, then shut it again without speaking. Mitch wasn't inclined to make things any easier on him.

Finally Dwayne spoke. "I just wanted you to know, I didn't mean for this to happen. I didn't mean for you to become a real suspect."

"Why don't I believe that? You sure never went out of your way to bail me out of any scrapes when we were younger. Like when I was a scrawny sixth-grader, and those high school boys cornered me and beat the crap out of me just 'cause they could?"

"I know. I could have stopped it and I didn't. I was too busy trying to be cool. I'd just made the football team. For the first time in my life, I realized I could be someone besides the town drunk's kid. And I was scared to death of losing that."

"What are you talking about? Everybody loved you."

"You're remembering things wrong. I struggled, same as you, trying to figure out where I fit in. I was the quiet kid who tried to be invisible. I got good grades so no one had reason to complain. It wasn't until I got a growth spurt and started to be good at sports that I saw a glimmer of hope for myself."

Mitch didn't like the squirmy feeling that came over him. He didn't want to feel any compassion for his brother. "At least Daddy was proud of you."

"I'm not sure where you got that idea, but if he approved of anything I did, he never let me know it. When I got an A in English, I was a pansy-ass Goody

Two-shoes. He thought I was a sheep, doing what everyone told me to do. You, on the other hand, thought for yourself. You built your own computer out of bubble gum and baling wire, to hear him tell the story. You, Mitch, were his favorite. At least, that was how he made it seem."

"Me, his favorite? Are you on crack? You were the award-winning athlete, focused, self-sacrificing."

"'What good is football?'" Dwayne did a remarkable imitation of their father. "'You can't make a career out of it, you're not that good. All being a football player does is make the girls drop their drawers for you so you can get 'em pregnant. Like your mama did to me.'"

"Jeez, you sound just like him. That's creepy."

"You know what's creepier? I'm starting to look like him. At least you were spared that."

Mitch had to agree, it was a blessing he'd taken after his mom in the looks department. He would hate to have to look at his father's face while he shaved.

"Did he really say that to you?" But Mitch already knew it was true.

"And a lot more. 'You should be more like Mitch. Now, there's a young man who's not afraid to speak his mind and think for himself. He'll be a senator someday.'"

"A senator?" Mitch nearly choked on his own spit. "He used to tell me I'd end up in a gutter somewhere. And you were such a born leader, you'd go on to be an NFL head coach."

"You gotta be kidding."

"Swear it on my grandma's grave."

They rode in stunned silence for a while. "He played us against each other."

"He liked having power over people," Dwayne said quietly. "And who better to manipulate than two boys desperate for their father's approval? One kind word. I never got it. Did you?"

"Hell, no." Mitch observed Dwayne from the corner of his eye, trying to figure out his game. But what he saw there convinced him, once and for all, that there was no game. Dwayne's eyes glistened with tears.

IT WAS AFTER EIGHT by the time Dwayne dropped off Mitch at his mother's house. His mom had waited dinner on him, but the thought of food still turned Mitch's stomach.

Poor Larry.

Billy had finagled an invitation to dinner, claiming he needed to be debriefed. But probably, he'd been lured by the prospect of a home-cooked meal.

His mom fussed around them, setting out plates and pouring iced tea. "Come on in and sit down, you must be famished."

"I appreciate your hospitality, Mrs. LeBeau," Billy said.

"Call me Myra, please. It's no trouble. I always make extra, just in case. I hope you like Frito chili pie."

"Are you kidding? I used to live on that stuff when I was a kid. I didn't think you could get it outside Texas."

"Well, we're close enough that some of the Tex-Mex influence drifts across the Sabine River. How about Cajun food? Do you like that?"

Billy clutched his heart. "I *love* Cajun food. Jambalaya, red beans and rice, boiled crawfish."

"Maybe we'll do a big crawfish boil this weekend."

"Mom," Mitch said, "this isn't a house party."

"Everyone still has to eat."

Mitch was mildly irritated at the way Billy just breezed in and charmed everyone. Not that Mitch couldn't turn on the charm when he wanted to, especially with the ladies, but underneath he knew he couldn't always hide the edge. His lazy drawl was something he'd worked on because his innate angry intensity hadn't won him any friends.

With Billy, Mitch suspected the charm came naturally. He didn't know what Billy's background was like, but he suspected he hadn't scrapped his way through childhood. Things seemed to come easily to him.

Or maybe Mitch was just jealous because he didn't like the way Beth smiled at Billy. Mitch preferred having all of her attention focused directly on *him,* selfish bastard that he was. Hell, Billy was here to help, yet Mitch had a hard time cultivating the appropriate gratitude.

Then again, gratitude had never been his strong suit. He'd never liked owing anybody anything and frankly, hadn't had many times when he'd felt anyone had it coming.

His mom scooped a mountain of her casserole in front of each of them. Loaded with fat, it wasn't the sort of meal he should be eating when he was supposed to be in training. But training for his upcoming fight had been pretty far from his mind the past couple of days.

He should call the promoter now and cancel. It was looking less and less likely that he would beat the charges against him so quickly. Hell, he wouldn't be all that shocked if he got *another* murder pinned on him. Once the cops reviewed his GPS history from last night he would have more explaining to do. Lieutenant Addlestein's questions hadn't been gentle. He'd gotten in Mitch's face, trying to force some kind of confession. But Mitch had kept his cool.

"Oh, man, this really takes me back," Billy said.

"I can give you the recipe," Myra offered. "It's easy."

"Um, I don't really cook much."

Billy was addicted to fast food. Mitch's diet had once been just as unhealthy, until he'd fallen into the world of MMA and learned the virtues of lean protein.

He took a couple of bites of the casserole, but his stomach rebelled and he laid down his fork.

"Is something wrong?" Beth asked.

"Just not very hungry." He wasn't about to admit to a weak stomach in front of Billy.

"First dead body, huh?" Billy jumped, and it was clear Beth had kicked him under the table.

"Billy, not at the table."

Mitch could feel his temper rising, and he didn't even know why. Maybe it was because he'd never felt so powerless. And he wasn't sure he trusted Billy Cantu with his life. Beth, yeah. But Billy was just so damn casual about everything....

"Excuse me," Mitch said. "I really don't have much of an appetite." He carried his plate to the sink.

"I can save that for you." His mom took the plate. Of

course she wouldn't want to waste good food. Although she was no longer living hand to mouth, the habits of poverty died hard.

"Sure, Mom, thanks." Although he didn't think he'd ever eat Frito chili pie again.

Beth cast worried glances at him, in between sharing looks with Billy.

"I'm fine," he said for her benefit. "I'll go tend to the livestock."

He didn't take a full breath until he was outside. He really needed to hit something, but though Daniel had thought of almost everything when he'd sent his belongings down here, he hadn't included a punching bag.

The chickens saw him coming and, perhaps sensing his mood, scuttled toward their enclosure before he'd even reached the outer pen. He checked that they had fresh water, then tossed them a few handfuls of grain.

The goats were next. As he tried to grab hold of the billy's halter, the goat skittered away and tried to butt him in the thigh.

"Come on, you idiot, I'm gonna feed you."

The nannies and the one tiny kid were easier—they just followed him docilely into the miniature barn and went right into their stalls. Finally the billy realized the error of his ways and trotted to his stall door.

Mitch fed them each a measure of oats. The kid nursed while his mother was occupied with her food, and Mitch paused to watch them, trying to draw some comfort from the sweet sight.

It wasn't working. Maybe a long, hard run was what

he needed. Or…he spied some bales of hay stacked in one corner of the barn. As a kid, with no proper training equipment, he used to pummel hay.

He took an experimental punch at the stack of dried grass. Hell, that would work. He gave it a right hook, a left uppercut, then spun around and kicked the hay in its head. But the hay was a tough bastard. He wouldn't go down.

Mitch ducked under his opponent's imaginary strike and hit him with a shoulder to the gut. Mr. Hay was up against the ropes now, feeling pain. Mitch yanked his T-shirt over his head and tossed it aside.

He punished his enemy with a chop to the neck, followed by a quick jab to the ribs. And just when the guy thought he had a chance, Mitch threw him to the mat, quickly straddling him.

"Had enough, mofo?" Mitch didn't give the guy an inch. He wedged a forearm under the guy's chin and went for the elbow joint. About this time, his opponent usually tapped out.

Mitch felt a searing pain on his forearm. At first he didn't give into it because he'd learned to ignore pain. But his opponent was a bale of hay, not a real fighter looking for weakness. Mitch reared back and saw blood on his arm.

Damn, the son of a bitch was fighting back. He'd been nailed by a piece of baling wire.

"Mitch?"

He looked up to see Beth, staring at him with horrified eyes, and he wanted to sink through the barn's dirt floor.

"Why are you beating up a bale of hay?"

He hopped to his feet. Why did she, of all people, have to come upon him like this? Twice?

"Just working off some frustration, that's all."

"You're bleeding."

He picked up his discarded T-shirt and held it against his bleeding forearm. It was just a scratch. "No big deal."

"How long since you've had a tetanus shot?"

"Honey, I'm fine, okay?" His impromptu workout had helped. The anger had seeped away, leaving in its place a pleasant physical exhaustion and a certain sense of misplaced satisfaction at having bested his sneaky opponent.

He touched Beth's shoulder. "Please don't worry—"

She edged away from him, just like the chickens had.

Oh, God. She was afraid of him.

"Billy wants to do the debriefing now." She turned and headed for the door. "I thought you'd want to—"

"Beth, Beth, wait." He wanted to grab her arm, to stop her from leaving, but he didn't dare touch her even in the gentlest way. He already knew she didn't take kindly to anyone physically challenging her.

She did slow down, though. "What?"

"You know I would never, ever hurt you, right?"

When she turned to face him, her eyes glinted with tears. "No, I don't know that. Vince used to say that to me all the time, and I believed him. He would throw a full beer can at the TV, or break a dish on purpose, but then he would promise me that he would never hurt me."

"Until one day he did."

"Yeah. Everyone was so shocked. Everyone said he was such a nice guy, sweet and funny. And he was, most of the time."

"Except when he wasn't. I get it, Beth. You think I'm like him."

"I don't know what to think. It seems every time I turn around you're wailing on something—punching bags, hay, not to mention the human beings."

"I've never in my life hit a woman. Never. I'm not like him. He had a history. I looked into it myself, after you pressed charges. It was a pattern with him. I'm different."

"There had to be a first time. With Vince, I mean. He had a temper. He *snapped*. Maybe you think you can control it, but three...four times now, I've witnessed something that has no relation to 'control.' You weren't seeing a wad of hay just now. You were seeing a human being, and I shudder to think what was going through your mind."

She had him there.

"Your dad?"

Not this time. But no way would he admit he'd been thinking about Billy, a man who was supposed to be his friend. A man who was trying to help him beat a murder rap.

"I wasn't thinking about anybody specific," he lied. "Just blowing off steam. It's something I do. It's something I have to do. But don't go lumping me with your loser-abuser ex. I'm not a bully. I don't hit people who don't hit me first. Maybe I have a temper, but I deal with it in a way that's worked for me for a long time. If you want to judge me for beating up punching bags and hay bales, go ahead."

For half a moment, she looked as though she was going to do just that. "What about Dwayne?"

"He threw the first punch. Anyway, that wasn't a serious fight. Okay, maybe a little bit serious. But if I'd wanted to hurt him, I could have, and I didn't."

Beth's face crumpled, and a sob came out of her that sounded like a wounded animal.

"Beth, don't cry." Crap, now what did he do? He was afraid to touch her, afraid anything he did would send her running, and he couldn't let her run from him.

She saved him from having to make any decision at all. She threw herself at his sweaty torso and wrapped her arms around him. "I'm sorry, Mitch," she said between sobs. "I don't know what came over me. It's no business of mine if you want to punch hay or leather bags, or homeless guys shooting at innocent people. And Dwayne…you have a right to defend yourself."

"Beth, I'm all sweaty…"

"Of course I have no idea what you're going through."

"It's a hot button with you. I get that. But you don't have to be afraid of me. I would never in a million years—"

"I know. I know. Just forget I said anything, okay?"

Maybe he could forgive the words she'd flung at him in an emotional moment. But he couldn't forget the way she'd shied from his touch. He stroked her hair, soft as a bird's feathers, calming her the way he might a skittish dog.

"I'm sorry I frightened you."

She gave a half laugh, half sob. "It doesn't take much. I'm pretty easy to scare."

He tipped her chin up until she was looking at him. "You're brave as hell. You stood up to that humongous man at the homeless camp. And you didn't let Lieutenant Addlestein intimidate you."

"Maybe I didn't look scared on the outside, but I was quaking on the inside."

"You were magnificent. I'm lucky to have you on my side."

"I'm so afraid I'll fail you."

"The system might fail me, honey. But not you. And if you don't let go of me and move away, like, now, I'm going to kiss you again."

She didn't move a muscle. She just stared up at him, her lips slightly parted. He could feel her breathing, her heart beating.

"Fair warning." He wanted to give her every opportunity to walk away from this.

Instead, she stood on her toes and closed the gap between them, pressing her delectable mouth against his.

Mitch had enough adrenaline floating around in his bloodstream that an alligator could swim through it. Now instead of fueling his anger, it all went straight to his libido. He was already half-naked, and ten feet away was a pile of hay, and all he could think about was getting Beth horizontal in that nice hay, which his fists had already softened, and getting down to her bare skin.

He broke the kiss long enough to push out a few strangled words. "I want you. And I don't want to even think about any more bullshit excuses why we can't be together."

"Billy's waiting for us." She still sounded dangerously close to crying.

"Is that your only objection?"

Her hands were all over him. "Yes. God help me."

"What about...you know."

Somehow, despite his lack of clarity, she understood. "I'm protected."

"Then Billy can wait."

CHAPTER ELEVEN

SOMEWHERE IN THE BACK of her mind, Beth knew she was making a colossal mistake. But she'd wanted Mitch for so long, and the tension between them was like a violin string tightened to the breaking point. Either they were going to have to have sex, or the string was going to snap.

Truly, it wasn't him snapping that worried her so much. It was her. She felt out of control. She needed to let off steam, and unlike Mitch, she didn't think punching a hay bale senseless would do the trick.

Before she knew what was happening, she was flat on her back in a pile of soft, dried grass. Mitch was considerate enough to remove the baling wire that he'd cut his hand on and toss it aside, but then all intelligent thought fell by the wayside.

There was no time for leisurely undressing. She yanked her shoes off without even undoing the laces and wiggled out of her jeans and panties. Mitch was even faster than she was. In seconds flat he was beside her in the hay, kissing the breath right out of her, and all around them was the pleasant, pastoral scent of alfalfa grass.

She'd managed to get her shirt half-unbuttoned.

Mitch finished the job and pushed it off her shoulders. For a moment her arms were trapped inside the sleeves and she felt a spark of panic. But then Mitch was so gentle as he helped her off with the garment that she let go of any lingering fear.

She quickly unclasped her bra and her breasts, achy and sensitive, sprang loose.

Mitch made a noise in his throat which she took to mean approval. His pupils darkened as he gazed at her, then gently, reverently caressed her breasts with his fingertips.

"You're more beautiful than I ever imagined."

It warmed her all over to know he'd pictured her naked, just as she'd done with him. And yes, the reality was far better. She felt his arousal against her hip, and she reached between their bodies to explore, wanting to experience him in every way possible.

As soon as she touched him he groaned, and all she could think about was having his erection inside her, filling her. She wanted not just the physical sensations of sex, but the intimacy.

She wanted him to be part of her.

Shifting slightly, she parted her legs and invited him inside, but despite the furtive nature of their coupling, he didn't rush. As he kissed her breasts, first one, then the other, and her nipples puckered into hard, rosy peaks, he trailed his fingers along her inner thigh.

When he finally touched her sex, she whimpered with the force of her red-hot desire. He brushed one finger between her slick folds and made another of those low growls of approval.

She tried to relax and savor his warm breath on her skin and the gentle exploration between her legs, but her body was primed for completion and she wanted him inside her when that happened. If he so much as touched her a quarter-inch to the left... She wiggled away slightly, then spread her legs wider, practically sobbing for him to put her out of her misery and enter her.

She didn't care if Billy wondered where they were. Right then, she wouldn't have cared if he walked in on them dragging the entire population of Coot's Bayou with him to have a look. She just wanted to join with Mitch, because she knew that for those few moments, he was hers.

Liquid heat pooled between her legs. "Mitch, I want you inside me," she whispered. "Now please!" Before they were interrupted. Or he came to his senses and changed his mind. She would die on the spot if anything stopped this beautiful, perfect moment.

"I can't refuse you when you beg, honey."

Finally, *finally,* he plunged inside her, and she took the length of him in one long, firm stroke. Nothing had ever felt so right. Before this moment, she'd thought she knew what good sex was, but nothing in her experience had prepared her for the delicious fusing of body and soul. With the suddenness of a pile of gunpowder igniting, they were one. He was in her body, in her head, in her heart, and her eyes filled with tears at the utter beauty of that singular moment.

His thrusts were not gentle; his control was slipping, and it should have scared Beth. But she didn't care. She raised her hips to meet each thrust, her arms wrapped around his neck holding him fast as if he might escape from her.

He would, she knew. She couldn't ignore the troubling thought that he wasn't hers to keep. Maybe his spirit was too wild for any woman to claim. But she had this moment, and no one could ever take that away from her.

I love you, Mitch. The thought came to her clear and clean as a cold morning breeze. He'd shown her his dangerous side, and she didn't care. Falling for him was probably the most knowingly reckless thing she'd ever done, and she didn't care.

The physical sensations built, bouncing off her emotions until it was all mixed up in one giant ball of hallelujah. She wanted to scream with joy when she climaxed, but still conscious of their less-than-private location, she pressed her face into the corded muscles of his neck and made a noise that sounded like a strangled groan.

I love you, Mitch, she thought again. *Don't say it aloud, don't say it aloud.*

"Sweet heaven," he murmured just before his whole body stiffened and he reached that same summit she'd just visited. She'd heard men make all kinds of outbursts during similar moments, but Mitch's words were the most moving of them all. If she could give him a little sliver of heaven during this awful episode in his life, she would make whatever sacrifices that entailed.

For him. "I love you, Mitch," she whispered. But she

did it very quietly, and she was pretty sure he was so far into his own world that he didn't hear.

WHEN MITCH AND BETH RETURNED to the house, Billy sat at the kitchen table with Myra, entertaining her with some wildly exaggerated yarn. Mitch couldn't recall ever hearing his mother laugh like that, and for a moment he just stood at the door and watched, his antagonism toward Billy melting away.

Billy could tease a laugh out of anyone.

"Guess we needn't have worried Billy would come looking for us," Beth whispered. "He seems perfectly content."

Billy and Myra both looked over when Mitch and Beth entered. "Oh, there you are," Billy said. "I was about to go on a search."

"Except you wouldn't want to get goat poop on your new boots," Mitch couldn't help saying.

"Is everything okay out there?" his mom asked. "Is Snowball…I mean the kid okay?"

"Yeah, fine."

"That baby goat is the cutest thing I've ever seen," Beth said, which served as a decent excuse for why she'd spent so long in the barn. "I need to go, um, wash my hands." She made her escape up the stairs.

Mitch washed his hands at the kitchen sink, using a dish towel to wipe his face and neck. He didn't recall if Beth had been wearing any lipstick, but he wanted to remove any traces of it from view.

He was still trembling with the enormity of what they'd just done. But he'd never felt an urge as powerful as that. The intensity of the encounter had fully dowsed Mitch's lingering anger, leaving a curious, mellow feeling.

Warm. Sweet. Dangerous.

She'd said she loved him. It had been barely a whisper, but he was almost positive he'd heard it. He'd been thrilled for about ten seconds. Then he'd come down from the physical high of his climax.

Lord in heaven, what had he done?

Beth reappeared. His mother, knowing they had business to discuss, retreated to the living room to watch TV with Davy.

"So, what's the scoop?" Beth asked Billy. "While we were stuck getting interrogated by Lieutenant Humorless, I assume you were running around collecting evidence to free our client?"

"I'm working down the list you gave me. Caught up with Amanda, the old girlfriend. Since the old days she's married, divorced, married again. Has a couple of kids. Seemed sad about Robby's death, in a nostalgic sort of way. I didn't sense any lingering anger, and she didn't seem to be hiding anything."

"She's had twelve years to prepare for the moment she would be questioned," Beth pointed out.

Billy just shook his head. "She's a nonstarter. The night he disappeared, she was working at her fast-food job. She's the kind of person who keeps *everything,* even work schedules from twelve years ago. She was at work that night."

"Could be faked," Beth said. "Who keeps a work schedule for twelve years?"

"She had boxes and boxes of records in a back bedroom, all neatly categorized and labeled," Billy said. "I could track down her supervisor, see if he remembers her going home sick or trading shifts with someone, but I think my time could be better spent."

Beth sighed. "Okay. What else?"

"I also talked to the original owner of the Monte Carlo, Harvey Clayton."

"Jeez, you get around," Mitch commented.

"When the car was stolen, he'd been hiding his key under the mat and leaving his door unlocked for months, telling anyone who'd listen that he'd done so, hoping the car would get stolen. He wanted the insurance money a lot more than he wanted the car, and he was ecstatic when it was not only stolen, but never recovered. Made his life easier."

Beth put her head in her hands. "Dammit, we need *something* to work with."

"This should cheer you up." Billy reached to the floor by his chair and produced a brown paper bag with an evidence tag. The tag had been carefully signed by Dwayne, then Billy.

"My Q-tip?"

"Yup."

Beth added her name to the card as she took possession, her spirits mildly buoyed. She couldn't wait to get back to the lab and find out what the stain was. Maybe it meant nothing; a homeless person's clothes were apt to be stained with anything. But the overall-clad man from the homeless encampment had made a point of mentioning that Larry had put on a clean T-shirt, so it was more than likely a fresh stain.

"What's on the agenda for tomorrow?" Beth asked.

"I have an address for Studs the Fence," Mitch said. "I emailed it to Billy."

"I'll try to roust him out of bed in the morning," Billy said. "What about you, Beth?"

"I'm hoping the police will release the crime scene and I can do my own search," Beth said. "Those guys couldn't find a clue if it jumped up and bit them in their collective butts. I want to return to the shack, as well. Wish I had a metal detector. There were a lot of areas that got skipped in previous searches."

"I think Davy's got one you can use," Mitch said. "Saw it in the barn."

"Excellent."

"Beth…" Billy looked like he had something unpleasant to say.

"What?"

"It's just that…there's a murderer out there somewhere. And you're not really trained for fieldwork."

"Daniel told you to keep an eye on me, is that it? I keep an eye on Mitch, you keep an eye on me?"

"Something like that. He worries."

"Like a mother hen," Mitch groused, leaning back in his chair and lacing his fingers behind his head.

"I don't think you should go to remote areas by yourself," Billy said. "That's all."

"She won't be alone," Mitch said. "I'll be with her."

"Mitch, you're supposed to steer clear of the investigating," she reminded him.

"Now, who's gonna know I was there unless you tell them, huh?" he pointed out.

She sensed this was an argument she wouldn't win. If Raleigh were here, she would take charge and sling orders. But if Beth tried to give orders, the two men would probably laugh at her.

"If you want to put the investigation at risk, I suppose that's your choice," she said tartly. "It's your neck on the line." What else was she going to do? Tattle to Daniel that the boys weren't playing nice?

"That's settled, then," Billy said. She'd been hoping he would take her side against Mitch. But the Y chromosomes were hanging together. "You want a ride to the hotel, or do you have your own car?"

"I'm, um…"

"She's staying here," Mitch said.

Billy raised one eyebrow. "That so doesn't look good. Would you stay at the home of any other Project Justice client?"

"Mitch isn't just a client. He's a friend. Anyway, Daniel said I should…" Hell, might as well admit it. "Daniel said I should keep Mitch out of trouble." Something she had so far been dismal at.

Billy and Mitch both laughed at her expense. All right, so she wasn't particularly suited to the job of enforcer. Did they have to make a big deal about that?

Especially Mitch. He shouldn't be laughing at her, given what they'd just shared in the barn. Unless it didn't mean as much to him as it did to her.

"I know I'm about as effective as a wet dishrag at making Mitch do anything, but I have to at least try.

I'm going to bed. It's been a long day. Mitch, give me your car keys."

"Wh-what?" He looked as if he was about to burst out laughing.

"I don't want you going on any more midnight rambles. If you can't sleep, read a book."

"Midnight rambles?" Billy asked.

"I went for a late-night drive last night, the night Larry was killed. It might have compromised my alibi."

Billy shook his head. "You have a GPS cuff that could prove you were home when a crime occurred, and you blew it?"

"I know, I know. Guess I should have known someone would get killed that night and I'd get blamed, right?"

"Give Beth your car keys."

Seeing that neither of them was going to back down, Mitch reached into his jeans pocket, extracted the keys and handed them to Beth. "I can get them from you anytime I want, you know."

Oh, she didn't doubt that. It appeared he could pretty much get anything he wanted from Beth.

FOR THE FIRST TIME since he'd been arrested, Mitch slept well. Maybe it was just knowing that Project Justice was on the case. Or maybe it was the mind-blowing sex with Beth, which had at least temporarily lessened the tension between them. Even knowing she was sleeping just a few feet away in the guest room didn't keep him awake for too long. His imagining what Beth might be wearing to bed transitioned pleasantly into erotic dreams, and he awoke rested.

But as he pulled on a pair of jeans, niggling doubts needled him. Making love to Beth might have eased the tension between them, but it had stirred up a hornet's nest of other problems. Like, where did they go from here?

He wasn't ready for a relationship with her. Maybe he would be if he could get out from under all criminal charges. But until then, it was totally unfair to grab on to Beth as some sort of lifeline to everything that was sane and beautiful.

If he wanted Beth, he needed to earn her, to become the sort of man she deserved. He wasn't sure he could do that; but what he could do was treat her with more respect.

Having his way with her in a barn was *not* respectful. Neither was coming on to her like a raging rhinoceros. He'd told her he wanted rose petals and a feather bed, yet he'd settled for hay.

Telling her he was sorry wouldn't be adequate. Actions spoke louder than words, which meant that he had to prove to Beth that despite what she'd seen of him lately, he was essentially a gentle person who wanted, above all, to treat her right. To do the right thing, for once in his life.

As he headed for the bathroom, he met Beth on her way out. She had just showered, and she wore only a thin robe. She was clearly damp and naked underneath. His resolve immediately started to crumble around the edges.

"Hey. Beth. Good morning." Under the circumstances, he thought that was pretty good, stringing four words together coherently.

"Oh, hi, Mitch." She looked down shyly. He wanted to capture her, put her up against the wall and press his body against hers. But he'd learned his lesson about manhandling her and wouldn't attempt it even in a playful way.

"Sleep okay?"

Good manners forced her to pause long enough to answer him. "Not the best."

"I'm sorry to hear that." What would that sweet, gentle, easygoing man of her dreams say? "Is the bed okay? Do you need an extra blanket or a different pillow?"

"No, the bed is fine." She lowered her voice. "It would have been better with you in it."

Oh, Lord in heaven. He could smell her soap now. Today it was a heady combination of vanilla and lavender that made him lick his lips.

Was she saying she was okay with what had happened last night? It would be so easy just to fall into a casual sexual relationship with her. But he couldn't. He simply couldn't allow that to happen. What if it leaked to the press? Being with Beth could compromise any work she did on his behalf.

Not to mention Daniel would have his job, if not his head.

But how rude was it to just pretend it never happened?

"I wish I could have spent the night with you, darlin'. But I think you and I both know it's not the right time."

Surprise flashed briefly in her eyes before she caught herself and schooled her face. "Of course. Of *course* I know that. I'm just saying it's…anyway…see you at breakfast." She turned on her heel and hurried back into her room, almost slamming the door.

Sometimes he just didn't understand women. He'd obviously handled that wrong, but he wasn't sure how else to do it. She had to know they shouldn't muddy the waters with a personal relationship when they had a lot of other balls to keep in the air.

When he came downstairs, showered and dressed, he found his mother and Beth making breakfast. His mom was cooking waffles, and Beth was stirring a pitcher of orange juice.

"Good morning, Mitch," his mother said with an almost forced cheerfulness.

"Morning, Mom. You don't have to go to all this trouble for me."

"Nonsense. I love making breakfast. Davy only likes his Grape-Nuts, so it's a pleasure to fix something different for a change. Besides, Beth confessed to me that she usually makes do with a carton of yogurt in the morning. A working girl needs something that'll stick to her ribs."

He could argue that Beth's high-protein yogurt had a lot more rib-sticking power than a pile of simple carbs in the form of waffles, and was probably healthier, but it wasn't what either of them wanted to hear.

"Well, I appreciate it. Beth, why don't you sit down

and let me do that? You're the guest here, and you did give up staying in a hotel with a free breakfast buffet."

Not to mention hot and cold running Billy.

Mitch couldn't deny he enjoyed the view of Beth's jean-clad bottom twitching back and forth as she vigorously stirred the orange juice. He wasn't used to seeing her in jeans. At work she usually wore dresses or skirts with lots of ruffles and bright colors, reminding him of a pretty doll that you would put on the shelf and admire, but not play with.

Dressed down in jeans and sneakers and a tank top, she was something with which he very much wanted to play.

"I'm not here to be waited on," she answered without looking at him.

"Let me pour you some coffee, then." He'd noticed that the coffeepot had just about finished its brewing cycle. "Cream and sugar, right?"

"Black. Thanks."

How was it that he'd never noticed how Beth took her coffee?

He poured all three of them coffee in the pale green glass mugs he remembered from childhood, but which probably dated back a lot further than that. His mother didn't tend to replace anything unless it broke or wore out, and these cups would never do either, apparently.

"Where's Davy?" he asked.

"Oh, he's usually up and out of the house before sunup. He eats his cereal, then drinks coffee with his farmer friends at the Primrose Café. As if a couple of goats and a half-dozen chickens make him a farmer."

Chuckling, Myra opened the waffle iron and added another golden square to a growing stack on a plate—more waffles than the Primrose Café had served today, probably. She set the plate in the middle of the table, along with a bottle of Aunt Jemima and a plastic tub of margarine. They all took their seats.

"So, Beth, are you making progress? Is Project Justice finding evidence to prove my son's innocence? I've seen on TV how you do it—the DNA and ballistics, surveillance video. Surely with all the scientific tests, you can prove Mitch was home in bed when Robby was killed."

"Unfortunately, TV makes it seem a lot easier than it is. Those shows condense an entire investigation into an hour, when in reality it might have taken weeks or months."

Myra didn't look happy about that prospect. "I wish it could be like on TV. You find the missing witness, and you trip him up and he confesses to the crime."

"I wish that, too. But we have made some progress," Beth said.

"We have?" Mitch had yet to see it.

"I had an email from Cassie this morning. She had a chance to look at the slug from the shack, and her findings are quite interesting."

"Really."

"The projectile was a 9 millimeter, 124-grain high-tech hollow point. It's the kind of bullet that's favored by law enforcement, and the amount of oxidation means it's been there at least a few years. We'll need to find out what kind of ammunition the Coot's Bayou police were using twelve years ago."

Mitch, who had just put a bite of waffle into his mouth, now struggled to chew and swallow it because it suddenly tasted like a wad of newsprint.

Beth didn't have to say what she was thinking, it came through loud and clear. She thought a member of the police force had killed Robby, then covered it up.

The same police who were now doing their damnedest to prove Mitch was the guilty party.

If that was the case, chances were good other members of the police knew. They would stick together, the cops—even Dwayne. Even if the guilty party was no longer on the force, even if he was dead, they would lie to protect him, one of their own.

How was Mitch going to fight that?

CHAPTER TWELVE

"Knock knock, are you in?"

Beth, who had been in her lab poring through a computer database of lipstick brands, jumped nearly out of her chair. "Raleigh. You scared me half to death."

Raleigh laughed. "Sorry. I tapped on the door several times."

Beth knew that when she was engrossed in something, she tended to shut everything else out. She pushed her chair away from the computer, removed her glasses and massaged the bridge of her nose. "How did your hearing go?"

"Score another one for the good guys. The judge overturned James Hattaway's conviction, and as soon as all the paperwork is done, he'll be a free man."

"That's excellent, Raleigh. I know how hard you've been working on that case."

"Now that it's done, I can devote more time to Mitch's case. How is our newest client doing?"

"In a helluva mood when I left him after breakfast this morning. You heard about the DNA?"

"No, what?"

"Cassie got the DNA analysis done on the blood from the floor splinters. She submitted it to CODIS, and guess whose name popped up?" CODIS was the national DNA database.

"Robby Racine."

Beth nodded vigorously. "Also, we've identified one of the bullets found at the shack. It's a 124-grain high-tech hollow point projectile."

"Cop ammo."

"In good enough condition to make a match, if we could find a gun to match it to. Although there's no legal chain of evidence on the bullet, so all it can do is lead us to a suspect, not help convict him."

"Mitch isn't happy about possible police involvement? No, of course not. That certainly complicates matters."

"Billy requested the duty roster from the police for that night, which might give us a list of possible suspects. They claim the records were lost."

"And what are you doing here?"

"I analyzed a stain that Dwayne obtained from Larry Montague's shirt. It's lipstick. Larry's friend said he was going to meet a woman. If we could find the owner of the lipstick, we might at least find a witness who saw him closer to when he was killed."

"Or the woman might be the murderer."

"There weren't any women on the Coot's Bayou police force twelve years ago, and there aren't any now."

"Don't get too married to the idea that a cop is responsible for Robby's murder," Raleigh cautioned. "Or Larry's. That's a big leap."

"I know. It's just that no other leads are panning out.

The girlfriend, the violent felon who owned the stolen car, the fence Robby used to work with—Billy has questioned them all and he feels pretty sure they had nothing to do with Robby's death. We've got a big, fat zero. The D.A. is going to file formal charges against Mitch any day, and it's going to be capital murder. We're all holding our breath waiting for someone to discover Mitch was out and about, alone, the night Larry was killed.

"I feel like I'm failing him." Beth had been holding herself together pretty well up until now, but she couldn't do it any longer. Her tears spilled over.

At least it was just Raleigh to witness her embarrassing breakdown.

Raleigh had her arms around Beth in an instant. "Oh, honey, don't cry. It's early yet. We still have lots of ways to shake loose something to help Mitch."

Beth grabbed a paper towel from the dispenser over her bench and mopped her face. "It's not just the criminal charges. I did something really stupid."

"You slept with Mitch."

Beth gasped. The shock of Raleigh's accurate guess checked the flow of tears. "Did he say something?"

"Beth, of course not. Billy told me."

"How did Billy know?"

"He said you both disappeared, and when you came back you had hay in your hair and it was written all over your faces. Both of you."

"And I thought I was being discreet. Oh, God, his mother probably knows, too."

"And why is this such a tragedy?" Raleigh asked. "Isn't this something you've been wanting?"

"Yeah, but…the next morning he said it was a terrible mistake."

"It's, um, not the best timing in the world," Raleigh said diplomatically.

"I know. It's a bad idea for so many reasons. But I don't regret what we did. Even if it's a never-to-be-repeated event."

"Maybe once we prove Mitch's innocence…"

Beth shook her head. "He was drowning, and I was the only life preserver within reach. He needed to connect with someone. Once he's free of the charges…he won't need me anymore."

Raleigh looked perplexed. "He's got a lot on his plate right now," she said.

"Don't make excuses for him. He did me because I was handy and available, and he had extra steam to let off despite beating up a bale of hay—"

"Wait. He beat up…"

"Hay. I can't even explain this, it's just too weird. Sweet, low-key, gentle Mitch has stockpiles of intensity I never dreamed of. He has a secret past and all this anger inside him…"

"So, he's not the right man for you anyway," Raleigh concluded. "If it only took you one sexual encounter to figure that out, you are way ahead of the game."

Beth took off her glasses and massaged the bridge of her nose. "That's just it. Despite everything that's happened, despite all I've learned about him, I still want him. I want him *more,* if that's possible." She put her glasses back on and looked at her friend. "Raleigh, why am I always attracted to the wrong men?"

"Are you sure he's wrong?"

"I'm not sure of anything." Beth got off her stool and started methodically tidying. "I thought a relationship with Mitch would be easy and uncomplicated. I couldn't have been more mistaken. And it's not even a relationship. It's probably just a one-time deal and now my head's all screwed up."

Raleigh, who *always* had good advice, patted Beth's shoulder in commiseration. "When it comes to men, it's never easy and uncomplicated. Let's focus on proving Mitch's innocence, okay? Then you can worry about whether you have a relationship or not."

Beth knew it was good advice. "Okay. I'm good now, I'm fine." She wiped the last of her tears away and chucked the paper towel into the trash bin. "Back to business." She picked up the report she'd generated earlier and handed it to Raleigh. "The lipstick from Larry's shirt is made up of wax, oil, alcohol, fragrance, preservatives and a particular dye called carmine. Carmine is made by boiling pigmented beetles."

Raleigh set the paper down and backed away from it. "Ewww! You're kidding."

"Nope. It's not even terribly rare. Several major brands use it for their red and orange shades. The list is in the report."

Raleigh reluctantly picked up the paper again and flipped to the second page. "Oh, my God, there's the brand *I* use! Why didn't you tell me?"

"You don't wear bright red or orange so you're probably safe."

"I'm checking the ingredient lists on all my lipsticks when I get home."

"I performed ultraviolet-visible spectroscopy on the sample, and I've sent the results off to a guy I know who can possibly give me an exact brand. Until then, I've narrowed it down to brands likely to be sold in southern Louisiana, and I'm looking at all the case designs. If I have to snoop in the purses of every woman in Coot's Bayou to find out what lipstick they use, I will."

"Hmm. A lipstick stain. That's so cliché."

"I know. And though I maintained a chain of evidence, it probably won't hold up in court. But if it turns out to be important, we could impel the police to do their own testing on the stain."

"Hmm," Raleigh said again.

"It's lame. But maybe I'll find some DNA in all that trash I collected from near Larry's body—cigarette butts, paper cups, tissues…"

Raleigh wrinkled her nose. "You're the only person I know who gets excited about garbage."

"…and I have a few things I found at the shack, though I didn't find any more bullets or shell casings. Just lots of beer pull tabs. So…what's our next move?"

"We're going to advertise for witnesses. Someone, somewhere, saw something. Oh, and here's what I really came in here to tell you. Larry Montague's autopsy is scheduled for tomorrow morning, 7:00 a.m., and they're honoring our request that you observe."

"That's a surprise."

"My guess is they want it to at least appear as if they were being cooperative with us. Dwayne is the one who called with the news. Whatever bad blood is between him and Mitch, he's been pretty cordial to us."

"I know. I wish I could get Mitch to see that. So, I guess I'm heading over to Coot's Bayou again." Viewing an autopsy wasn't her favorite pastime, but her presence could mean the difference between uncovering helpful evidence, and losing it forever.

Plus, she'd sort of been hoping for an excuse to see Mitch again. Like a moth to a flame.

She should probably check into the Sleepy Time Motel where Billy was staying. But as she packed her things into her car after work that day, she knew she would head straight for Myra's house.

"YOU KNOW I DON'T MIND you using my car," Myra said, "but I don't understand why you don't just take your own."

"Because if anyone does a casual check to see if I'm home, I want them to see the El Camino in its usual parking space."

"Mitchell Bernard Delacroix, you're up to no good. I could always spot the signs when you were a teenager, and nothing's changed." She looked down at his feet and sighed. "Where's your monitoring cuff?"

"Don't worry about it. Just pretend you didn't see that, okay?"

"Just tell me where you're going. Is it illegal?"

"Mom, of course not. I don't do illegal stuff anymore. All I'm doing is bending the rules of my bail a little."

"Oh, Mitch…"

"It's something I have to do," he said. "Something I'm contractually bound to do. There's a lot of money at stake, a lot of people counting on me." His trainer and his promoter would have his head on a platter if he didn't show up tonight. He'd already tried to get out of appearing, and short of admitting he was under suspicion of murder, which he hadn't wanted to do, he couldn't convince them to find a replacement for the match tonight. Too much had already gone into promoting his fight against Ricky "Quick Death" Marquita, who would be the real star.

It was an important step for Mitch, though. For the first time, he would be participating in a headline match. And even though he was heavily favored to lose, the fact he'd even gotten the match meant his popularity was on the rise.

Myra reluctantly handed over the keys. "When will you be home? In case someone does come around looking."

"If someone comes looking, you didn't even realize I was gone. I took your keys without asking."

"I'm not going to lie."

He didn't want to get his mom in trouble. "I'm gonna hang out with some friends, okay? And I should be home by one in the morning." He kissed her on the cheek. "Don't worry."

"Self-destructive. Davy says you're self-destructive, and he's right."

That was a low blow—and surprising, coming from a woman he'd almost never seen initiating a confrontation. But he didn't have time to argue with her, or explain that he was trying to preserve the one thing in his life that was still okay. In the cage-fighting world, they didn't know he was Mitch Delacroix, a Project Justice employee under suspicion of murder. He was just the Cagey Cajun who would fight anyone—and usually win.

DESPITE HERSELF, BETH FELT a slight thrill of anticipation as she drove her yellow Ford Escape up the dirt road and Myra's house came into view. There was Mitch's El Camino in its usual spot.

Raleigh was right. Mitch had an awful lot to contend with right now, and looking after Beth's precious feelings shouldn't be one of them. What had happened in the barn had been a purely biological reaction when two people who were attracted to each other spent too much time together under too much stress.

During the drive, she had put this into perspective. She oughtn't to have any expectations regarding what would happen in the future.

The front door of the house opened almost before Beth's car came to a full stop. Myra wiped her hands on her apron, then shaded her eyes against the setting sun and gave Beth a small wave. Beth supposed she should have warned Myra she was on her way back, but Myra had told her the door was open any time she needed to stay in Coot's Bayou.

Beth grabbed her overnight bag from the passenger

seat and exited her car, waving back. But she could tell something was wrong just by the tight way Myra smiled back.

"Beth, sugar, I'm so glad you're here." Myra trotted down the front steps, a worried frown putting a crease between her thin eyebrows.

A dozen scenarios played through Beth's mind, none of them pleasant. "What happened? Oh, God, they didn't take Mitch back to jail, did they?" Had they found out about his late-night ramble?

"No, but I'm worried sick they will. Mitch is gone."

"Gone?" Alarm shot through Beth's veins like an injection of pure adrenaline. She glanced at the El Camino parked in the driveway, then back at Myra. Had the prospect of prison finally gotten to him? Had he fled custody?

"He took my car. I mean, God help me, I loaned him my car because, whatever he's doing, I guess he didn't want the police to spot him…" She shook her head. "I never could say no to him."

"Where do you think he's headed?" She already had her cell phone out, scrolling through her contacts to find Daniel's number. "Would he go for the border? Did he take any survival stuff with him, tents or food—"

"No, no, you've got the wrong idea. He's coming back. At least, he said he would be back before 1:00 a.m."

Beth paused just before she hit the dial button. "Do you think he was telling the truth?"

"Well, Mitch has never lied to me before. He never had any reason to, since I had no control over him whatsoever. He said if anyone should come looking for him, I should say I don't know where he is and that he took my keys without my permission, but I told him I wouldn't lie."

Beth sank onto the steps, the wind out of her sails. She hadn't realized how much she'd been looking forward to seeing Mitch again until she found he wasn't home.

"Did he give any indication where he might be going?"

"Absolutely none. But, Beth…he wasn't wearing the cuff. He got it off his ankle somehow."

"Then he's probably left the parish," Beth said dully. "How long ago did he leave?"

"It's been at least two hours. I probably should have called you or his attorney right away, but I guess I was clinging to the hope that he would think better of his plans and turn around."

Two hours? If he'd had the cuff off for two hours, the monitoring company should have noticed by now.

"I'm expecting the police to show up any minute," Myra confessed. "I'm so scared. Why did he do it, Beth? With you and the other Project Justice people on his side, he stands a good chance of beating the murder charge. But he's just making a bad situation worse."

"I don't know." Beth shook her head. "I wish I did."

"You've got a hankering for him, don't you?" Myra didn't sound like she was guessing. Beth supposed she wasn't very good at hiding her feelings.

"A hankering…that's a good way to put it," she said, figuring her protests would sound lame.

"You'd be good for him, I think," Myra said. "A settling influence."

"I used to think we might be good together because we had so much in common." Maybe it wasn't the best idea in the world to spill her guts to Mitch's mother, but she sensed a sympathetic listener. And right now, her feelings were so desolate she needed to unload on somebody. Since Raleigh, the usual shoulder she cried on, wasn't available, Myra was the lucky substitute.

Maybe Myra could give her some insight into her son that would help Beth understand him.

"Mitch is a computer geek, I'm a science geek. We're both addicted to true-crime TV shows. But those are just surface qualities. There's a lot to Mitch that I don't understand at all. Way below the surface."

"He's not always easy to understand."

They lapsed into silence. For a few minutes, the only sounds were the leaves rustling with the evening breeze and the insects and frogs that started their incessant buzzing and croaking the moment the sun went down.

Finally Beth spoke again. "He admitted his father mistreated him."

"His father used to beat him black and blue," Myra clarified. "I oftentimes had to keep him home from school until the bruises faded."

Beth shuddered.

"I'm sure you think I'm a terrible mother for allowing it to happen. For not *doing* something."

"Actually, that thought never crossed my mind. You were afraid that no matter what you did, you would only make things worse."

"Why, yes, that's exactly how it was!" Myra sounded surprised to find someone who understood. Had she never confided to anyone? Beth supposed group therapy for victims of abuse wasn't readily available here in the sticks, or at least it hadn't been years ago.

Beth wasn't sure what else to add. She wasn't a therapist, and she couldn't undo years of abuse with a heartfelt declaration of sympathy. The last thing she felt like doing right now was recounting her own brief episode of living with a bully whose temper escalated to violence against her.

She was too emotionally fragile to be the strong one.

Not knowing what else to do, she reached out to Myra's hand and squeezed it.

"Do you think he could ever forgive me?" Myra asked in a small voice. "When we talked, he seemed to understand, a little bit."

"Sounds like he's taken the first step. Even if he knows, in his head, that you did the best you knew how to do, it might take his heart a while to catch up with his brain."

"That's good enough for now, I expect. He has more important things to worry about than soothing his mama."

Yeah. Like being a fugitive.

"Did you try to call him?" Beth asked.

"No. Even if he answered, he wouldn't tell me anything different than he already told me."

Beth already had her phone out and was dialing Mitch's cell. It went to voice mail, of course. Hey, at least he wasn't driving and talking on the phone at the same time.

"I can't answer the phone," came his recorded voice. "But just so you know, I *will* be back before 1:00 a.m. and I'm not making a break for Mexico. I'm keeping a promise I made a long time ago, and it has nothing to do with the charges against me. I'm not doing anything illegal or immoral. And, Beth, if you're listening to this…I'm sorry I…" He was silent too long, and his outgoing message ended with a beep.

"Sorry?" Beth yelled into her phone. "You think 'sorry' is going to make up for abusing the faith of everyone who is working their asses off to prove your innocence *and* worrying your mother sick? Sorry isn't gonna cut it, you miserable son of a—" She quickly cut herself off, since his mother was sitting right next to her.

She disconnected with an angry jab of her thumb.

"Dang, girl, I hope I don't ever get on your bad side," Myra said. "When you catch up with him, I hope you give him a good talking-to. Maybe you can straighten him out."

Beth suspected the Coot's Bayou Police would straighten him out before Beth ever got the chance. Except…if he removed his cuff, why hadn't the police shown up here?

"What do you suppose he did with the cuff?" Beth asked Myra.

"I have no idea. But the thing is run by a computer chip, right? Monitored by other computers, communicating with yet more computers."

"Yes..."

"If anyone can figure out how to outsmart a chip, Mitch can."

That had to be it. He had somehow figured out how to hack into the cuff's communication feedback loop long enough that he could get it off his ankle, then fasten it closed again.

But that would only provide a temporary fix. The cuff could sense whether it was attached to a warm, mobile human being. If it cooled off and didn't move at all, an alarm would go off somewhere.

Beth searched Mitch's room but couldn't find the cuff. His computer was password protected, so there was no way to see what he'd been doing in cyberspace, not that he would ever be stupid enough to leave a trail.

"Did you find it?" Myra asked, standing uneasily in the doorway.

"No."

"Are you going to report him?" Myra asked. "I don't want you to get in trouble."

"He said he would be home by one," Beth said. "Let's just see if he shows up." Besides, Beth couldn't bear the thought of telling her Project Justice colleagues about Mitch's transgressions. What if they lost faith in him? What if Daniel washed his hands of Mitch's case? It wouldn't be the first time Daniel had pulled the plug on a self-destructive client who wouldn't play by Daniel's rules. The one thing he required of a client—besides their being innocent—was honesty.

Mitch was obviously hiding something.

"I need to go feed the goats and put the chickens up," Myra said. "Then we can have some dinner. I put a broccoli-cheese casserole in the oven a few minutes ago."

"I'll help you with the animals," Beth said. "I want to see the baby again."

"She sure is a cutie-pie," Myra said. "I find it comforting to watch the cycle of life continuing, no matter what else is going on in my life. The goats eat and have babies and give milk, the chickens lay eggs and raise chicks. They're not bothered by all the drama."

"Maybe they've got the right idea," Beth said. "I could do with a little less drama in my life."

It seemed to Beth as if the baby goat had grown just since yesterday. It was so cute, pure white with just the hint of gray highlights on its head, feet and tail, very different looking from its brown mama. It hid behind its mother when Beth approached.

"Come on, you two, let's go to the barn and get some oats, hmm?" Beth thought she would take the mom goat's halter and lead her into the barn, but that turned out not to be necessary. The second Myra opened the door, all of the goats turned and trotted toward the shelter and dinner.

That was when Beth saw that the billy goat wore a fetching new black collar made out of Gore-Tex.

CHAPTER THIRTEEN

"In this corner, weighing in at one-eighty-nine, Mickey the 'Cagey Cajun' Croix! Let's give it up for the Cajun, undefeated in his last six fights!"

A roar rose in the Houston Memorial Arena, the largest venue Mitch had ever fought in. He raised his hands and bared his teeth at the crowd like a madman, quivering with anger that was only a little bit faked. He'd risked a lot to come here, and defeat was not an acceptable outcome.

"And in this corner, weighing in at one-ninety-nine, the current light-heavyweight champion of South-Southeast Texas, Ricky 'Quick Death' Marquita!"

The volume of applause and screaming cranked up a notch. Marquita had certainly found a fan base, and Mitch could see why. The guy was a solid wall of muscles with a gleaming white smile in a pretty-boy face. Looked as if he'd never had his nose broken.

But Mitch wasn't fooled by the movie-star looks. Marquita was tough. Rumor had it that early in his career he'd bitten half a guy's lip off—back when he was a back-alley brawler, before he'd gone legit.

Mitch knew that world. Anybody who had come to

MMA via that route knew how to play dirty. He would be prepared for anything.

At first, the two men just circled, with Marquita in the center and Mitch dancing around him. Mitch didn't like that dynamic, so he moved in, doing a few one-two-one-two punches toward Marquita's head. Marquita counterpunched, mixing a few body shots in with his jabs, but Mitch rolled to the side, avoiding serious contact. He ducked under a left hook, feeling the rush of air over his head as Marquita missed, and lunged for Marquita's body, trying to find a takedown off the other man's punches, but Marquita was faster than he looked. He slid out of Mitch's grasp like a greased pig.

Mitch punched straight to Marquita's middle, but Marquita parried with an elbow. Mitch stepped back and fired off a roundhouse kick, making solid contact with Marquita's ribs. But the guy was hard as a rock, and the kick didn't seem to faze him.

Knockouts were showy, but Mitch realized the only way to defeat Marquita was to get him on the ground and force a tap-out. Brazilian jujitsu grappling was effective no matter what the size of the opponent, depending on leverage and torque to deliver excruciating pain—and serve up an opponent's surrender.

Mitch targeted Marquita's body and legs with kicks, still looking for entry but pleased he was holding his own.

The bell signaled the end of the first round, and Mitch retreated to his corner of the cage where his trainer, Craig McGee, blotted the sweat from his body and squirted water into his mouth.

"You're doing great, kid," he said, sounding surprised. "Spend the next round tiring him out. He'll get sloppy and you can go for the takedown. Don't try to ground-and-pound him, he can take an amazing amount of pain. Use that naked rear choke we've been working on."

Mitch happened to glance at the clock. Hell, if he had any prayer of making it back to Coot's Bayou by one, he'd have to end this thing sooner rather than later. To hell with tiring out Marquita.

Just before the match had started, he'd made the mistake of listening to the message Beth had left for him. His stomach tightened every time he thought about it. He should have known he wouldn't be able to get away with this stunt and have no one find out.

But he damn well wasn't going to make it worse by being late. He couldn't lose the support of Project Justice, but especially not Beth.

The bell rang, and he and Marquita were back at it. Mitch landed a right hand kick that snapped Marquita's head, but Marquita, snorting like an angry bull, landed a couple of left kicks of his own.

Mitch took a shot to the eye. He could detect it swelling, but with all the adrenaline pumping through his body, he felt no pain.

When Marquita took him down, Mitch didn't see it coming. Suddenly he was flat on his back with Marquita in his guard, attempting to ground-and-pound.

Mitch fought back with double underhooks and double butterflies, looking for an opportunity. There, just the slightest release of pressure on his hips, and

Mitch had the opening he needed. He swept his legs out and levered himself on top of Marquita, catching him in a half guard, looking for the arm triangle choke. Marquita turtled and tried to get up. Mitch was about to go for the joint manipulation that would end this thing when the bell rang again.

He hardly listened as Craig jabbered advice into his ear about Marquita's weak spots. He was pissed now, and he was going to get this guy. When the bell rang, Mitch rushed Marquita like an out-of-control bullet train, getting his opponent into a clinch against the fence. Mitch landed double underhooks, then a right elbow. The two men traded a few heavy punches. Mitch landed a knee, but Marquita got hold of Mitch's ankle and grounded him again with a single-leg takedown.

But Mitch didn't go all the way down. He managed to wedge himself partly against the fence, from where he could throw some short right hands. Marquita tried to pull him away from the cage, which gave Mitch the opening he needed to regain his feet. Marquita tried for another takedown, but Mitch was having none of it. Fueled by the urgency of the clock, he literally saw red as he got a grip around Marquita's midsection, lifted him into the air, and slammed him facedown into the mat. It was dangerously close to spiking, but since Marquita landed more on his chest than his face, the ref didn't call it. Mitch sank on top of Marquita and went for the kill...the rear naked choke.

Within three seconds, Marquita tapped out, and it was over. Mitch was a champion...of something. Not the world, or the state of Texas, but some universe this particular fight franchise had carved out for itself.

Mitch helped Marquita to his feet. The two men embraced briefly. "Helluva fight," Marquita said. Then the ref grabbed Mitch's wrist and lifted his arm into the air, and the crowd went crazy.

Mitch accepted the fickle crowd's approval with another growl. Then he was heading for the dressing room.

"Hey, where ya going?" Craig demanded, trailing after him with towel, water bottle and the silk robe he'd had made with the Cagey Cajun logo emblazoned in red on black.

"I have to get back home or I'm in a shitload of trouble, Craig. I'll sign autographs next time." Maybe his disappearing act would add to his mystique.

Ten minutes later, he was in his mom's station wagon headed out of the parking lot. He'd managed to beat most of the traffic, and within a few more minutes he was on the freeway headed back to Louisiana.

He drove a consistent nine miles over the speed limit the whole way because if he got pulled over by any law enforcement, it would all be over.

It might all be over anyway. There might be an angry posse waiting for him at his mom's, ready to cart him off to jail.

He'd known the risks going in. And his victory tonight in the cage might be all for nothing. If he ended up sentenced to prison for life, tonight was his swan song.

But he'd done it. He'd needed the victory. His body

hummed pleasantly at being pushed to its absolute physical limit. He felt more at peace than he had in a long time. His ass was in a sling, and he felt at peace. This was something he would never be able to explain to anyone, least of all Beth, who would run screaming into the night if she ever saw him in a cage, beating someone to a pulp.

The traffic was light as he bombed down I-10 toward the Louisiana border, and he opened the window and let the cool, moist night air riffle through his hair.

As he turned down the dirt road where his mother lived, he felt only momentary apprehension over what might await him. He half expected to see a cluster of cop cars, dome lights flashing angry red, blue and white, sitting in the driveway. But as the house came into view, no glaring lights assaulted his senses. All looked quiet...

Except there was Beth's yellow Escape. His gut tightened. What was she doing here? His body went to war with itself. He felt he should dread the coming confrontation. But he also felt a liberating sense of exhilaration at the prospect of seeing her again.

As he pulled into the driveway, the car clock said it was ten minutes to one. He'd kept his word to his mother, at least. For what that was worth, after he'd abused everybody else's faith in him.

The lights were on. He supposed it was too much to hope that everyone had gone to bed. He wouldn't get off that easily.

He eased the station wagon into its usual spot, ran up the window and turned off the engine. As he got out of the car, the absolute quiet struck him. After the noise of the cheering fans, then the Houston traffic, sirens and horns, the peace wrapped him up like a pig in blanket.

He'd always hated Coot's Bayou. But maybe this place had its strong points. The quiet, the freshness of the air—when you were upwind of the refinery, at least—brought you a little closer to God.

The peaceful feeling lasted only until he went inside, placed his mother's car keys in the bowl by the door, and entered the kitchen where the lights blazed.

His mother and Beth sat at the table playing a card game. He knew they heard him come in; it wasn't like he'd attempted to be quiet. But at first they didn't look at him.

Beth laid a card facedown into the discard pile. "Gin."

"You got me again." His mom shook her head, then finally looked at Mitch. Her eyes widened in alarm. "Oh, my God."

That made Beth turn and look. Her mouth fell open, and she was out of her chair, grasping his arm, standing on her toes to peer into his face. "God, Mitch, are you okay?"

"I'm fine." Then he remembered the blow he'd taken to the side of his face. He probably had the makings of a black eye. He stepped around Beth to the kitchen counter, where his mother's ancient chrome toaster sat, and leaned down to have a look.

His reflection gave even him a start. He looked like something out of a horror movie, his face covered in dried blood, his left eye swollen and starting to bruise.

"You should go to the emergency room." Beth's voice trembled, though he didn't know whether she was afraid or angry or some combination of the two.

"Now, hold on. It's not that bad. Just a small cut. I didn't realize it was bleeding, that's why it looks so bad." He tore off a paper towel, soaked it in cool water from the sink and wiped off his face.

"I'll get you an ice pack," Myra said quietly as she went to the freezer and rummaged around. "Here, I think this will work." She handed him a bag of frozen peas. "Did you wreck my car?" She sounded really disappointed in him.

"No, the car is fine."

"Then what happened?" Beth demanded hotly. "Hell, never mind, it's obvious. You got into a brawl with someone. Couldn't you have done that inside the parish? Did you have to break the law?"

He should tell her. She believed he'd been involved in a bar fight, and wasn't that way worse than the reality? But somehow, he couldn't get the words past his mouth.

"I'm going to bed," Myra said. "I'll leave you two to sort things out."

"There's nothing to sort," Beth said. "Mitch appears to be intent on ruining any chance he has of beating the charges against him—"

"That's not true."

His mother left the kitchen without looking at him. She'd been angry with him before; he'd been a more-than-troublesome teenager. But she'd never given up on him.

And Beth…

"The only law I broke was to violate the terms of my bail," he said. "I didn't drink and drive, I didn't assault anyone." Not illegally, anyway. "I didn't even drive fast."

"Are you going to tell me where you were and what you were doing?"

"I was in Houston. I was keeping a promise."

"And you ran into a door," she said flatly.

He'd thought about lying—telling her he fell, or that he was mugged. But he wasn't going to add lying on top of everything else. "No, someone hit me."

"Was there a woman involved?"

So that's what this was about? She thought he'd gotten into a fight over a woman?

"No. Not even close. You're the only woman in my life." As he said the words, he realized how strong and emphatic they were—and how true. He was involved with Beth, whether he wanted to be or not. She'd sneaked under his skin somehow.

Her face softened, but she looked wary, too. "I'm in your life? Is that what you call it?"

"'Fraid so. I never intended for that to happen. But I care about you."

"Oh." She sat back down in her chair. "That's what guys say just before they tell you you deserve someone better. Or, 'It's not you, it's me.'"

He could have easily said either of those things, and they'd have been true.

"Why won't you tell me where you were, and what you were doing?" she asked.

"Because I'd rather have you angry with me than..." Than what? Repulsed? "Would it help if I said it won't happen again?"

"You won't go out at night and get beat up, or you won't lie?"

He hadn't lied. He just hadn't volunteered the whole truth. But he sensed Beth didn't want to quibble about semantics.

"I won't mess with the cuff anymore," he clarified.

"So you're done with your contractual obligations?"

"Yes, for now." He'd told his manager he couldn't appear in any more fights until he was free of the charges against him. "Does Daniel know about—"

"That you outsmarted your monitoring cuff and disappeared? No. I was going to call him if you hadn't shown up before one. But I didn't want to admit I'd lost track of you. That was my job, you know. Yes, I was supposed to be evaluating evidence, but as your friend, I was supposed to keep you in compliance with your bond. I failed at that."

"I'm sorry I worried you. But you have to believe me—it won't happen again."

"I want to trust you." Her eyes brimmed with tears. "I wish I could."

That hurt. But he had only himself to blame. Because it mattered what Beth thought about him. It mattered a lot. His mother's disappointment bothered him. But Beth's was like an ice pick straight through his heart.

Did that mean he loved her? Would it make her feel better if he told her that?

No, he couldn't. He'd burdened her with enough; he wasn't going to try to guilt her into further loyalty to him by telling her he loved her, especially when he wasn't a hundred percent sure *what* he was feeling.

He only knew he didn't want to hurt her again.

"Can you put the cuff back on without setting it off?" she asked suddenly.

"I think so."

"Good. Tomorrow, I have to view Larry Montague's autopsy. Then I have some work to do with Billy. Can I count on you to stay here, and stay out of trouble?"

"Yes." He still felt tiny quills of jealousy making his skin prickle. But he'd forfeited any right he had to object to her spending time with anyone she wanted, for any reason.

For years now, he'd been working toward becoming an elite MMA fighter. Now that he was finally making headway, he had to ask himself: Was it worth it? Was it worth tossing aside the finest woman who'd ever crossed his path?

Unfortunately, the answer didn't matter. He'd blown it with Beth. He was history.

WHEN BETH ARRIVED at the parish morgue at 6:45 the next morning, Larry Montague was already laid out on the dissection table. He'd been bathed and photographed, so she'd missed that part.

Dwayne was up in the observation room with her. He was out of uniform, in worn khaki shorts and a red YMCA T-shirt.

"What happened to his clothes?" Beth asked. Her

voice sounded raspy; she'd spent a good part of last night crying into her pillow like a jilted teenager. A cool shower and lots of concealer had made her puffy eyes look respectable, but she couldn't shake the frog in her throat.

"Sent to the lab for processing, I imagine."

"So they'll test the stains for DNA? Will they look for seeds and pollen that might tie him to another murder scene? And dirt—they should take samples of the dirt. Each area has its own signature of minerals, shells and diatoms that can be matched like a finger-print, you know. And insect larvae—"

"The lab is good," Dwayne said, uncharacteristically sharp. "I'm sure they'll do all the necessary testing."

"I only ask because I tested the lipstick stain. There was a small amount of DNA present, but it was too degraded to give me a profile. Maybe with a larger sample, your lab could get better results."

"I already pointed out that stain to one of the physical evidence squints," he said.

"Good. Because I've narrowed it down to only a few brands and colors. If we find a witness, or even a suspect, who wears one of the matching lipsticks we can compare—"

"I got it, Beth."

"Okay. I just want to be thorough."

"You give a whole new meaning to that word."

Maybe Dwayne had taken some flak for cooperating with his half-brother's team of investigators. She tried not to take his sour mood personally.

Larry's autopsy didn't produce much in the way of

surprises. His death was due to a single gunshot wound to the head, which had bled out. The bullet had gone all the way through his skull and out the other side and hadn't been recovered, but judging from the size of the wound, the M.E. thought it was a small caliber.

Time of death was estimated at between 1 and 4 a.m. the night before the body was found.

"Do the police have any leads on where the actual killing took place?" Beth asked Dwayne casually.

"Nothing yet. But don't be surprised if someone shows up at Myra's house with a search warrant. The current theory is that, if Mitch killed Larry, he did it without leaving home. So the victim must have come to him."

"And, what, his mother disposed of the body? Come on, Dwayne."

"Maybe not his mother. Could have been...you."

An uneasy sensation wiggled up Beth's spine. "So now *I'm* a suspect?"

Dwayne just shrugged.

Apparently the cops didn't know Mitch had left the house that night. Had they simply not checked with the monitoring company?

The rest of Larry's autopsy had revealed Larry to be a man in very poor health, from the years of drinking, drugs and living on the street.

"If a bullet hadn't killed him," the M.E. said, "his liver would have given out within six months."

"Somebody actually did Larry a favor," Dwayne commented. "At least it was quick."

"I doubt he'd see it that way," Beth said coolly. She

was still miffed at Dwayne's insinuations. Whose side was he on?

One of the lab assistants who had left after taking some samples came back in. "Good news," he announced. "The scrapings from under the deceased's fingernails yielded DNA. I'm pretty sure I can get a profile from it."

Finally, something was going their way. If the profile turned out to be someone other than Larry himself, and if that person had previously been in the system, they could find a match.

"I'm not sure how helpful that will be," Dwayne said. "God knows how many people Larry struggled with over the last few days. Me and Mitch, for sure. And I doubt he cleans his fingernails on a regular basis."

"But he did!" Beth said. "His friend at the homeless camp told me he'd spiffed himself up before meeting the mystery woman, and that he even cleaned his nails."

"He specifically said that?" Dwayne asked.

Beth noticed, then, that Dwayne had several fresh scratches on his arms. An icky feeling squirmed under her skin, and suddenly she wondered if she was standing in the same room as a murderer.

What if Mitch was right? What if Dwayne was only pretending to be helpful, and instead was insinuating himself into the investigation so that he could be privy to what evidence the police and Project Justice were coming up with?

Beth had gotten sidetracked about the lipstick, thinking a woman was involved, when maybe that stain was irrelevant.

She needed to get out of that room, away from Dwayne, before she said or did anything that would give away her suspicions. Her cell phone rang, giving her the perfect excuse to step outside.

Caller ID told her it was someone at Project Justice. She answered as she stepped outside into the stairwell that led downstairs. "Beth McClelland."

"Beth, it's Cassie. We got a report back on the lipstick. It's an off-brand called Genevieve Stay Put Color Glo. The shade is Youthful Coral. The case is very distinctive, gold with copper stripes."

"That's good work. Thanks."

"You don't sound that excited."

"It's just that I'm not really sure a woman is responsible for killing Larry Montague."

"But she could be a witness, right? And she hasn't come forward. So maybe she's guilty, too."

"Yes, you're right." Beth had to remember that she wasn't trained as an investigator. A few weeks of the police academy and years spent collecting and analyzing evidence didn't make her a detective. She needed to turn over what she'd discovered to Billy and let him lead the investigation.

Just as she disconnected, Dwayne exited right behind her. "Are you done observing?"

She nodded. Anything further, she could get from the official autopsy report.

"Good. I promised Linda I'd put in a full day in our garden." He seemed in a hurry to get away from Beth.

He certainly wasn't as friendly toward her as he'd been on other occasions.

She'd just gotten into her car when the cell rang again. It was Raleigh.

"Hey. What's up?" She tried to sound upbeat. If her depressed mood showed up in her voice, Raleigh would want to know what was wrong, and she simply wasn't up to telling her about the latest fiasco with Mitch. Daniel didn't tolerate clients who didn't want to help themselves; there were many prison inmates on the foundation's waiting list.

She was terrified of the thought that Daniel might cut Mitch off and apply their resources to someone who wasn't skating on such thin ice.

"I'm on my way into town to meet with Buck Michoux again." She sounded impatient.

"Is the local lawyer not working out?"

"He's okay, just nervous. He's never defended a death penalty case before. Don't worry, Beth. If we end up going to trial, Daniel will hire a whole herd of top defense lawyers. I called you for another reason."

"Oh?"

"I want to meet you for lunch, if you're free. I have something to show you. It's something you might find…unpleasant," she warned.

"Something about Mitch?"

"I'm afraid so."

Beth's stomach fell. How much more could she take? She'd already decided to back off from any relationship, no matter how much it hurt. Did she need to know anything else?

But curiosity got the best of her. "Where do you want to meet?"

At twelve-thirty, Beth and Raleigh were seated at the Conch & Crab, the family-friendly bar and grill where Mitch and Beth had been looking for Larry only two days ago. Raleigh ordered a club sandwich, but Beth was still full from the huge breakfast Myra had cooked for her, so she settled for a side salad. She wasn't really hungry after viewing the autopsy, anyway.

"I skipped breakfast," Raleigh said after the waitress left.

"I wish I had. Remind me not to eat bacon and eggs before an autopsy."

"How did it go?"

"No huge revelations, but there was biological material under Larry's fingernails. They're searching the database for a match. But I have to say, Dwayne Bell started acting real weird when he heard that news. And he has fresh scratches on his arm."

Raleigh looked disturbed by that news. "He did struggle with Larry when he arrested him at the shack."

"Yeah, but Mitch had control of Larry's arms. I don't remember any scratching or bleeding."

"You think Dwayne…no. He's been helping us to clear Mitch."

"Or just pretending to."

Raleigh took a sip of her soft drink and mulled that over.

"So what is it you have to show me?" Beth asked, knowing she would have to face whatever this "unpleasant" news was sooner or later.

"It's a video. Griffin was watching some cable sports show last night. Cage fighting."

Beth felt her nose wrinkling in distaste. She liked and respected Raleigh's new husband, a former investigative reporter who was now on the Project Justice staff. "What would he want to watch something like that for?"

Raleigh shrugged. "I don't know, but it seems to be a popular sport these days."

"So, what exactly is cage fighting, anyway? The bartender I met here the other day was talking about it, too. Is it where they throw two guys in a cage and see who comes out alive? Is that even legal?"

"It's nothing like that, really. It's more like boxing, but using martial arts and wrestling, too. They have timed rounds and a referee."

"So why are you telling me this?"

Raleigh pulled her phone out of her purse. "One of the fighters last night was…well, I told Griffin it was impossible. But then I started watching and saw for myself. This is a clip we got off YouTube after the fight was over."

Beth had a sick feeling in her stomach. She knew what was coming. And now everything that had happened last night made sense. And those two times she had seen Mitch beating up inanimate objects—he was training.

She almost told Raleigh she didn't need to see, that Mitch had gone AWOL last night. But some part of her *had* to look. She had to know the worst.

Raleigh handed the phone to her after starting the

video. Even on the small screen, she could see that one of the fighters was unmistakably Mitch Delacroix. He called himself Mickey Croix, the Cagey Cajun, but it was him.

She watched, mesmerized, as the two men beat each other up. Even squinting, peering through her lashes, it still was enough to make her want to throw up.

The blow that had cut Mitch's forehead came toward the end of the video. As soon as she'd seen blood, she'd almost thrust the phone away. But only a few seconds remained; Mitch, roaring like an enraged animal, picked up his opponent and slammed him facedown into the mat.

Beth thrust the phone back at Raleigh and made a run for the restroom. She lost what was left of her breakfast. Maybe it was the gory sight of the autopsy catching up with her, and watching that fight had been the final insult to her stomach.

Or maybe it was watching someone she'd thought she loved in a homicidal rage. And the terrible certainty that, if a rage like that had come over him, he might be guilty of murder.

CHAPTER FOURTEEN

MITCH KNEW HE WAS IN DEEP trouble when the two women strode across his mother's front yard toward him as if they wished they had guns.

They knew. No doubt about it. He couldn't imagine who'd told them, because absolutely no one knew his real name except Craig.

He was sitting on the front porch, shelling peas for his mom the way he'd done when he was a kid. The simple act of keeping his hands busy had helped prevent him from going slowly nuts, wondering if he'd jeopardized his case by fighting last night.

The more he'd thought about it, the more he'd realized that driving to Houston had been a boneheaded move. Yeah, his fighting career had taken a big leap forward with last night's victory. But what good would that do him if he was sitting on death row?

He put the bowl of peas aside and stood up, trying to muster a smile. But no amount of charm was going to help him now.

"Hello, Beth. Raleigh." He nodded a greeting to Raleigh while his gaze remained on Beth, looking daisy fresh as usual in a short, peach-colored skirt and dainty white shirt with tiny peach flowers. He tried to gauge her mood. But her expression was shuttered, like one of the vacant storefronts in Coot's Bayou's struggling downtown.

"You risked going back to jail for a cage fight?" Beth said when she'd mounted the steps to stand in front of him. "Really?"

"It seemed like the thing to do at the time," Mitch said. "I'd signed a contract. I was a headliner. Backing out would have cost me a lot of money and done a lot of damage to my reputation."

"Your reputation is exactly what I'm worried about," Raleigh said. She didn't sound all that angry, just concerned. "If that YouTube video ever gets in front of a jury, they're not going to doubt you have violent tendencies. And I hope you plan on that black eye being better the next time you have to appear in court."

"I hadn't thought about that," he said.

Beth flopped onto the porch swing, refusing to look at him. "You didn't think about much of anything, did you, except the childish need to beat some hapless guy senseless."

"Not just 'some guy.' I beat the champion," he said. "As of last night, I'm the reigning light-heavyweight MMA champion of the south-southeast district of Texas."

"And this is something to be proud of?" Beth asked incredulously.

"As a matter of fact, yes." He paced the porch in front of the swing, a little bit irritated by her lack of understanding. "I shouldn't have ditched the cuff and violated the terms of my bail, I can see that now. Although I was pretty sure I wouldn't get caught, and I couldn't see any harm in it at the time, I can see that I've betrayed your trust. Raleigh's and Billy's and Daniel's, too."

"Ya think?"

"For that, I am sorry. Truly."

"Apology accepted," Raleigh said cheerfully. "Can we move on to damage control?"

"But I'm not sorry about winning a fight. It's something I've been working toward for years. This was my first televised fight—well, the first one to go on a real cable TV channel. I was the total underdog, and I won! That means something to me."

"Okay," Raleigh said, "I'll just go inside and visit with your mother, Mitch. I'll let you two debate the merits of cage fighting versus other hobbies."

"It means something to me, too," Beth said bitterly. "It means that you're a violent human being. It means that gentle, funny, sweet, kinda nerdy guy I fell in love with is a phony."

Fell in love with? Then he hadn't imagined those hasty, whispered words in his ear when they'd made love. His heart was buoyed for a few seconds. Surely if Beth loved him, he was worth saving. But his hopes fizzled at her next words.

"The guy I shared pizza with, the one who laughed at my collection of ceramic bunnies, the one who freaks out if he sees an anchovy on his pizza, the one who will stay up till four in the morning tracking down some elusive clue that will help some innocent person get out of prison—that guy doesn't exist."

"Of course he exists. Although I'm *not* nerdy, thank you very much."

"My ex-boyfriend could pour on the charm, too. But he was nothing but a violent bully with an uncontrollable temper. You're no better than him."

Hearing her compare him with that bastard who'd broken her jaw, Mitch felt that illustrious temper flaring. But he tamped it down. If he showed any emotion but calm reasoning, he would lose Beth forever.

He suddenly realized that he really, really didn't want to lose her. He wanted a chance to make things work.

She loved him. Or she had, until she'd learned about his secret life. A hobby, Raleigh had called it, but it was more than that.

"I'm not like Vince," he said. "I don't hit women. I don't hit children. I'm not a bully."

She said nothing, just looked down at her lap.

Mitch sat on the porch railing. "I don't deny that I have a temper. That's what happens when you spend your childhood getting beat up on a daily basis with absolutely no way to stop it. The anger builds up inside you, with no way to release it. And then it spills out."

She hopped to her feet and paced, her platform sandals clunking against the wood planks. "So you get help. You go to therapy. You learn anger management. You don't start beating people up."

"I *went* to therapy. The last shrink I saw told me to find a socially acceptable physical outlet for my temper. So I did. I signed up for jujitsu classes, and I discovered I had a knack for it. Fighting in a cage, with a referee, is my therapy. Fighting is what allows me to be the laid-back guy you know.

"I don't assault people. I participate in a sport that obviously isn't to your taste, but that's all it is—a sport. If you want to condemn me for outsmarting my monitoring cuff and breaking the rules, fine. I'll take my lumps for that decision. But martial arts is part of who I am."

Finally she looked at him, and she did seem to be trying to understand.

He tried again. "I don't particularly like your ceramic bunnies, but I don't condemn you for collecting them. Or insist you get rid of them."

As an exit line, it was laughable. But Mitch had run out of argument. He wanted to go punch some hay, but that would have to wait until Project Justice was done with him.

He hopped off the railing, grabbed the shelled peas and went inside, where his mom was putting together some kind of dessert in a casserole dish and Raleigh sat at the kitchen table with a glass of tea.

"Just set those in the sink, Mitch, thank you."

"You're welcome." He pulled out a chair and sat across from Raleigh. "So, how badly have I screwed myself? Is Project Justice going to abandon me?"

"Oh, heavens, no. My last client threatened to assault me, and I didn't drop him. Emotions are running high, and sometimes bad decisions run rampant. We'll deal with it. Hopefully, your prosecutor isn't a big fan of mixed martial arts. And if he should try to get a video of your fight admitted as evidence, I'm pretty sure he won't succeed.

"But I need to know, Mitch—are there other videos floating around?"

"Maybe, but nothing as alarming as last night's fight. A takedown like that doesn't happen every day. That's the only televised fight I've ever been a part of."

"Is there anything else you haven't told me? Please, I don't care how bad it is, it's better if I know about it now, rather than later."

"I haven't been arrested since the car theft thing. I did some not-strictly-legal street fighting before I got smart and went legit, but nothing that involved the police. Nothing that resulted in serious injury."

"But the local cops—they could probably dig up a few people who will testify that you beat them up?"

He nodded, conceding the point. "Maybe. But you won't find anyone who'll testify that I ever owned a gun, or shot a gun. Robby and Larry were both shot."

"One more thing…does Daniel know about the cage fighting?"

He looked away guiltily. "No."

"I find that hard to believe, given how he vets his employees."

"I've never used my real name."

"And how did you beat the psych evaluation every Project Justice employee has to go through?" she asked without missing a beat.

"I'd like to think I didn't have to beat it—I'm perfectly sane."

"Okay." Raleigh patted him on the arm. "We'll get through this, Mitch. Did you and Beth sort things out?"

He only wished.

BETH PULLED HERSELF TOGETHER and headed indoors. She wanted to mull over what Mitch had told her, but now wasn't the time. There were other considerations—such as breaking the news to Mitch that she thought they should seriously consider Dwayne as a suspect, at least in Larry's murder. His demeanor at the M.E.'s office had bothered her, and her instincts about such things were usually dead-on.

She smoothed her hair off her face, took a deep breath and opened the door. She met Myra in the hallway, having come from upstairs. She had just freshened her makeup and fixed her hair, looking much better than she had the first day Beth had met her. Maybe having her son around had given her something to live for, something to fight for. She hardly resembled that hopeless, defeated woman who had answered the door five days ago.

She also, Beth noted, wore a bright pink-orange shade of lipstick.

"Oh, hello, Beth," Myra said pleasantly. "I hope you'll be staying for dinner."

Beth had lost any semblance of an appetite, but dinner was still a few hours away. "Yes, I will, thanks. Myra, that's a lovely shade of lipstick. Do you think it would look good with my coloring?"

Myra smiled shyly. "Thank you. Are you an autumn? I'm an autumn."

Beth felt a prickling of guilt for asking a trick question. Myra had been so sweet through all this...although she *had* been cagey when asked about Willard Bell's guns.

"I think I'm a winter." She'd once taken the what-season-are-you test in a magazine, anyway.

"You're welcome to try it," Myra said. "I have a new tube in my purse—I'll get it for you."

Beth's guilt increased. No one had ever considered Myra a suspect, but who knew for sure what family dynamics were going on back then? Myra had already admitted she thought Robby was a bad influence on her baby boy. Maybe, after the car theft incident, she'd decided to get rid of that influence once and for all.

Myra went to the hall tree, where her purse was hanging, and dug around in a small zipper pouch until she found a tube of lipstick. Beth's breath caught in her throat—the tube was gold with copper stripes. Myra took off her glasses and squinted at the bottom of the tube. "It's made by Genevieve. The color is Youthful Coral." She handed the tube to Beth.

Her hand shaking, Beth opened the tube and, using the hall tree mirror, applied a touch of the lipstick to her bare lips. The color actually didn't look bad on her.

"That's right pretty," Myra said. "I think it looks better on you than me. You want to keep it?"

"Oh, no, that's okay."

"I can get another one." She chuckled. "Debbie at the drugstore meant to order ten of these lipsticks and she added an extra zero and ordered a hundred. She has them on sale for a dollar apiece. I think every woman in town is stocking up on extra lipstick."

The tightness in Beth's stomach eased, although her suspect pool just widened considerably. She and Myra entered the kitchen together. Myra went to work emptying the dish drainer, opening and closing her battered oak cabinets and drawers to put the dishes away. Beth avoided looking at Mitch, keeping her eyes aimed squarely at Raleigh.

"Is that a new lipstick color?" Raleigh asked, looking perplexed that Beth would primp at a time like this.

"I borrowed it from Myra. The color is Youthful Coral. Should I stop by the drugstore and buy a tube? I understand they have a whole bunch of it on sale for a dollar, and every woman in town is stocking up."

Raleigh grimaced, obviously understanding the implications. "Well, that was a whole lot of money wasted on chemical analysis and database comparison."

Mitch looked from one woman to the other. "What are you talking about?"

"Just that the lipstick stain found on Larry's clothes won't be much help if dozens of women in Coot's Bayou wear this same shade."

"Wait a minute. You thought my mother—"

"No, Mitch, of course not." Beth found herself fibbing again. She was doing that a lot lately. "I just happened to notice the lipstick and wanted to know if she'd bought it around here. If it was unusual, that could have helped us find a suspect. But it's not rare."

Myra didn't seem fazed by the idea she might be considered a suspect. She didn't act like a guilty person…except about those guns. This, Beth decided, was a matter she should put to rest.

"Myra, you're not considered a suspect. But I do think you know more about Willard's guns than you're telling us."

"You gotta be kidding." Mitch sounded disgusted.

"No, Mitch, Beth is right." Myra turned to face them, wiping her hands on an old linen dishcloth. "I didn't tell the truth when she first asked. I needed money, and I sold Willard's guns at a flea market. I sold them to anyone who had the cash, and some of those men might have been criminals. There, now, I've said it, and I'm glad I've gotten it off my chest."

"Myra, don't worry," Raleigh said. "You didn't do anything illegal. But do you happen to remember who might have bought a small revolver?"

She thought for a moment. "I only remember one handgun. It was a big thing, though." She indicated a span with her hands far larger than a .22. "The rest were all shotguns and rifles."

"So Willard might have disposed of the .22 before his death," Beth said.

"I'm afraid so. Anything could have happened to it."

Beth quietly sighed. She was glad to put any lingering suspicions about Myra to rest, but the new information didn't help with the investigation at all. Unless…

"Mitch," Beth said, "remember when you said you thought Dwayne might be trying to sabotage your case?"

"Yeah, but I've been doing a lot of thinking about that. I didn't want to cut him any slack at first."

"No, you certainly didn't." She shivered, recalling how angry he'd become over her suggestion that Dwayne had been abused.

"From everything I've seen, Dwayne's a lot different than he was when we were kids. He's been pretty cool about this whole thing. Even when he picked the fight with me—I think he did it for my own good, so I could work through some old resentment. I just read him wrong. He really was trying to give me a heads-up when he came to see me at work. Now that I think about it, he probably didn't have a current home address for me—"

"Mitch, wait…" How inconvenient that he'd changed his mind, just when she'd changed hers. "Dwayne behaved very suspiciously at Larry's autopsy this morning. He had fresh scratches on his arm. I think he might know something about Larry's death."

Mitch rolled his eyes. "First you think my mom did it, now Dwayne?"

"I never really thought your mom—"

"That's it. I don't want to hear any more." He stood up and pulled a set of keys from his pocket.

"Is that your solution? You get angry, so you walk away rather than talking things out?"

"I'm not angry." His tone of voice said otherwise. But he took one deep breath, then another, and a steely calm came over him. "I'm not angry," he said again. "But I'm gonna go talk to Dwayne. I'll extend him the same courtesy he did for me. I'll give him a heads-up. Dwayne might be a jerk sometimes, but he's proud of that badge. Can't see him breaking the law."

"I'm going with you," Beth said. If Dwayne really was a murderer, she didn't want Mitch confronting him alone. Maybe she couldn't defend him, but she could try to keep the calm if things got crazy. She could at least call 9-1-1.

"Wait, both of you. No one do anything right now, okay?" Raleigh said. "I need to go. I have a meeting scheduled with Buck. Can I please depend on you—both of you—to stay out of trouble?"

"Nothing I do is going to cause trouble," Mitch said, actually offering a smile. "I've learned my lesson after last night, okay?"

Beth noted that he hadn't actually said he would stay put, or that he wouldn't go see Dwayne. Which meant it was Beth's job to make sure he didn't. As if she'd been so effective in the past convincing him to do anything.

"Thank you, Myra, for the iced tea," Raleigh said as she gathered up her things. "I've never been a fan of sweet tea before, but you've turned me into a convert." She gave Beth's shoulder a meaningful squeeze before departing. She knew Beth was struggling, but she obviously had no sage words of advice.

Mitch sat at the kitchen table, nibbling on a cookie from a plate Myra had put out and flipping through the paper, looking unconcerned.

"So you're not going to see your brother?"

He didn't answer right away; at least he didn't seem intent on lying to her. She supplied an answer for him.

"You're waiting until I'm distracted, then you're going to take off."

She knew by his expression that she'd guessed correctly.

"It's not like going to see my brother would be violating the terms of my bail. He lives well within the parish. And don't tell me I'd be interfering with a police investigation. So far the police don't view him as a suspect. Only Project Justice." What he meant was, *only you*.

"I could very well be wrong," Beth said. "But you'll turn him against Project Justice by telling him."

Mitch seemed to be weighing her words.

"You should listen to her, Mitchell," his mother said, proving that even when she appeared to be minding her own business, she was listening intently.

"I want to see him," Mitch said. "I won't tell him what you think. Maybe I can figure out why he was acting weird this morning. I'll ask him about the scratches. Maybe there's a logical explanation."

Beth thought about arguing. But Mitch was the classic immovable object, and she was nothing like an irresistible force. "I'll go with you," she said in a voice that she hoped made it sound like a done deal.

CHAPTER FIFTEEN

AMAZINGLY, HE NODDED. Maybe she was getting better at standing up to men. Or maybe, deep inside, she knew that with Mitch, she didn't have to be afraid. His words were sinking in—he wasn't the same as Vince, or his father. Yes, he hung on to anger he should have let go a long time ago. But he didn't channel that anger into hurting innocent people.

"He wasn't actually on duty today," Beth explained. "He was dressed in civilian clothes. He said he had to get home because he'd promised Linda he would help her in the garden."

"Good. I'd rather talk to him without his cop buddies all around him."

"Why don't you take them this peach cobbler?" Myra suggested. "It'll give you a good excuse to stop by. I bought a whole lot of peaches on sale yesterday, so I overbaked. I was going to freeze the extra."

"That's a great idea, Myra," Beth said.

Minutes later they were in the El Camino, roaring out of the driveway and down the dirt road, raising rooster tails of dust behind them. Tension between them was thick as cold syrup.

"I might have overreacted about the cage-fighting thing," she said carefully.

He shook his head. "You have every right to be furious with me. It's *better* if you stay mad at me."

"Better for whom?" No one had ever confused her the way this man did. Just when she thought she would be placating him, saying something that would make him happy, he changed his stance.

"For you."

"You don't know what's better for me." She rolled down her window to get some air into the car, now that they were off the dirt road. "I'm a big girl, and I can make my own choices. Right now, I'm choosing to overlook my personal abhorrence for violence and agree that there's nothing morally wrong with the sport you've chosen to participate in."

"But—"

"Violence is violence. And being around it is not for me."

He glanced over, looking startled. How could her stance surprise him, given everything he knew about her, everything she'd said to him on the porch?

"Does that mean you don't want to be friends with me?"

Friends? She hadn't even thought about their friendship, she'd been so focused on their more personal, intimate relationship. She didn't have a ready answer.

"It would be nice if *somebody* visited me in prison," he said. "I'll be the most popular guy in Huntsville if a Project Justice evidence analyst shows up on visiting day."

"Don't joke about that, okay?" At least he was back to joking. That was the Mitch she knew...knew and loved, dammit. She vaguely recalled that she'd blurted out something about loving him during their argument on Myra's front porch. How stupid could she be?

"Humor is one way of coping. I've developed lots of ways."

Beth didn't have an answer for that. She understood coping mechanisms. After the climactic end of her relationship with Vince, she'd done a lot of crying and sounding off in therapy. But men usually didn't feel comfortable with that option. They had to channel their pain and hostility some other way.

She was still trying to wrap her mind around the whole fighting thing.

Before long they were cruising through a nice section of Coot's Bayou where the houses stood on large lots with mature trees bright green with new spring leaves.

"How does Dwayne afford to live in such a nice area on a cop's salary?" Beth asked.

"He inherited his mom's house. She died young. Actually, my dad probably was the original owner. He made pretty good money working at the refinery before his drinking lost him his job."

"It must have been sad watching him decline. I was starting to see that in Vince—he was drinking too much, angry too much. He'd skip work sometimes when he was hungover. But before all that...he was a good guy, you know?"

"There's no way I can picture my dad as ever being

a 'good guy.' I never saw him when he wasn't drunk, mean or both."

"But did you ever wonder what turned him into a mean drunk? Was *his* father a mean drunk? Vince lost his job and had to take another job at a lower pay scale. It ate at him. That was what started him down the self-destructive—"

"Beth, I don't know and I don't care. He's dead, I never knew his father or anything about him. I don't want to understand what made him such an SOB."

"But if you understood, maybe you wouldn't hate him so much. Maybe you wouldn't be so angry." She knew she was overstepping. Vince hadn't reacted well when she'd tried to get him to talk about feelings and such. But when she saw someone in pain—even if he thought he was "dealing" with it—she couldn't help herself.

"You can't make excuses for him."

"I'm not. Really I'm not. I just don't want you to hurt anymore. Forgiveness is one way to stop hurting."

She expected an angry comeback. Or sarcasm. Or at least a joke. But Mitch just looked at her. "Have you forgiven Vince? The last time I asked you that, you couldn't answer."

She paused. She'd always *thought* she'd forgiven him, but had she really? If she was going to confront Mitch about this, she owed him a completely honest answer.

She pictured Vince's face, twisted in anger, and waited for the sharp pinch of pain. But it wasn't so bad. What she felt more than anything was regret that she'd allowed him to control her long after he was out of her life.

"Maybe not completely," she finally said. "I still hate what he did to me, and I'd be the first one in line to put him in jail to prevent him from hurting some other woman. But I'm not nearly as angry as I was. By holding on to my anger like a security blanket, I let him hurt me over and over and over again. It feels good to loosen my grip on those memories." She took a deep breath, certain she spoke the truth. "I'm making progress, at least."

"You're a better person than me."

The discussion ended, because Mitch pulled into the driveway of a brown, brick ranch house, circa 1970s. It wasn't the biggest house on the block, but the structure and the yard were immaculate. The grass was an emerald carpet, and azaleas blossomed in pink profusion all along the front of the house and the brick walkway.

"Try to give me some time alone with Dwayne, okay?" Mitch said. "You and Linda can do the girl bonding thing. Make lemonade with her or something. Maybe Dwayne will be more open with me."

"All right. Just don't provoke him, okay? What if he really is a murderer? He has guns. We don't."

"He's also a cop. He's not going to shoot us in his own house, not in front of his wife. Not when my mother knows where we are, and my GPS cuff telegraphs my location every minute of every day."

"Good point."

They mounted the two steps to the front porch and rang the bell. Something small and yappy barked at them, and Mitch chuckled. "I never figured Dwayne to have an ankle-biter dog. He always said those little dogs don't even make for good roadkill."

Though the dog barked and barked, no one came to the door.

"Maybe they're in the backyard," Beth said. "Dwayne did mention something about gardening."

They walked around to the side of the house and met up with a chain-link gate, locked.

"Hey, Dwayne!" Mitch yelled, sounding less than cordial. "You back there?"

Beth thought she heard the murmur of voices, but the breeze hummed through the tall trees just then, so she wasn't sure. "We come bearing gifts," Beth added, so they would understand it was a social call.

"I'm gonna go see if they're back there." Mitch grabbed on to the top of the fence, obviously intending to vault it, but Beth grabbed his arm and stopped him just in time, bobbling the cobbler and nearly dropping it.

"No. That's technically breaking and entering. Or at least trespassing. Don't give anyone a reason to— Oh, hi, Dwayne! Myra sent us over with a cobbler."

Dwayne had just rounded the corner of the house, looking perplexed. At the mention of dessert, however, his guarded expression changed to one of curiosity. "Peach?"

"Mmm-hmm. Isn't it nice how we can get fresh peaches all year round? She said the store had a sale and she bought more than she can eat."

"Linda?" Dwayne called over his shoulder. "Mitch

and Beth are here and they brought dessert." He pulled a key out of his pocket and unlocked the padlock that secured the gate.

Dwayne was still in his shorts and T-shirt, dirtier than they'd been this morning.

"Pardon my attire," Dwayne said as if he'd noticed Beth's examination. "Working on that honey-do list."

When Beth came around the corner and got her first look at the huge backyard, she was awestruck. She'd expected to see a little patch of flowers and maybe some tomato plants and strawberries. But the Bells' garden was enormous, probably a quarter acre, with neat rows upon rows of small, healthy plants from the nursery. Several more rows had been tilled, and flats of everything from squash to cucumbers to peppers waited in flats to be put into the ground.

"This is beautiful!" Beth exclaimed. "You must spend an awful lot of time on it."

Linda, who wore a wide-brimmed hat tied under her chin, a denim work shirt and pink capris, smiled proudly. "It's kinda my thing." She turned her attention to the large glass casserole dish Beth held. "What did Myra send over?"

"A peach cobbler."

"That was so sweet of her. And very nice of you to bring it over. Come on inside, Beth, and I'll show you around. I'm ready for a break."

Well, that was easier than Beth had thought it would be. No need to invent a reason to get Linda away from the menfolk so the brothers could bond. But Beth intended to stay close to a window and keep Mitch and

Dwayne within view. No matter what Mitch said, if a killer got cornered he was apt to forget all good sense and do something crazy.

Now that she was here, though, in this domestic oasis, she had a hard time picturing Dwayne as a killer.

Linda led Beth up a set of wooden stairs onto a screened-in porch that housed a picnic table and propane grill. "We use this as a mudroom in the spring and summer," she said, pulling off her gloves, hat and sunglasses and laying them on a bench. She slipped off her pink Crocs. "We don't wear shoes in the house, if you don't mind. It saves the carpets like you wouldn't believe."

That was Beth's cue to take off her shoes. Was Linda the kind of woman who put down carpet runners and clear plastic furniture protectors?

The door they went through led them into the kitchen, which had that Tuscan look that had been all the rage a couple of years earlier. Everything was warm brick and oiled bronze, with granite counters and a flat cooktop. The refrigerator was behind custom cabinets painted a distressed gold-green, and the floor was hand-scraped cypress planks.

"I love your kitchen," Beth said. "Do you cook a lot?"

"Every day, practically." Linda tucked the casserole onto a glass shelf. Everything in the refrigerator, Beth noted, was arranged with geometric precision in matching plastic containers, labeled.

Beth was getting the feeling that Dwayne's wife was a bit...particular about things, and she had to smile. Raleigh was that way, though perhaps not to this degree. Linda even had a little dog like Raleigh did. The fluffy white thing had met them at the door and was sniffing around Beth's feet curiously.

"That's Oscar. Noisy, but wouldn't hurt a flea."

"Hello, Oscar." Beth leaned down and let the dog sniff her hand, then scratched him behind his fluffy ears.

"I'll just give you a quick tour," Linda said, assuming Beth would be interested in her decor, as most women would be. And, frankly, Beth was a little curious to see if the rest of the house lived up to the spectacular kitchen.

She wasn't disappointed. The floors were covered in cream-colored Berber carpet. Beth didn't even want to think about how hard that was to keep clean. No wonder Linda didn't allow shoes indoors, and thank heavens they didn't have kids.

The kitchen flowed into a great room that looked like something out of a magazine, right down to the fresh flower arrangements. A den off to the side looked slightly more lived in, but still tidy enough to show off.

The house had a master suite on one side, and two smaller bedrooms on the other.

"Ordinarily I wouldn't show company into the bedroom," she said, "but I just had the bath redone and I love showing it off."

It was, indeed, worth showing off, every surface covered in blood-red tile. The glassed-in shower had two spigots and was plenty big enough for two. There was also a whirlpool tub and a double-sink vanity with a row of black wrought-iron lights.

"It's gorgeous," Beth gushed, though personally she thought it was a tad overdramatic. All that red reminded her of blood and made her sick to her stomach.

"Oh, my goodness," Linda said, obviously focused on her own image in the mirror. "I look a fright. Let me freshen up. I'll just be a minute."

"O—" Beth choked on her words as Linda shoved up the sleeves of her shirt to wash her hands. She had four deep, parallel scratches on one forearm.

Beth's gaze automatically moved to Linda's array of cosmetics, neatly organized in a compartmentalized Lucite tray that sat on the counter. Among the lipsticks was a gold-and-copper-striped case, and it was the one Linda reached for. Beth knew before Linda even opened the case that it would be Youthful Coral.

Linda met Beth's gaze in the mirror. "Is something wrong?"

"No, no, nothing. I'll just, um, wait in the kitchen." She ducked out of the bathroom, telling herself over and over it meant nothing. Lots of women in town had that lipstick—Myra had said so. But those scratches—undoubtedly made by human fingernails.... No wonder Dwayne had gotten nervous about Larry's fingernail scrapings. He knew...or suspected...

No, surely it didn't mean anything. She was jumping at—

An arm went around her neck, and Beth found herself in a choke hold with one arm twisted behind her back. "It was the damn lipstick, wasn't it?"

Adrenaline surged through Beth, fueling her panic. Her scream came out as a gurgle. She clawed at Linda's arm with her free hand and flailed her legs, but in bare feet her struggles had no effect at all as Linda dragged her toward the kitchen like a rag doll.

Once again, she was completely at someone's mercy.

CHAPTER SIXTEEN

"WANT SOME HELP WITH THOSE?" Mitch gestured toward the flat of squash plants.

Dwayne looked as awkward as Mitch suddenly felt. "Yeah, sure. I guess. We have to dig the holes exactly eighteen inches apart, though. If they're seventeen, or nineteen, I'll hear about it."

"Ah. I do seem to remember Linda liking things a certain way."

Dwayne expelled a breath through his teeth. "You don't know the half of it."

They worked in semicompanionable silence for a few minutes, with Dwayne measuring and digging the holes and Mitch coming behind him to drop in the plants.

"You didn't come over here just to deliver a cobbler," Dwayne said.

"No. Beth said you were a little bit agitated at the autopsy this morning. It bothered her. A lot. So much that she's wondering if you had anything to do with Larry's death."

Dwayne went still. "Really."

"How'd you get the scratches on your arms?"

"Huh?" Dwayne looked down at his arms as if

seeing the scratches for the first time. "Oh. The roses." He gestured toward a row of rosebushes along the fence, just starting to bud. "I weeded that bed yesterday. I had nothing to do with Larry Montague's death."

Mitch was relieved to have such an easy explanation. "I guess we're all jumping at shadows. You're a lot of things, but I can't see you murdering someone in cold blood. But something spooked you at the autopsy."

"Look, right now it's just a hunch. Something I need to look into. It's an open investigation, and I can't share everything with you."

Mitch felt the frustration welling up in him again. "This is my life we're talking about."

"I know. And I promise, if I find out anything I can use to clear you, I will."

"Can you at least tell me if they consider me a suspect in Larry's murder?"

Dwayne leaned back on his heels and blew out a breath. "Yeah. 'Fraid so. But they're nowhere near ready to press charges. They figure they got time to develop a case against you, and you're not going anywhere."

"They won't find any evidence I did it." Mitch mashed one of the plants into its hole a little more forcefully than necessary, breaking off one of the leaves.

"Easy with that plant." Dwayne picked up the broken leaf, dug a little hole with his finger in the soft soil and buried it. "Linda's OCD. I guess you figured that out. But I love her. She's had my back for a lot of years."

"It's good to have someone you can count on," Mitch

said, thinking of Beth and wondering if there was any way to fix what was broken there. She already had his back. Even after she'd learned about the cage fighting and tampering with the cuff, she was still looking after his interests.

Loyalty like that wasn't easy to find.

"Given who we had as role models, it's a miracle either one of us ended up with a decent marriage. And it's not too late for you, Mitch."

"If I can beat a murder rap." He paused, pinching off a brown leaf and burying it like Dwayne had done. "Yeah, if I beat this thing, I'm gonna try for what you have."

"Parts of it are real good." Dwayne sounded a little wistful. "You just have to learn to accept the parts that aren't so perfect. No relationship is perfect."

Mitch's mother had said something similar, about her and Davy. Something about every relationship being about give-and-take, compromising here and there, picking your battles.

He suspected that if he wanted Beth, he was going to have to give up fighting. Could he do that?

The sound of a slamming door made him look up. Beth and Linda were returning from inside. He looked back down at the plant he'd been about to drop into a hole, but something registered in his mind as wrong, wrong, wrong.

He looked up again.

Linda had Beth in a headlock, a gun to her temple.

"Jesus!" Mitch sprang to his feet, grabbing the first

thing he saw that could reasonably become a weapon—a small shovel.

"Oh, my God," Dwayne murmured right behind Mitch.

Mitch's instinct was to charge. He had to get to Beth—had to save her.

"Stop right there!" Linda commanded in a strangely guttural voice. "Do as I say."

"Linda, what are you doing?" Dwayne nearly strangled on his words. "Let her go! Put the gun down, are you crazy?"

"She knows, Dwayne. About the lipstick."

Mitch couldn't help noticing that Linda had put on a fresh coat of a peachy-orange color on her lips. Was it the Youthful Coral Beth had mentioned? Had she seen the lipstick and made some sort of accusation?

Given Linda's reaction, she had something to do with Larry's death. Was that what Dwayne had suspected? Or had he known for sure?

"Linda," Dwayne tried again. "Put the gun down. This is only going to make things worse. We had a plan, remember? We need to stick to it."

"I'm not leaving this house!" Keeping her stranglehold on Beth, who appeared too terrified to move any muscle she didn't have to, Linda dragged her victim closer. Mitch gauged how close he would have to get. He could knock the gun out of her hand with a high roundhouse kick. If he did it fast enough, she wouldn't have time to react and pull the trigger.

But could he do it fast enough?

He didn't know, and he couldn't risk Beth's life finding out.

"You killed Larry Montague," Mitch said, hoping the exact right words would come to him, words that would convince Linda Bell that killing anyone else wouldn't help her cause. "We were just waiting for the lab to confirm the match to your lipstick."

"Honey, it's over," Dwayne tried one more time in a wheedling tone. "Please, baby, put down the gun. Everything's going to be okay."

"Okay?" Linda screeched. "With both of us going to prison? I don't think so. I busted my ass helping you cover up Robby Racine's death. I lied for you all these years, and now you want to throw all that away?"

"There's still—" Dwayne tried again, but his wife cut him off.

"We agreed that if the murder ever came to light, everyone would think your brother did it. But now you're going soft on me, aren't you?"

Dwayne glanced over at Mitch. "It was an accident." He silently pled for understanding. "I was a rookie, and I was gonna be a hero, finding the stolen car and bringing the thief into custody. But Robby said he had a gun. I panicked..."

"Dwayne, just shut up!" Linda screamed.

"I thought he was going to shoot me. But when it was over, Robby was dead, and there was no other gun. I saw my career going in the toilet before it had even begun. So I called Linda to help me. I had an old gun of Daddy's in my glove box, and I shot a couple of rounds into the shack, then planted the gun in the car. We sank the car and buried Robby, and I honestly thought that would be the end of it.

"And it was—until Robby's body was found."

"Great, just spill your guts," Linda said, "and implicate me while you're at it."

"It's over, Linda," Dwayne said. "Just let Beth go, and give me the gun." He inched toward his wife, his hand outstretched.

Suddenly Linda thrust Beth away from her, shoving her to the ground, hard. "Don't you move!"

She turned the gun on Dwayne and pulled the trigger.

PAIN RADIATED FROM Beth's shoulder and her head felt as though it had been split in two, and for one crazy moment she thought she was the one who'd been shot. But then she saw a red circle blossomed on Dwayne's shirt.

"Linda, honey..." Dwayne collapsed, and Linda slowly turned the gun and pointed it at Mitch. Beth swallowed the urge to scream, fearing any sound she made might cause the unbalanced woman to twitch. All she could do was watch, helpless.

Mitch had crouched in preparation to launch an attack, but now he froze, probably realizing that martial arts were no match for a loaded gun in the hands of someone who fully intended to use it.

"You killed Larry?" Mitch asked.

That's good, Beth thought. *Keep her talking.*

"He was there that night. He was trying to blackmail us. I couldn't let him do that. I didn't want to kill him…" A single tear coursed down her cheek. Still, though she was obviously distraught, her hand was steady, her gaze never wavering.

"I'm sorry, Dwayne." Linda started to sob. "But better the widow of a hero than the wife of a disgraced cop."

"Linda, give it up," Mitch said. "Please. By now, the neighbors heard the gunshot. They'll be calling the police."

"You're probably right." She sniffed back her tears. "So this is how it's gonna go down. You and Dwayne got into a terrible argument. You pulled a gun and shot at Dwayne. You missed the first time, hitting Beth by accident, but the second shot hit Dwayne. Dwayne made a grab for the gun. You struggled, and it went off accidentally, fatally wounding Mitch. I saw the whole thing from the porch."

The woman was a monster! Beth tried to think of some way to stop her. But Linda had a gun. How could Beth and Mitch argue with a gun?

Beth should say something. Reason with her. But she was so terrified, she couldn't even formulate words. And maybe it was better if she said nothing. Right now, Linda discounted Beth as a threat. Who would be afraid of a small-statured woman cowering on the ground with an injured shoulder?

That was when she saw movement out of the corner of her eye. Dwayne…it was Dwayne moving his hand, one inch at a time. He wasn't dead.

Did he have a gun? He probably didn't carry one around to do yard work. His hand closed over the blade of the shovel, which Mitch had dropped on Linda's command. Did Dwayne have enough strength left to do anything useful with the shovel?

Dwayne pushed the shovel toward Beth, and that was when Beth realized that if anyone was going to use the shovel, *she* would have to. Three people's lives hung in the balance, and she didn't have much time to act. She could see the wheels turning in Linda's mind, visualizing the scenario she would tell the police, calculating how to shoot Mitch and Beth in a way that would match up with her story.

Seconds. Beth had only a few seconds to act.

Courage surged through her, fueled by her anger at this woman's savagery, her utter disregard for anyone's well-being but her own. Well, Linda had made a critical error when she'd pointed that gun at the man Beth loved.

It's over, bitch.

In one fluid motion, Beth grabbed the shovel, surged to her feet and swung that shovel in a wide arc toward Linda's head. Linda had time only to turn, eyes wide with surprise, before the shovel made contact with a sickening thwack.

At the same time, Mitch made his move. His right foot seemed to blur as it circled through the air and made contact with the gun in Linda's hand, knocking it a good twenty feet away.

Linda went down, but Beth didn't stop there. She leaped on top of the woman and, utterly untrained in how to subdue someone, simply lay down on top of her with her arms and legs spread wide so she couldn't wiggle out.

Mitch went for the gun. And though he never did anything awkwardly, he held the gun as if it were a snake and pointed it at Linda.

"You move a muscle and I'll shoot you through the head," he informed her in a steely voice. With his left hand he reached into his pocket for his cell phone.

Beth wanted to go help Dwayne, but she didn't dare move. If she let Linda up, the woman might realize Mitch would never shoot her, and flee. Thankfully, Linda stopped struggling.

"Officer down," Mitch said into his phone. Nothing brought the police faster than those two words. He rattled off the address and a rather garbled version of what had just happened.

"The police are never going to believe you," Linda said, her voice muffled by Beth's shoulder pressing against it. "If Dwayne is dead, and you're the one holding the gun—"

"And you're the one with gunshot residue on her hand," Beth said. "Nice try." She was amazed she could string words together. She'd just hit someone in the head with a shovel. A human being. In the head. With a shovel.

Thank God Linda was at least conscious and talking. She could just as easily be dead. Beth hadn't given her just a little tap; the blow had vibrated all the way through Beth's body, and her hands hurt like they'd been hit with a hammer.

It seemed like forever until the cops arrived, but

probably only two or three minutes passed. Finally, though, Beth heard sirens. She could feel it when the cops actually arrived, feel their eyes on her, but she didn't see them.

"Sir, lay down your weapon and put your hands behind your head."

"He means you," Beth said to Mitch. "Just do it— we'll sort it out later."

Mitch lay the gun gently on the grass, then slowly stood and put his hands at the back of his neck, as instructed. *Then* she saw cops—lots of cops, all over the place. Every cop on duty for twenty miles must have responded to the call.

She didn't move until two pairs of hands, one on each arm, pulled her to her feet. She yelped at the pain in her shoulder.

"Are you okay, miss?"

"Hey, I'm the one who's hurt," Linda said. "That crazy bitch hit me in the head with a shovel."

"Because she shot her husband, and she was going to kill us, too!" Beth babbled. "Do a GSR test on her, on all of us. She's the only one who did any shooting."

"In self-defense!" Linda cried, sounding panicked now. "It was an accident. She hit me in the head with a shovel. I was trying to shoot her and I hit my husband instead!"

Her tears appeared genuine, and Beth felt stirrings of a new panic. What if they didn't believe her and Mitch? Mitch was a murder suspect, she was part of his defense team. What if they didn't do the proper tests? A small-town police force sometimes made mistakes.

Two other cops had gone to help Dwayne. One was using some kind of pack to apply pressure to the chest wound. The scene was chaotic as officers shouted to each other, calling for paramedics, securing the scene and overexcited at being so close to an attempted murder. Stuff like this didn't happen in sleepy Coot's Bayou very often.

Then a new voice joined the babble of excited cops and crackling police radios. "My wife…shot me." It was Dwayne.

"What?" one of the cops asked, leaning down and putting his ear close to Dwayne's mouth. "What did you say?"

Dwayne's voice was barely above a whisper, and each labored breath sounded as if it might be his last. "Linda shot me… No accident… She killed Larry… I killed Robby… Mitch and Beth…innocent…" His eyes closed, and he went silent.

It was a deathbed confession, which she and at least three cops could attest to, and in the legal world, it was golden. Admissible in court whether Dwayne survived or not because clearly he *thought* he was dying.

Mitch was home free.

But she didn't want Dwayne to die. "Can't you do something?" Beth asked.

"Paramedics are on the way," the cop who appeared to be in charge said, then added, "Let her go."

It took a moment for Beth to realize she was wearing handcuffs. She hadn't even been aware. Moments later, her wrists were freed. And as the adrenaline in her body ebbed away, the pain in her shoulder was like a knife.

She wanted to find Mitch. The cops had moved him out of her line of vision. But she couldn't take her eyes off Dwayne, either. He wasn't moving. Was he dead? But when the paramedics arrived, they worked on him for a while, then loaded him up and took him away on a stretcher, pale and still. That meant he was still alive. If he were dead, they would leave him at the scene, and he would fall under the venue of the crime scene investigators and the medical examiner.

"Ms. McClelland?" Lieutenant Addlestein addressed her. "Could you come over here, please?" He treated her gently, guiding her to the patio where he sat her down in a chair. She felt dazed, stupid, and it wasn't until one of the paramedics came to check her out that she realized she was bleeding from her elbow where she'd hit the ground. She'd gotten blood all over her clothes.

"Tell me what hurts," the handsome young paramedic asked, as if she were five years old.

"I'm okay," she insisted. "Where's Mitch? What happened to Mitch?"

"He's fine," the lieutenant said. "I'm sure you know the drill. We take your statements separately."

"But you know he didn't do anything wrong. You heard Dwayne?"

"Yes, ma'am. If you could just tell me what happened?"

Pulling her scattered thoughts together, she told her story, starting with her suspicions about Dwayne, and

Mitch's insistence that they talk to his brother and find out what was going on. She moved on to what her lab had uncovered about the lipstick stain, and spotting that specific brand of lipstick in Linda's bathroom.

"I guess I said or did something to give myself away," Beth said, feeling guilty over that part. Raleigh, or any of the Project Justice investigators, would have handled that moment a lot better than she had.

"It's okay. You did fine."

She moved on to the more difficult parts, about Linda assaulting her, and the fact she was such an easy hostage. "I couldn't do anything to stop her, even before she had a weapon," Beth said. "I remember clawing at her arm— Oh! You have to take fingernail scrapings."

Addlestein made a note. "We'll do all that at the hospital." He looked at her neck and jaw. "I expect you'll have bruises, too. And that shoulder will need X-rays."

She'd thought she was hiding her injuries, hoping to avoid the hospital. The longer this took, the longer it would be before she could see Mitch. She had so much to say, so much to tell him.

"I hit Linda in the head with a shovel," Beth said miserably. "She said she was going to kill us all, and I didn't see any other way."

Addlestein actually smiled. "You probably saved three lives today. It's nothing to be ashamed of."

Shouting from behind her made Beth turn her head. "Enough, all right? You can take all the statements you want in five minutes." Mitch, with two uniforms trailing behind him, strode toward Beth. Neither of the cops was brave enough to try to physically detain him.

Beth came out of her chair. "Mitch!"

He pulled her to him and enveloped her in a crushing hug that set her shoulder on fire again, but she didn't care. "Beth. Oh, honey. You scared me half to death."

"I'm sorry. I gave away the game—"

"Shh. It's okay."

"I'm such a wimp."

"What are you talking about? What you did was amazing. Where did you find the courage?"

"I don't know. I knew she was going to shoot you, I knew it was only seconds away, and I just did it. I didn't really think about it. I mean, where did that violence come from? I've never hit anyone, ever."

"Helluva way to start."

She pulled back to look at him. "You actually approve of what I did?"

"If there'd been any other way to stop Linda, then, no. Of course I couldn't approve. But you did what you had to do, and I'm nothing but proud of you. Not just proud—in awe of your courage. And your brilliance in figuring out who really killed Larry."

Beth was still processing this new, weird reality—that under the right circumstances, she could be a violent person. Murderously, lethally violent. It made Mitch's bout with a bale of hay pale by comparison. Even his cage fighting—that was just a sport. A competitive sport with willing participants, with rules and a referee and safety precautions. It wasn't like anybody in a cage fight got to use a shovel.

"I've been so stupid," she said on a sob.

"Don't, Beth. You're the smartest person I know."

"Smart in the lab, maybe. Stupid when it comes to relationships. I judged you, all sanctimonious, thinking I was somehow better because *I* never was violent—"

"Beth, it's okay."

"It's not okay. I love you and yet I pushed you away for something so trivial—"

"It's not trivial if you're afraid of me."

"But I'm not. Maybe I was a little bit afraid because I had this picture of you as gentle and sweet, but I understand so much more now."

"I am gentle and sweet. With you. Always. Give me a chance to prove that. I still think you deserve better than me, but I'm gonna be selfish and insist that you take me anyway."

"I'll take you if you'll take a dangerous Shovel Woman. But you'll have to promise me one thing."

"You want me to stop cage fighting? I could do that."

"No, that's not it at all! I want you to teach me to defend myself. It was pathetic, how easily Linda controlled me. She didn't even break a sweat."

"Deal." He started to kiss her, but stilled just before their lips made contact. Beth gradually became aware that a third party had never left their conversation.

Lieutenant Addlestein stood right next to them, looking as if he wanted to puke. "Can we continue this later, little lovebirds? I've got an investigation to conduct. If you want me to nail down a case against Linda Bell, you'll cooperate."

Beth and Mitch parted self-consciously, and Beth realized the detective had overheard everything. Mitch took her hand and pressed his lips to her knuckles. "Go to the hospital. Get yourself checked out, okay? I'll see you there."

"It's a date."

EPILOGUE

"SMACK HIM IN THE HEAD, that's it!" Celeste was standing on her chair, screaming encouragement to Mitch at the top of her lungs. She'd worn one of her most fetching outfits—a leopard print minidress with a belt made from rifle cartridges, and thigh-high snakeskin boots—for the occasion of Mitch's first fight as the reigning light-heavyweight champion of South-Southeast Texas—and his first official fight using his real name.

Daniel had purchased an entire section of the arena, and everyone at Project Justice had been given free tickets. He'd also sent tickets to Myra and Davy, at Mitch's request. Dwayne had wanted to come, but his health, not to mention the conditions of his bail bond, made that impossible. But he'd promised to watch on TV.

"Run away!" Raleigh called out, but not loud enough for anyone but Beth to hear. When she'd seen Mitch's muscle-bound opponent with his neck-to-ankle tattoos, shaved head and fierce expression, she'd been more unnerved than Beth. But Beth, who'd watched Mitch train and spar with practice partners, knew more about what was going on than Raleigh did.

"Size and strength don't matter nearly as much as

leverage," she'd explained. "Watch, see how Mitch is looking for an opening? The other guy is just punching blindly. Mitch is wicked accurate with his kicks. You won't see it coming—there!"

Mitch had just spun so fast he'd become a blur, whacking his opponent in the ribs with a powerful kick. As the guy reeled, Mitch was on him and had him on the ground.

"Now he's gonna ground and pound," Beth said proudly. Her shoulder injury hadn't been serious, and after a couple of weeks to recuperate, she'd signed up for Brazilian jujitsu lessons from Mitch's trainer. To her surprise, she actually enjoyed it. If Linda ever tried to put a choke hold on her again, Beth would be able to easily escape. If Vince or any man tried to break her jaw, she knew how to defend against that, too.

Theoretically, anyway, but she felt confident she would gain more skills, in time.

Mitch's opponent wasn't done yet. He wiggled out and somehow managed to flip Mitch onto his back.

"Kick him in the family jewels!" Celeste shouted.

"That's not allowed, Celeste," Beth shouted back, laughing at her coworker's antics. She'd never seen Celeste cut loose like this before—which was saying a lot because Celeste wasn't known for holding it back.

"They oughtta let me in the ring with that slimy snake. I'd show him what-for."

Beth didn't doubt that Celeste could hold her own in a fight. She was solid sinew, and rumor had it she'd collected black belts in several disciplines.

Beth watched, literally chewing her nails, as Mitch

struggled to get out from tattoo man, who was sprawled with all four limbs spread, just like Beth had instinctively done with Linda.

But Mitch somehow swiveled around, wrapping one of his arms around his opponent's shoulder and neck, and all of a sudden the guy was wincing in pain and tapping the mat, signaling the fight was over. He was crying uncle.

Mitch immediately loosened his grip. The two men parted, and Mitch popped to his feet and gave his opponent a hand up. The two men quickly embraced. MMA was a small world, and though the guys might look like they wanted to kill each other when they competed, out of the ring most of them were friends.

Only then did Mitch clasp both of his hands together and raise them into the air in the classic victory gesture.

Mitch had successfully defended his title, and the crowd went wild for the Cagey Cajun, who smiled broadly, then blew a kiss to Beth and mouthed, "I love you."

"Did you see that?" Celeste said excitedly. "He loves me. I knew this new lipstick would do the trick."

"Don't tell me," Beth said. "Is it Youthful Coral?"

Celeste climbed down from her chair. "How did you know? I stopped at the drugstore on the way out of Coot's Bayou, after I delivered Mitch's car, and they had these lipsticks on sale for a dollar!"

Beth had become intimately familiar with the color. It turned her stomach every time she looked at it. "Truthfully, Celeste, I like your signature fire-engine-red better."

"Hmm." She took a compact out of her purple, faux lizard purse and inspected herself critically.

Mitch headed out of the ring and toward the dressing room, and Beth went after him. He'd said if he won tonight, he had a very special present he wanted to give her, and she was hoping it was her engagement ring.

They'd already decided to get married. The ring was just a formality, but Beth felt a giddy, girlish thrill at the prospect of wearing that symbol of their commitment for everyone to see.

They'd also agreed that he should keep fighting, so long as he was winning. He wanted to see how far he could take it, because each victory meant a bigger paycheck—to be socked away for some future child's college education. But his attitude about fighting was completely different than it had been.

Part of it was gaining new insight into his mother—and his brother. Mitch had put himself inside the head of that scared rookie cop. Though hiding the fact that Dwayne had killed Robby was an awful crime, Mitch realized Dwayne might have done the right thing if he hadn't been pushed by the woman he loved to hide that he'd shot Robby.

Whatever the reason, Mitch no longer felt he had anything to prove. The angry beast inside him was now more of a quirky family pet—with sharp teeth. He'd been a little worried that without the anger he might lose his edge. But he obviously still had it—in the cage, at least.

Beth found a crowd of groupies waiting at the dressing-room door, but the guy standing guard there recognized her and let her past. "Go on in, Beth, if you don't mind a few half-naked guys."

"Nuh-uh." Mitch came out the door, his hair damp from a shower and wearing only a pair of jeans and carrying his shirt. A couple of young boys thrust MMA magazines for him to sign, and he obliged them. Then he swept Beth into a hug. "Sorry, darlin', but I'm the only half-naked guy you get to see tonight."

"Don't forget the party Daniel and Jamie are having for you. We have to put in an appearance. Then we'll see about half-naked. Or maybe even full naked."

"Wouldn't miss it. I told you if I won, I was gonna give you a present." He released her and pulled her farther into the hallway, out of earshot from the fans as he continued to dress, shoving his arms into the sleeves of his bowling shirt. "I want to give it to you in front of everybody."

"What if you'd lost? Would you have taken the ring back to the store?"

His face fell. "You know?"

"For someone who maintained a secret identity for years, you're not very good at keeping secrets." She buttoned his shirt for him. "You showed the ring to at least half the staff."

"I couldn't help it." He grinned. "I'm like a little kid."

Maybe the little kid he never got to be when he was young.

He stroked her hair, then leaned down and whispered in her ear. "Let's fly to Vegas tonight. We could be married by morning."

Tempting though the invitation was, she shook her head. "My mother and sisters would take out a contract on us if they didn't get to plan this wedding."

"C'mon, champ," said the security guy from the door. "We gotta clear out of here in ten minutes so they can mop the floor. Unless *you* want to mop it."

"Glamorous life I lead."

Mitch took Beth's hand and they strolled out the back exit toward the El Camino, parked in its reserved spot. She knew their future still had a few rough patches to navigate through. They would both have to testify in Dwayne's and Linda's trials, if they didn't plead out.

But their lives were intertwined now, just like their fingers were. Neither of them would ever again have to face a challenge alone.

She squeezed Mitch's hand, as she'd done dozens of times since they'd pledged their love to each other. Beyond the momentary clouds on the horizon, she saw a future that burned bright with hope.

* * * * *

HEART & HOME

◆ Harlequin®

Super Romance

COMING NEXT MONTH
AVAILABLE APRIL 10, 2012

#1770 THE CALL OF BRAVERY
A Brother's Word
Janice Kay Johnson

#1771 THAT NEW YORK MINUTE
Abby Gaines

#1772 PROTECTING HER SON
Count on a Cop
Joan Kilby

#1773 THE WAY BACK
Stephanie Doyle

#1774 A RARE FIND
School Ties
Tracy Kelleher

#1775 ON HIS HONOR
The MacAllisters
Jean Brashear

You can find more information on upcoming Harlequin®
titles, free excerpts and more at www.Harlequin.com.

HSRCNM0312

REQUEST YOUR FREE BOOKS!
2 FREE NOVELS PLUS 2 FREE GIFTS!

Harlequin

Super Romance

Exciting, emotional, unexpected!

YES! Please send me 2 FREE Harlequin® Superromance® novels and my 2 FREE gifts (gifts are worth about $10). After receiving them, if I don't wish to receive any more books, I can return the shipping statement marked "cancel." If I don't cancel, I will receive 6 brand-new novels every month and be billed just $4.69 per book in the U.S. or $5.24 per book in Canada. That's a saving of at least 15% off the cover price! It's quite a bargain! Shipping and handling is just 50¢ per book in the U.S. and 75¢ per book in Canada.* I understand that accepting the 2 free books and gifts places me under no obligation to buy anything. I can always return a shipment and cancel at any time. Even if I never buy another book, the two free books and gifts are mine to keep forever.

135/336 HDN FC6T

Name	(PLEASE PRINT)	
Address		Apt. #
City	State/Prov.	Zip/Postal Code

Signature (if under 18, a parent or guardian must sign)

Mail to the **Reader Service**:
IN U.S.A.: P.O. Box 1867, Buffalo, NY 14240-1867
IN CANADA: P.O. Box 609, Fort Erie, Ontario L2A 5X3

Not valid for current subscribers to Harlequin Superromance books.
**Are you a current subscriber to Harlequin Superromance books and want to receive the larger-print edition?
Call 1-800-873-8635 or visit www.ReaderService.com.**

* Terms and prices subject to change without notice. Prices do not include applicable taxes. Sales tax applicable in N.Y. Canadian residents will be charged applicable taxes. Offer not valid in Quebec. This offer is limited to one order per household. All orders subject to credit approval. Credit or debit balances in a customer's account(s) may be offset by any other outstanding balance owed by or to the customer. Please allow 4 to 6 weeks for delivery. Offer available while quantities last.

Your Privacy—The Reader Service is committed to protecting your privacy. Our Privacy Policy is available online at www.ReaderService.com or upon request from the Reader Service.

We make a portion of our mailing list available to reputable third parties that offer products we believe may interest you. If you prefer that we not exchange your name with third parties, or if you wish to clarify or modify your communication preferences, please visit us at www.ReaderService.com/consumerchoice or write to us at Reader Service Preference Service, P.O. Box 9062, Buffalo, NY 14269. Include your complete name and address.

HSR11

Harlequin® Romance

*Get swept away with a brand-new miniseries
by* **USA TODAY** *bestselling author*

MARGARET WAY

The Langdon Dynasty

Amelia Norton knows that in order to embrace her future,
she must first face her past. As she unravels her family's secrets,
she is forced to turn to gorgeous cattleman Dev Langdon for
support—the man she vowed never to fall for again.

Against the haze of the sweltering Australian heat Mel's
guarded exterior begins to crumble…and Dev will do
whatever it takes to convince his childhood sweetheart
to be his bride.

THE CATTLE KING'S BRIDE

Available April 2012

And look for

ARGENTINIAN IN THE OUTBACK

Coming in May 2012

www.Harlequin.com

HRI7799

Taft Bowman knew he'd ruined any chance he'd had for happiness with Laura Pendleton when he drove her away years ago...and into the arms of another man, thousands of miles away. Now she was back, a widow with two small children...and despite himself, he was starting to believe in second chances.

Harlequin Special® Edition® presents a new installment in USA TODAY *bestselling author RaeAnne Thayne's miniseries,* THE COWBOYS OF COLD CREEK.

Enjoy a sneak peek of A COLD CREEK REUNION

Available April 2012 from Harlequin® Special Edition®

A younger woman stood there, and from this distance he had only a strange impression, as though she was somehow standing on an island of calm amid the chaos of the scene, the flashing lights of the emergency vehicles, shouts between his crew members, the excited buzz of the crowd.

And then the woman turned and he just about tripped over a snaking fire hose somebody shouldn't have left there.

Laura.

He froze, and for the first time in fifteen years as a firefighter, he forgot about the incident, his mission, just what the hell he was doing here.

Laura.

Ten years. He hadn't seen her in all that time, since the week before their wedding when she had given him back his ring and left town. Not just town. She had left the whole damn country, as if she couldn't run far enough to get away from him.

Some part of him desperately wanted to think he had made some kind of mistake. It couldn't be her. That was just some other slender woman with a long sweep of honey-blond hair and big, blue, unforgettable eyes. But no. It was definitely Laura. Sweet and lovely.

Not his.

He was going to have to go over there and talk to her. He didn't want to. He wanted to stand there and pretend he hadn't seen her. But he was the fire chief. He couldn't hide out just because he had a painful history with the daughter of the property owner.

Sometimes he hated his job.

Will Taft and Laura be able to make the years recede...or is the gulf between them too broad to ever cross?

Find out in
A COLD CREEK REUNION
Available April 2012 from Harlequin® Special Edition®
wherever books are sold.

Celebrate the 30th anniversary
of Harlequin® Special Edition® with a bonus story
included in each Special Edition® book in April!

Copyright © 2012 by RaeAnne Thayne

HSEEXP0412

Love Inspired®
SUSPENSE
RIVETING INSPIRATIONAL ROMANCE

Bakery owner Shelby Simons can't deny a stalker is after her, but admitting she needs a bodyguard is another issue. Bodyguard Ryder Malone is too big, too tough and way too attractive...but he won't take no for an answer. As Ryder and Shelby get close to answers—and each other—the killer closes in....

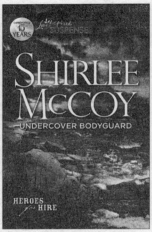

UNDERCOVER BODYGUARD

by SHIRLEE McCOY

HEROES *for* HIRE

Available April 2012
wherever books are sold

www.LoveInspiredBooks.com

LIS44484